By day I dress in cargo pants and boots for my not-so-glamorous job of making movies. But at night I come home to my two little Princesses, and we dress up in tiaras and pink tulle … and I get to write Happy Ever Afters.  Since I believe every girl is a princess, and every princess deserves a happy ending, what could be more perfect?

Follow me on Twitter @romy_s.

# To Catch a Star

## ROMY SOMMER

HarperImpulse an imprint of
HarperCollinsPublishers Ltd
77–85 Fulham Palace Road
Hammersmith, London W6 8JB

www.harpercollins.co.uk

A Paperback Original 2014

First published in Great Britain in ebook format by HarperImpulse 2014

A catalogue record for this book is
available from the British Library

ISBN: 9780008108168

Automatically produced by Atomik ePublisher from Easypress

*To Barbara and Sarah, Terry and Sue, for friendships that have spanned decades, continents and countless film productions.*

# Chapter 1

One woman tearing your clothes off was fun. Five at once? Not so much.

"Please, ladies..." Christian was only half laughing now.

Rip. There went an Armani sleeve. He shrugged away from the grasp, but there were still other hands pulling at him, tugging at him.

He'd known adoring fans before, but they seldom pawed him. And this had gone way beyond pawing.

"I'll sign autographs, but you really don't need to take souvenirs." He had to raise his voice over their squeals. This was definitely not fun. In fact, it was getting downright scary. The crowd surrounding him pressed in tighter. There seemed to be more of them now too.

Another rip. This time his shirt. The excited squeals increased in volume.

"He's mine!" shouted one over-eager fan.

"Mine!" the others echoed.

"Well, actually, ladies..." He belonged to no one. But in the grip of mob mentality, they neither heard nor cared.

He had to get out of here.

With another rip, this time the rear seam of his evening jacket, he pulled away from the knot of admirers. One young woman tumbled to her knees with the impetus. Fighting every instinct to be a gentleman, he didn't pause. He ran.

The sound of their pursuit spurred him on. He ran blindly. Now he knew how it felt to be the fox in a fox hunt.

A block or two further and the number of feet behind him seemed to diminish, but he still didn't look back. He only hoped no one had been trampled in the ruckus. Though if one or two of the fanatics broke a heel in the process, justice would be served.

He reached an intersection and looked both ways. This foreign city had turned into a maze and he had absolutely no idea where he was. Back where he'd been accosted, the streets teemed with life. He paused. He stood now in a deserted residential street, a terrace of imposing townhouses lined with trees stark against the night sky.

And no way out.

Cul-de-sac either side and a dead-end straight ahead.

Damn.

He looked back over his shoulder. There were only three women left in the race, but they were gaining.

A car pulled out of a driveway within the cul-de-sac to his left, picking up speed as it approached his street corner. An open-topped sports car with only one occupant. Blonde was all he had time to register. Drawing on a lifetime's worth of instinct, he took a running leap and landed face-first in the rear seat, just as the roof began to unfold and close over them.

The driver screamed, more ear-splitting even than the fans who, thwarted of their quarry, howled as the car sped past.

Christian sprawled on the back seat until the adrenalin rush waned enough that he became aware of aches and pains. He was winded too. He struggled upright.

The convertible roof clicked into place, sealing them in. Mercifully, the scream stopped as the driver drew in a fresh breath. He braced himself against another, but it didn't come.

While the white knuckles grasping the steering wheel still

revealed her terror, the driver seemed to have composed herself remarkably well. Her chin lifted and her shoulders straightened.

"What are you going to do with me?" she asked in local dialect, her voice icy, betrayed by the barest tremor. She turned her head to look at him in the rear-view mirror and he glimpsed an intriguing profile, beautifully arched eyebrows, long eyelashes, full lips, and a pert nose.

"Keep driving," he urged, glancing out the back window at the group of young women receding into the distance. He looked down at his clothing. Great. The jacket sleeve fluttered loose and his shirt had been torn and gaped open across his chest, enough to reveal dark skin through the crisp white broadcloth.

The shirt had been hand-crafted in Milan.

He swore again.

The only thing he could rectify was the skew bow-tie. He removed it and stuck it in his pocket, then climbed into the passenger seat beside her. She gasped, as if about to scream again.

"It's okay," he said. "I'm not a…" he struggled for the word in her language "… hijacker."

She glanced at him, long enough this time to be able to recognise him. Her eyes, Arctic blue, rounded with awareness, recognising him, struggling to place how she knew him. It would only be a matter of time. He relaxed.

But she didn't. The white knuckles tightened their grip on the wheel and her gaze whipped back to the road. "I know your face… you were on television…" She choked. "Oh my God! You're…" A single tear slid down her cheek.

He was used to women screaming, fainting, or losing the ability to speak when they recognised him, but that panicked tear was the most perplexing. Was she one of those crazies who believed actors really were the characters they played? Not that he'd played many villains. He was usually typecast as the charming rogue. The role fit him like a glove.

But she didn't look crazy. She looked… terrified.

3

What was with this place? Fans who mauled him, women afraid of him…

His mother had told him a great deal about Westerwald. Sometimes, instead of bedtime stories, she'd reminisced about the place and its people. Bitter-sweet as her departure had been, she'd loved her time here and the people she'd met.

Right now he couldn't figure out why. These Westerwaldians were mad.

The street grew busier around the car, a restaurant and a late-night corner-shop now amidst the residential buildings. He was worse than lost. He had no idea where the hell he was and had lost all sense of direction. Why had he said he'd walk to the damn party?

Because he'd wanted to see the city where he'd been conceived. Without an entourage.

Now he'd seen more than enough. Maybe he'd even agree to that local PA the producers kept trying to foist on him.

The woman was still driving way too fast.

"Slow down," he instructed.

She nodded, a stiff movement, her gaze riveted ahead.

"What do you want from me?" She sounded calmer, but the ice was still there.

He opened his mouth to answer that he wanted nothing now he was safe, then the thought occurred that a lift to the party would be nice. He smiled with all the charm he could muster in his current sorry state.

The smile didn't last long.

He slammed into the dashboard as the driver jammed on the brakes.

"Help!" she called. Without even cutting the engine, she leapt from the car. It stalled.

A man on the sidewalk turned at her voice. A uniformed police officer.

"I'm being abducted! This man jumped into my car… "

The policeman stepped up to the car, leaning in to look at

4

Christian. "You're Christian Taylor!" He took in Christian's dishevelled attire and frowned. "You weren't really trying to abduct this young woman, were you?"

He sounded sceptical. At last – a rational-sounding local. And one who spoke English. Christian breathed a sigh of relief and winced, winded again.

"Of course not." His voice sounded amazingly stable considering he felt as if he'd been punched in the gut. Twice. "I was attacked by a group of fans and this young lady unwittingly provided the getaway car."

Saying it out loud made it seem even more bizarre than it was, but the policeman nodded, as if rabid fan attacks were an everyday occurrence in Westerwald.

Perhaps they were.

The policeman opened the passenger door and Christian stepped out gingerly, holding his bruised ribs.

"Oh, you're hurt!" The young woman hadn't gone far, though her stance screamed fight or flight.

The policeman's eyes widened as he took in Christian's state. "Do you need a hospital?"

Christian shook his head. "I'm fine." Battered, shaken, but fine. He turned to his rescuer with another of his trademark smiles. "I'm sorry I frightened you."

He hadn't noticed before, but she was a real stunner. Classically beautiful, with high cheekbones and blonde hair, almost white beneath the street lights, swept back into one of those elegant twist things. She was dressed in a short, dark swing coat, buttoned up to conceal whatever lay beneath.

Like a model, she was thinner and less curvy than he preferred, but her stockinged legs, revealed now she was out the car, were the clincher. Perfectly shaped legs that went on forever. Legs he could see bare and wrapped around him in his very near future.

He grinned. Maybe he was going to like Westerwald after all.

Her classy attire was in stark contrast with his own, however.

He glanced down at his torn suit. There was no way he could arrive at the party like this. It was a charity banquet and there was sure to be a press presence, and he really wasn't in the mood for lengthy explanations.

Not when there was a much more pleasant diversion available than speeches and shaking hands.

"A lift back to my hotel for a change of clothes would be much appreciated." And once he got her back to his hotel room…

"I'll take you," the woman offered, in lightly accented English. Where she'd looked pale moments before, now she looked flushed. "It's the least I could do for not giving you a chance to explain."

The policeman beamed. "All's well that ends well, then." His eyes twinkled as he turned to the young woman and addressed her in dialect. "This is your lucky day. Do you have any idea how many women would like to be in your shoes right now?"

Christian flinched. He'd just found out the hard way how popular he was in this little country.

His getaway driver didn't look as if she felt particularly lucky either, but she nodded and climbed back into the car. Christian followed suit, this time buckling himself in. His ribs couldn't take any more abuse.

She took a shaky breath, as if pulling herself together, and re-started the engine.

"I'm Christian Taylor," he said as she put the car in gear and pulled off.

"I gathered." That touch of ice was still there. So knowing who he was hadn't melted any of her stiff attitude. "I assume I should know who you are?"

"I'm an actor. And you are?" He smiled, warming up for a charm assault, but she didn't even glance his way. If anything, she seemed to freeze up even more.

"Teresa."

Sheesh. Glaciers were warmer.

"Thank you for coming to my rescue, Teresa."

"Were you really attacked by fans, or were you just pulling some stunt?"

"You didn't see them – the girls on the sidewalk?"

Her brow furrowed and she pursed her lips, troubled. "Which hotel are you staying at?"

"The Grand. It's on… "

"I know where it is."

He'd never worked such a hard crowd. But there wasn't a woman he couldn't seduce when he set his mind to it. He upped the smoulder. "I thought you recognised me. Who did you think I was?"

"I don't watch much television, but the story's been all over the news lately… Two prisoners escaped from their transit van on the way to court. I thought you were one of them."

Another punch to the gut – an emotional one this time. "You thought I was an escaped con? Why – because I'm black?"

"Of course not." She turned her head to look at him, as if seeing him properly for the first time.

He was a little mollified she hadn't judged him by the colour of his skin. Even in his adopted homeland, which had made him far more welcome than his own people ever had, that still happened all too frequently.

But this woman, looking down her regal nose at him, had still judged him and found him wanting. Something started to sizzle inside him, something old, dark and unhealed.

They paused at a traffic light. "I knew I'd seen your face somewhere before," she said.

"Which of my movies have you seen?"

"I don't know, but I suppose I must have seen one once."

*One once?* His face had been on the cover of more magazines than he could count, he was a household name on at least five continents, and she'd seen *one once?*

"I told you, I don't watch much television."

Nor was he some two-bit TV actor. His movies were Hollywood tent poles and their marketing alone cost millions of dollars. *Time*

7

magazine called him the world's most bankable star, and *Vogue* had voted him the world's sexiest. And this woman didn't know who he was?

"Besides, when you've seen one of those action movies, you've seen them all. It's not real acting," she said.

The punches just kept on coming. He frowned. "So if you don't watch movies or television, what do you do for fun?"

"I read. Or I go to the opera and the ballet."

He rolled his eyes. Bor-ing. "People don't do those things for fun. They do those things to impress other people."

"Maybe in Hollywood. But here in Westerwald we're not cultural philistines. We have brains and we use them."

Ouch. Two hits in one perfectly enunciated sentence. She spoke better English than the Queen.

The swift sensation that accompanied her words was one he hadn't felt in years. His hackles rose. "You wanna bet? Clearly there are a few philistines here who watch my movies. I've never been attacked by fans in California before."

"They were probably Americans."

"So now you not only have a problem with movie-goers and Hollywood, but with Americans too?"

She lifted her chin. "When were you last even inside a theatre? The kind with a proscenium arch, not a screen?"

"Do the Academy Awards count?"

Her lips pursed. No sense of humour, then.

Her gaze fixed firmly back on the road as she indicated and turned into a wider street that looked vaguely familiar to him. "You Americans place so much emphasis on entertainment and beauty. On your own immediate gratification. Nothing lasts, movies are quickly forgotten. Who will even remember your movies five or ten years from now? Audiences will have moved on to the Next Big Thing and what difference will you have made in the world?"

Forget the fact that he'd been wondering the same thing these past few months. His blood boiled, the temper he usually kept in

8

check flaring like a Californian wildfire.

What did she know about him? He'd given nearly a third of his income to Los Pajaros over the years. Not that the people there deserved it. The happiest time in his life was *after* he left the islands and moved to California.

"So what difference are *you* making in the world?" he bit out.

He eyed her tailored coat and the diamonds on her wristwatch that twinkled as she moved. It was easy to talk about making a difference in the world when you didn't have to fight for your place in it.

"I do volunteer work for several local charities."

And that confirmed it. Only the idle rich had time to spare to volunteer for charities. She'd probably never had a real job in her life, had never had to make it on her own or prove her worth to anyone.

She continued, her gaze still on the road ahead: "If only half the money spent on frivolous things, like movies and actors' lavish lifestyles, were used to help the less fortunate this world would be a much better place."

Great, a Greenpeace Evangelist. The vision of those long legs wrapped intimately around him flickered out and died.

"Are you always this judgie about people you've just met?" He crossed his arms over his chest and leaned back against the window. "You think you know me, but I'll have you know I was on my way tonight to a charity banquet to raise funds for a new children's hospital in Los Pajaros."

Teresa flicked him a contemptuous glance. "A society event packed with pretentious people all showing off their designer wear and eating gourmet food? That's not helping others. That's helping yourself."

She was right, of course. Tonight was all about him, not about the charity. His appearance as guest speaker tonight had been arranged by his publicist. And even free publicity hadn't been his real incentive. He'd only agreed to attend when he'd heard his latest co-star was going to be there too.

But he wasn't going to admit that this prissy bitch was right.

He forced a crooked smile. "And what's wrong with that?"

The look she cast him could have out-frozen the Antarctic. "Do you even care about anyone other than yourself?"

Not any more.

Teresa pulled the car to a stop. Glancing out the window, he recognised the forecourt of his hotel.

Then she turned her clear, frigid gaze on him, and every repressed childhood memory, every insult and every torture he'd endured rose up. He kept his fury in check and resisted the urge to fist his hands. He thought he'd left the past behind, but clearly it still lingered beneath the surface, waiting for a moment just like this. He wanted to lash out, to take revenge on this superior ice queen, who suddenly represented every person who'd ever slighted the outcast mixed-race child from Los Pajaros.

But he was an actor. He could control his emotions. And he would die before letting her see how she'd got to him.

He opened the door and the chill night air rushed in. "I'm a narcissist and proud of it. But before you judge another person, Miss High and Mighty, you should take a walk in their shoes."

A slight smile tugged at the edge of her full lips. "Are you upset because I haven't fallen at your feet?"

He stepped out the car. "Thank you for the ride, Princess." He slammed the door shut and the trailing tail of his evening jacket caught in it, but he didn't care. He heard the fabric rip as he stalked away, head high, shoulders back, barely seeing the doorman as he pushed past into the plush lobby.

Tessa sat for a long moment, her hands on the steering wheel, which vibrated with the engine's purr. Now he was gone and the adrenalin rush faded, reaction set in.

Her hands began to shake.

She'd been unpardonably rude.

It wasn't like her.

Blood thundered in her ears and she laid her forehead down on the steering wheel. She could blame it on the shock of having a strange man jump into her car, invading her personal space, but it was so much more than that.

She was angry with herself.

If Daddy found out about her lapse tonight, she'd never hear the end of it. She'd been raised better than that. *Remember your manners, keep your temper, and don't be rude.* She'd broken all three tonight.

Not to mention that he'd warned her that danger could come when you least expected it and that she needed to be vigilant. But she'd been so wrapped up in her own thoughts, in herself, she hadn't even seen Christian until he'd leapt into her car. Nor had she noticed the women chasing after him. She'd been as self-absorbed as she'd accused him of being.

If her father heard of this incident, he'd have a security detail on her in a heartbeat, and she hated having eyes and ears trained on her. How could she go about planning the biggest day of her life with a bodyguard stalking her every move? She felt claustrophobic enough in her life as it was.

She could only pray that by then the escaped convicts would be back behind bars and they could stop living in fear. And that this dreadful feeling of being caged would go away.

She lifted her head and put the car in gear.

Still, neither fear nor anger was an excuse. She'd behaved insufferably tonight. Christian was right – she'd been judgmental and condescending. Just because he represented everything she distrusted and despised didn't mean she had to say it out loud.

She'd lied too. She'd pretended not to know who he was. But even she, enclosed in her ivory tower, had heard of Christian Taylor, the man who'd made his fame playing the ultimate superhero.

She sucked in a deep breath and pulled away from the hotel forecourt.

11

The last thing she felt like right now was a charity banquet. Especially one where she'd just insulted the guest of honour. She turned the car in the opposite direction to the banquet hall and headed home. She'd have a bath and curl up in bed with a book. And if her father wanted to know if she'd done as he asked and met Christian Taylor, at least she could answer honestly that she had.

And she'd send up a prayer that it was over and done with and she never need see him again.

# Chapter 2

"You may go straight in. Your father's expecting you."

His executive assistant waved her in, and with only the barest pause in her stride to acknowledge the older woman, Tessa headed towards the closed office door. Her heels beat out a firm rhythm on the parquet floor. She hesitated at the door; her hand suspended a centimetre from the solid wood door.

Did her father know what had happened last night? He always knew everything. Was he disappointed in her? Or had he summoned her here today to insist on a bodyguard? Whatever it was, his assistant had said it was urgent. So urgent she'd left one of the world's leading dress designers standing open-mouthed in the bridal boutique.

She steeled herself with a deep breath, straightened her back, and knocked on the door.

"Come in."

She opened the door and stepped in.

Her father stood in the bay window, which overlooked one of Neustadt's numerous squares, a leafy oasis amongst the eighteenth-century buildings, his back to her and his hands clasped behind his back, like a king surveying his domain. Which wasn't far off.

Victor Thomas Adler, Twelfth Count of Arelat, former Supreme Court Judge and new head of the nation's Intelligence Service, wielded almost as much power in the little European nation as the Archduke or the Prime Minister.

He turned as she closed the door behind her. "Thank you for coming so quickly." He waved her to the seat across the desk and she sat, folding her hands demurely in her lap. Her hand felt bare where her engagement ring usually sat. She'd barely had it a few months and already it felt like a part of her. As soon as this interrogation was over, she needed to collect it from the jeweller's, along with the insurance valuation certificate.

"Your assistant said it was urgent."

Please, please don't let him have heard about last night... she hated to disappoint her father.

"Did you enjoy the banquet last night?"

She blinked.

He never indulged in small-talk. So why did he want to talk about some charity event? She crossed her fingers in her lap, careful they were out of her father's line of vision. She nodded. "It was a lovely evening."

"Did Stefan go with you?"

"I told you last week that he's away. He has meetings in New York."

He wasn't happy with that. He'd already made his feelings known on that score – he didn't think Stefan would make a good husband for his only child. *He's too wrapped up in his work. He should take better care of you.*

Her father was a good one to talk. He was married to his job.

She was used to being alone. And tough if he didn't think Stefan was good enough. The man he'd thought suitable – the man they'd *both* thought eminently suitable – now lived in exile half a world away and she had to move forward with her life.

She didn't want to be alone. She wanted a family. And since Fredrik's departure, she and Stefan had seemed inevitable. She'd known Stefan since they were children. They'd grown up in the same social circles and his family lineage was almost as impeccable

14

as her own. They were friends.

"You met the American actor?"

"I did." At least that wasn't a lie.

Her father moved to the chair behind his desk and sat, steepling his fingers together.

Oh-oh, she was in trouble. She just didn't know what for, yet. For lying to him, or for paying so little attention to her safety that she'd endangered herself? Or both?

"I spoke to him."

His eyes narrowed. Worse, then. Did he know how rude she'd been to a visiting celebrity? He might not be big on small-talk but he was big on manners. And for reasons she couldn't fathom, he'd wanted her to meet the man.

"What did you discuss?"

She'd replayed the conversation enough times in her head since last night to be able to answer that. But somehow she didn't think 'I mistook him for an escaped con' or 'I insulted him' would rank highly in her father's estimation.

"We spoke about opera and ballet … and the Los Pajaros children's charity, of course."

"Of course. And what was he wearing when you had this scintillating conversation?"

He wanted to talk men's fashions? Something was going on here she couldn't quite see. Did he know she hadn't attended the banquet last night? Did he know she was lying? He always knew everything… but she was in so deep now.

She closed her eyes briefly and summoned up an image of Christian Taylor. Torn evening jacket, crisp white shirt ripped to reveal bare, hard chest beneath. Smooth, muscled chest… skin a rich cappuccino colour. "He wore an evening suit, like everyone else."

Her father leaned forward in his seat. "Very interesting… in view of the fact that he never made it to the banquet last night."

Oh-oh. She cleared her throat but couldn't think where to start.

"Which means you never attended either."

She lifted her chin. "It's a long story."

He waved his hand, not interested, and she breathed an inward sigh of relief at not having to divulge the entire sorry story.

"You have the opportunity to redeem yourself. After last night's stunt, the film production company is looking for a PA for Mr Taylor. Someone local who knows their way around this city and who can ensure he gets to where he's needed on time. I suggested you."

Tessa choked. "I'm not a PA!" And it wasn't as if she needed a job.

She flinched as Christian's words reverberated, still sharp in her memory. "*So what difference are you making in the world?*" Spoken in a tone so scathing, it had burned at her all night.

"It's not much different from being a social secretary. You have plenty of experience at that." Her father relaxed a fraction and almost smiled. "You've been doing it for me long enough."

She tried to think, but her head had turned to mush. See Christian Taylor again? Oh no! Not after last night... "I'm planning a wedding."

"You have an assistant," he pointed out.

Precisely. She had an assistant. "You can use Anna. I could pull her off the wedding preparations for the next week, and she's an excellent PA."

And Anna would probably love the idea of being around movie people all day.

Her father shook his head. "Not just anyone can do this job. I need *your* help."

She shut her mouth. He never needed help from anyone. Her father was the most self-assured, most formidable man she'd ever known. She'd often had reason to be grateful she was his daughter, the one person in the world he cared about, and not on the receiving end of his less-merciful side.

Even so, he wasn't above manipulating her or trying to control her life. Her eyes narrowed. Was this a ploy to keep tabs on her?

An actor as famous as Christian Taylor no doubt had an entourage of drivers and bodyguards. People who could just as easily watch over her too. If she'd thought her life was suffocating before now, it would have nothing on *that*.

She pictured herself, trapped in the back seat of a limousine with the man she'd insulted last night, watched over by beady-eyed security men. It was enough to make her break out in hives.

But not for nothing was she her father's daughter. She summoned up her own most formidable expression. "Why me?"

His gaze bore into her. "Because I need someone I trust to get close to him. I need to know everything about him. It's a matter of national security."

She couldn't keep the surprise from her face. Since when was a frivolous Hollywood actor a matter of national security?

Her father rose from his chair and paced back to the window. "You've seen Fredrik's ring – the Waldburg ring?"

She nodded. Of course she had. Her former boyfriend had worn that ring as a symbol of who he was. She swallowed against the lump in her throat. The last time she'd seen him, at his brother Max's engagement party, he hadn't worn it.

That night had been one of the hardest she'd ever had to endure. Almost everyone there had known she and Fredrik were dating before he'd been summarily exiled. Most had expected them to get engaged. She certainly had.

She'd been so grateful for the protection of Stefan's engagement ring on her finger that night, even though he'd been away on business and she'd had to brave the lion's den alone.

It should have been even worse for Fredrik. He'd lost so much more than she had. Instead, he'd been so wrapped around his new girlfriend Kenzie he'd scarcely noticed anyone else.

She frowned. Fredrik had disappointed her. She'd believed he was above vulgar public displays of affection. That's what one expected from a Hollywood actor, not from a European prince.

"You would recognise the Waldburg ring again if you saw it?"

She forced the past back where it belonged and lifted her chin. "Of course."

"Did Fredrik ever tell you there are three rings?"

She shook her head. They were the rings of the heirs of the Archdukes of Westerwald. Fredrik had one. His brother Max, the new Archduke, had one. Of course there could be another, locked away in safety in the event of a third son and heir being born, though that hadn't happened in over a century.

Her father contemplated the view beyond the window. "It's not known outside the royal family, but the third ring disappeared more than thirty-five years ago. Fredrik believes he saw it on a chain around Mr Taylor's neck a few nights ago."

Tessa tried hard to remember what she'd seen last night. She had to struggle past the vision of toned, dark-skinned chest.

A flash of silver.

It was possible. A lot of men wore jewellery these days. But if the ring was genuine – and she trusted Fredrik implicitly – then how had Christian Taylor come by it? A royal heirloom like that must surely have been as closely guarded as the crown itself.

Her father smiled, answering her train of thought. "Yes, that's what I need to know. Christian told Fredrik that he got it from his mother. I checked her out. She worked as a political intern in the palace here in Neustadt many years ago, on a policy think-tank. She left before he was born. I need to know how she got that ring, and anything else she may have taken. It shouldn't take more than a week or two at most. Then we can send Anna in to replace you."

She thought quickly. An intern would never have had access to the royal vaults. Christian's mother must have had inside help. But who, and how deep did this go?

Her father was right. This wasn't a job for any ordinary PA. And this way she could restore her father's faith in her too. Wedding or not, she'd do whatever she could to help. Even lose her independence. Even face Christian Taylor again.

She wouldn't only be doing it for her father, or out of friendship for Fredrik, but out of love for her nation. This was her home, her security, and she loved Westerwald more than she'd ever loved any man.

"I'm sure I don't need to tell you to keep this strictly between us. Fredrik has asked me to keep this from Max until we have real evidence." Her father slid a file across the desk to her. "Read this before you leave. The address is inside. You're expected there in an hour."

"How did you persuade them to hire me?"

He smiled. "I didn't. Kenzie did."

The film's production office was in the warehouse district on the outskirts of town. Though it was another balmy day, unseasonably so for January, and the sky an enticing blue, Tessa kept the top firmly closed as she drove. She wasn't taking any more chances.

A security guard signed her in and she circled the enormous car park looking for an empty space. Half the car park was filled with trucks and motor homes. People scurried between buildings and vehicles with an almost frenetic sense of urgency.

She sat in the car for a long moment, hands gripping the steering wheel. She wasn't sure which was worse. Having to face Christian Taylor again, or having to make nice with Fredrik's new girlfriend. No, not girlfriend. Fiancée.

Sucking in a deep breath, she climbed out of the car.

The offices were above a voluminous warehouse space, where a construction team hammered and sawed and raised voices echoed. Up a narrow flight of stairs she found the reception and was shown to a waiting room with faux-leather sofas, a water cooler and a pile of outdated magazines. Beyond the door she heard voices, phones ringing, laughter.

Suppressing the urge to pace, she sat with her ankles crossed and her hands clasped in her lap. And tried very, very hard not to imagine how abjectly she'd have to apologise to Christian for her behaviour last night before he'd even give her the time of day.

She would do or say whatever it took. Though for someone who always knew all the right words, who wasn't fazed in any company, the sudden attack of butterflies in her stomach was disconcerting.

"Would you follow me, please?"

Tessa followed the young receptionist down a long hall lined with offices and into a nondescript glass box identical to all the others. The redhead behind the desk rose with a ready smile and waved the receptionist away. "Thanks for coming, Teresa."

Fredrik couldn't have chosen two women more different if he'd tried. Where Tessa was tall and fair, Kenzie was petite and freckle-faced, her face as open as any book – not an accusation anyone would ever make of Tessa.

People usually described Teresa as competent. Kenzie was more "damsel in distress", fragile and delicate. Tessa could understand what Fredrik saw in her.

Kenzie came around the desk, and as she moved, her hand caught the sunlight from the bare windows. Tessa rubbed the empty spot where her own ring should have been. She still hadn't managed to get to the jeweller's to collect it, and without it she felt naked. Unprotected.

Kenzie wrapped her in a hug and Tessa stiffened. She wasn't a hugging type of person. Especially with a woman she'd only met once in her life.

"Try to look as if we're old friends," Kenzie whispered. Then she moved to close the door and waved Tessa to sit. "No one here knows who you are. I've told them you're a friend of mine and you're looking for a job."

"I didn't know you worked in the movies." Tessa hadn't made much effort to find out anything about Fredrik's new woman. About her replacement.

And yes, she was perfectly aware this was a case of pots and kettles. Just because she was now engaged to Stefan and would soon be married herself didn't mean she wasn't hurt Fredrik had moved on so quickly too.

"They're calling me the location liaison, but really it's just a fancy title they've given me because the mayor of Los Pajaros refuses to deal with anyone else. Rik and I are headed back tomorrow. The production team there have hit a few snags." Kenzie bit her lip. "In fact I've never known so much to go wrong on a shoot before."

Which explained why Kenzie wasn't the one doing the snooping. "No one's wondering why I'm being given the job over someone more experienced?"

Kenzie laughed. "That's the thing. Westerwald doesn't have much of a film industry, certainly nothing like the scale of this movie. There are no film-experienced PAs here." She dropped her voice. "And the work permit application to bring in someone from London has been held up by red tape."

Highly unlikely. Westerwald's bureaucracy functioned like clockwork. But Tessa had a very good idea *who* had held up the application. "So what do I need to do?"

"It's very simple. You'll be the main contact person between Christian and this office. Every day you'll be issued a call sheet for the next shooting day. You let Christian know what time he needs to be on set, then in the mornings you check that the driver is ready and waiting on time. If there are any delays, you let the second AD know, and if there are any changes to the schedule, you let Christian know."

Tessa raised an eyebrow. It sounded like a lot of hand-holding. Most grown men she knew were quite capable of setting their own watches without their PA's help. Stefan certainly was.

No wonder celebrities turned into such arrogant monsters if they didn't even have to take responsibility for getting themselves to work on time.

And Christian was definitely a monster. What rational person would slam the car door on her and stalk off just because she hadn't fawned all over him?

Kenzie handed her a folder. "This is from Christian's publicist back in LA. He has a few promotional commitments you'll need to

21

manage: you'll need to coordinate the arrangements for a premiere in Paris after filming here in Westerwald is done, and there are a few press interviews, a photo op or two… that sort of thing."

Like the charity banquet he hadn't attended last night.

"Anything else?"

"You might be expected to make dinner reservations, perhaps do a little personal shopping… " Kenzie looked apologetic. "I'm sorry, Teresa. I know this is a terrible imposition, and I'm so sorry to ask it of you, especially since you have your wedding coming up."

Tessa gave a cool smile. "It's no problem. And my friends call me Tessa."

Relief blazed in Kenzie's face. "We can't thank you enough. With everything that's going on back in Los Pajaros I just don't have time to look into this, but Rik is very concerned. He's very grateful for your help."

But not enough to pick up the phone and talk to her himself.

Kenzie escorted her along the corridor, introducing her to a dozen people along the way, the casting director, the production people, the assistant directors.

She still had to pass an interview with Gerry, the unit production manager. While she'd never had to interview for a job in her life before, this one was a walk in the park compared to the grillings her father subjected her to.

"Christian's easier than most," Gerry said, leaning his elbows on the desk between them. "He's not one of those stand-offish stars with an entourage around them who won't look you in the eye or who'll treat you like his skivvy. He's very approachable and easy-going."

Which didn't gel with the first impressions she'd got. He'd exuded so much testosterone that "easy-going" was the very last thing she'd have described him as. She hoped Gerry was right and the man she'd met last night was nothing like the man she was about to meet.

"I've worked enough diplomatic parties to be able to handle

whatever he throws at me," she replied. Her voice sounded way more sure than she felt.

"I like you," Gerry leaned back in his chair and steepled his fingers, just as her father did. But that was about where the resemblance ended. Gerry looked like a cuddly teddy bear – not something her father could ever be compared to. "I was worried about hiring a female PA for Christian, but I think you're going to work out just fine."

She arched a questioning eyebrow and Gerry laughed. "He has a bit of a reputation with women, but you look like someone who can hold your own. Somehow I don't think you're going to go all fangirl on him and fall into his bed."

"I should hope not!" Perhaps it would not be such a good idea sending Anna in to finish this job when she'd got the information she needed. Not that her personal assistant was in the habit of falling into bed with men, but it would be like sending a lamb into a lion's den.

But finding a replacement was a worry for another day.

"What is the movie about?" she asked.

"The usual. A little romance, lots of action. It's about the bastard son of a king and a slave girl who becomes a pirate. You're in luck. Today's a day off for the shooting crew, but Christian's downstairs in the costume department doing some final fittings so you can meet him straight away. If you don't mind waiting a few minutes, I'll walk you over and introduce you. There's just one call I have to return before we go."

"I'd like her to meet Lee first," Kenzie said, rising from the chair beside Tessa. "So we'll meet you down at Wardrobe in ten."

"Who's Lee?" Tessa asked as they headed downstairs. She'd learned a few tricks over the years and was good at remembering names and faces, but she was starting to reach saturation point.

"My best friend. He's an art director and he's supervising the set-build downstairs."

In the vast warehouse space Kenzie had to shout to be heard

23

over the din of construction. "Principal photography started a few days ago. The first couple of weeks are all location filming, mostly at the palace, then they move in here and shoot the interiors of the pirate ship for a few days before the entire production moves to Los Pajaros. You have three weeks to find out what you need."

Tessa nodded. And she had four weeks until her wedding. The quicker she could get this job done, the better.

From the outside, the set looked like nothing more than make-shift wooden walls on wheels, but passing inside was like moving from one world to another. From a dirty warehouse into the captain's cabin of a pirate ship.

Smoke and mirrors, like everything else in the film business where nothing was real.

Lee was bent over a table littered with drawings and schematics. He straightened with a grin, dimples flashing. He might easily be the most beautiful man Tessa had ever seen.

"How's my best girl?" He winked at Kenzie and pulled her close into his side.

"This is Tessa," Kenzie said, hugging him back.

"Ah, the super-spy."

Tessa frowned. "You told him?"

"I tell Lee everything. You can trust him too."

Lee turned the full wattage of his grin on Kenzie. "If you ever need anything, just ask."

Tessa cast a glance over the drawings on the table. "Did you do these?"

He nodded, pride shining in his eyes. "I designed this set. It's kind of what I do. Interior design with a difference."

"Any chance you do weddings too?"

"Tessa's getting married soon," Kenzie jumped in.

"It's been a whirlwind," Tessa explained. "I wanted a spring wedding, but Stefan's so busy and the only break he has is over the St Valentine's weekend. It's all terribly last-minute, but my biggest challenge has been finding Valentine's themed decor that

24

isn't a cliché."

Kenzie grinned. "If it's spring you want, you've come to the right place. Ask Lee to tell you sometime how he decorated a St Pancras station platform with fresh frangipanis in October for Rik."

They exchanged a look. "I didn't do it for Rik," he said, then he turned to Tessa. "I've never done a wedding scene before. Could be fun."

"Just promise me no pink hearts. I fired my wedding-planner because she insisted on hearts and cupids."

Lee grinned. "No pink hearts. Cross my heart. Are you and your fiancé free for dinner tonight so we can thrash out ideas?" He pulled his mouth down. "I've got nothing planned since my best friend's ditched me for a better offer."

Kenzie smacked his shoulder. "It's Rik's farewell dinner with his family. I told you."

Tessa ignored the pang in her chest. She'd once been a part of that family. "Stefan's out of town on business, but my assistant and I are available for dinner."

Lee pulled her in against his free side and gave her a squeeze. "It's a date."

She tried hard not to flinch at the touch, and extricated herself as quickly as she could without being rude. "So when do I get to meet Mr Taylor?"

Kenzie smiled, mistaking her question for enthusiasm. "Right now."

In the adjacent building, they passed a warren of dressing rooms, props workshops and store rooms before they reached the costume department.

Feeling very much like that lamb being led into the lion's den, Tessa followed Kenzie through a set of wide double doors into a bright space lined with rail upon rail of period clothing. To one side, beneath the light of the tall windows, seamstresses beavered away behind clattering sewing machines. Straight ahead, in a cleared open space, stood a couple of battered sofas and a table

25

with a tray of coffees. Tessa could smell the fresh coffee clear across the room.

Her stomach flipped. She'd skipped lunch too in the hurry to get here.

Beyond the sofas, reflected half a dozen times in the bank of mirrors behind him, stood Christian Taylor.

He wore full eighteenth-century costume, complete with ruffled cuffs and pantaloons. There weren't a lot of men who could look masculine in an outfit like that. Christian did.

He laughed at the stylist, who unknotted the cravat around his neck. His laugh travelled clear down Tessa's spine. Even the bones in her heels vibrated at the sound. If a sound could personify sex, then Christian's laugh was that sound.

"Okay, try the next one," the stylist said, waving Christian towards the cubicle with louvered doors which stood open to reveal more costumes hanging ready.

Christian turned towards the cubicle and as he turned he caught sight of Tessa in the mirror. Their gazes locked. Recognition dawned. Her heart skipped a beat or three.

# Chapter 3

Thank you, merciful fate! Christian didn't believe in God, but if he did he'd be on his knees and saying 'Amen'. Since he'd stormed into the hotel last night without a backward glance, he'd thought of a few choice things he'd like to say to Miss High and Mighty. Top of the list was that she should take a look in a mirror sometime.

And now fate had delivered her here. He'd get that chance to vent after all and hopefully exorcise the demons that had kept him awake all night. The fact that she'd hit on a sore spot, on something that had been nagging at him for months, hadn't helped.

Whatever she wanted here, she wasn't going to get it. This was his chance to turn the tables and send *her* packing.

"This is a private area," the Wardrobe Supervisor said, hurrying to intervene.

"They're not fans." Gerry, the UPM, pushed through the doors behind the two newcomers. "Sorry I'm late, just putting out fires." He waved at the redhead. "This is Kenzie, our Los Pajaros liaison." She was pretty, perhaps older than she looked. At least Christian hoped she was older, or she'd be a serious case of jail-bait.

Then Gerry gestured to Miss High and Mighty. "And this is her friend, Teresa Adler. Christian, meet your new PA."

Like hell. He'd already told the producers he didn't want an assistant. And this was who they'd hired? Just how small was this

27

country?

He set his hands on his hips. "Over my dead body."

Gerry ran distracted hands through his hair so it stood up at all angles. "We've already had this argument once today." He turned to the delicate redhead beside Teresa. "There's a genuine fire on Tortuga. No one's hurt and they've got it under control, but we've lost a large portion of the set. We're going to need to bring in more labour if we're going to get the build done on time. You need to speak to the mayor and ask him to give us some local labourers. We just don't have the budget to bring in more people from Florida."

Christian's eyes narrowed as he followed the conversation. "Good luck with that. You won't get a single islander to set foot on Tortuga. Not now that you've triggered the curse."

Every face in the room turned to him. Gerry's expression was one of annoyed disbelief. The redhead looked intrigued. The Wardrobe Supervisor and his stylist both simply looked lost. His friend Dominic, who'd been dozing on the couch beneath an upside-down newspaper, sat up. Only Miss High and Mighty showed no emotion whatsoever.

"You've heard of the curse?" the redhead asked.

"Of course. Every child on Los Pajaros knows the legend. Until the pirate and his princess return to Isla Tortuga, any person who steps foot on the island is doomed to life-long grief and heartache."

"The pirate and his princess died several hundred years ago. They won't be coming back." The redhead looked almost sad. "So you're from Los Pajaros?"

He ignored the question. His past wasn't open for discussion. He faced Gerry. "I don't need a babysitter."

"She's not a babysitter, she's your assistant. And your publicist insisted."

Screw his publicist. Or perhaps that was the problem. He already had. This was no doubt her revenge for the fact that he'd slipped out in the middle of the night without saying goodbye. But what

28

had she expected? She'd done enough damage control on his reputation to know what he was.

"If you don't want her, I'll take her." Dominic's voice drifted up from the sofa. He grinned at Teresa, looking her up and down. "You can assist me any time."

Christian glared at him. "I'd like a moment alone with Teresa." He used his most imperious tone and it worked. Everyone in the room, including the stylist, backed away. Even Dominic, though Christian had to send him another glare before he dragged himself off the sofa and followed the others, unread newspaper still in hand.

Teresa remained unmoved. He circled her, checking her out. She was as pretty as he remembered, in that Scandinavian super-model way. An Ice Princess out of legend, with her white-blonde hair swept up into a knot at the back of her head, not a strand out of place. In the bright light of day, her complexion was pure peaches and cream, her eyebrows perfectly sculpted, her make-up professional but subtle.

She wore an elegant pants suit that hid those long legs he remembered so well, and a conservative white blouse buttoned up to the neck that was no doubt intended to conceal the swell of her breasts. It failed utterly.

What kind of a PA dressed in Ralph Lauren anyway?

Only when he stepped close did she betray herself with a startled breath.

"So you've come to slum it here among us philistines, have you? Or are you here to help out the *less fortunate*?"

Another woman might have blushed. But Teresa's cool gaze swept over him, evaluating, unimpressed. It was last night all over again. She made him feel two feet tall, like the bastard kid he'd once been, blamed for every schoolyard prank within a mile, and made to feel like dirt for no other reason than that he had no father.

Or perhaps because the colour of his skin betrayed the fact that his father had been a white man, making him an outsider twice over.

But this was no dusty playground on Los Pajaros. They were on his turf now. And for once he had the upper hand.

"Why do you want to work for me?"

"Because I'm star-struck?" She was mocking him now. He held her gaze and waited.

She let her breath out on a sigh. "Because last night I was told I needed to walk in someone else's shoes for a while."

She kept her head high and held his challenging gaze. He admired a woman with spunk. She would definitely be fun to break.

"And just like that you decided to get a real job?"

"Until then I thought I'd slum it here in La-la land."

She was either mocking him or flirting with him, but he couldn't decide which since her face gave nothing away. Either way, she piqued his interest. There was more going on beneath the picture-perfect surface this woman portrayed to the world. As an actor, he knew one when he saw one.

"Give me one reason why I should hire you."

She met his gaze, more like an equal than the usual deferential, sycophantic assistants he had back in LA. "Because I'm efficient, I can multi-task and I know my way around this town. I can get you a table at any restaurant at the drop of a hat and tickets to any show in town. That's five reasons. Do you need more?"

So she was a still a smart ass. But in spite of himself he smiled. "You understand you'll be on call to me twenty-four-seven? There'll be no time for volunteer work." Or a life. "And when I say jump… "

"I ask *how high?*"

He grinned, enjoying himself. "No sweetheart. You don't need to ask. You jump as high as you possibly can, with everything you have in you."

He was sure she was going to tell him to take the job and shove it so she could go back to having her hands manicured, or whatever the idle rich did to while away the time.

And just like that he changed his mind. The idea of owning her for the next three weeks was much more appealing than watching her walk away with her pretty tail between her legs. No, he wasn't going to send her packing. He'd give her the job. And he'd get his revenge in the most pleasurable way possible.

He wouldn't just crack that damned composure. He'd see her completely undone.

Once again he imagined those long legs wrapped around him. Naked, unbuttoned. She wouldn't call him a philistine when he was inside her.

He grinned, with all the charm he was famous for. "Shall we start afresh? Hi, I'm Christian Taylor." He held out his hand.

"Teresa Adler." She shook his hand. Her touch was as cool and impersonal as her voice. She tried to pull her hand out of his as soon as it was polite, as if the contact stung her delicate pale skin. "I am really, really sorry for the things I said last night. It was inexcusable and I apologise."

"You had a very good excuse. It's not every day, I'm sure, that a stranger jumps into a moving car beside you." He could afford to be magnanimous, but he wasn't above teasing. He gripped her hand tighter, refusing to let go. "I assume you've never worked as a personal assistant to an actor before?"

She shook her head, and he wondered if that spark in the cool, contained depths of her eyes was amusement or anger or fear. "I've never worked as anything before. Will you be gentle with me?" Definitely amusement. But she wasn't flirting with him. More like playing with him, like a cat playing with a captive mouse.

So much for his turf. Even so, he couldn't resist flirting back. He wrapped her hand in both his, daring her to pull away.

Her breath stuttered and her gaze flicked down to their joined hands, hers so small and white between his larger, darker ones.

"Since we're going to be spending a lot of time together over the next few weeks, how about we get to know each other better. Tonight – over dinner?"

"I already have a date for tonight."

"Break it."

31

She shook her head and yanked her hand out of his. "I think dinner would be crossing a line. It wouldn't be professional."

That hadn't stopped his publicist. Or his previous two assistants.

"Suit yourself." He stepped away and waved the others closer. "Okay, I'll go for this. On one condition." He held Teresa's gaze. "You're mine for the next three weeks. This isn't a game. I need you to take this job seriously."

She nodded slowly. "Agreed."

"As soon as this fitting is done, Dominic and I are heading to rehearsals. You can go with us, and on the way I'll fill you in on what I expect from you."

"Great!" Gerry clapped his hands together in relief. "Play nicely."

He and the redhead headed for the doors, heads bent together in earnest conversation.

Dominic settled himself back on the sofa, looking much more awake than a moment ago. "We will!" he called after their departing backs and patted the open space next to him for Teresa to sit.

Christian sent him a look that his old friend couldn't miss: *Hands off. She's mine.*

This fitting was a far cry from the one she'd left in such a hurry this morning. The bridal boutique had been pristine and uncluttered, smelling of roses, with hushed voices, champagne, the soft strains of classical music drifting through, and the designer himself dancing attendance on her.

The costume department was noisy, with people coming and going, and a faintly musty smell. But it wasn't as dull as Tessa had expected. Not with Dominic serving her coffee and pastries, and keeping up the banter.

Unlike Christian, who glowered in their direction between costume changes, Dominic had no problem sharing his life's story. It was surprising that Christian had become the star when Dominic was the born entertainer. Within the space of half an hour she learned that the two of them had been friends since high school.

They'd started in the movie business together as stunt men, before Christian had been "discovered" and turned into a star. Dominic still worked as stunt coordinator on all Christian's pictures.

Which explained how Christian had managed that flying leap into her car last night with the top already half-closed. Fleetingly she wondered what else that athleticism would be good for, but she shut the thought down before it could take root. He flustered her enough already without indulging her imagination. And she never indulged her imagination.

Listening to Dominic chatter was not only a mine of information, far more so than the "official" biographies she'd read in the file her father showed her, but also a much-needed distraction. It was incredibly hard not to stare whenever Christian stripped off to try on a new shirt, and the stylist seemed to have rather a lot of shirts for him to try.

In the darkness of her car last night she hadn't fully appreciated just how lean and muscled Christian was. He made Stefan look positively soft in comparison, and Stefan was no lightweight in the looks department.

"If Dominic has finished monopolizing your attention, we need to run through tomorrow's schedule," Christian said, frowning at his friend.

Tessa pulled out a notebook and pen, and the call sheet Robbie, the Second Assistant Director, had provided her with, and scribbled notes. Christian was very specific about what he ate, when he ate, and how he liked his life run. If this was easy-going, she'd hate to know what a more demanding star would be like.

She was almost relieved when the fitting was over. The three of them left the wardrobe ladies bagging up the costumes to ship to Los Pajaros, and headed back through the maze of corridors to the rehearsal room.

Her relief was short-lived.

This wasn't a group of people sitting around a table reading from a script. The rehearsal was a sword-fighting practice. With both men barefoot and stripped down to their jeans.

Tessa sat mutely in the corner, eyeing them over the top of the folder of printed-out emails from Christian's publicist that remained unread, and tried to look as if two half-naked men trying to smack each other with dulled swords was an everyday thing.

The swords may not have been lethal, but they weren't playthings either. They looked heavy, and the sound that rang out when they struck was pure metal on metal.

The two men were equally matched. Dominic's skill was greater, but Christian was quick on his feet. There was something familiar in the way he moved: light and graceful, but she couldn't quite place it. She rubbed her brow and the sense of *déja-vu* disappeared.

She hadn't yet learned anything that wasn't in the file her father had shown her. The first few pages, Christian's official biography according to Wikipedia, IMDB and a dozen other websites, held no mention at all of his family or his childhood. Transcripts of various press interviews were less than helpful. They frequently contradicted one another and never asked the important questions. The gaps had been filled by the woefully short single-page report gathered by her father's intelligence people.

Christian had been born on Los Pajaros, only child of a single mother, which was still a stigma in the islands. There was no father named on his birth certificate. He'd been in and out of trouble from a young age. Then mother and son had suddenly moved to Los Angeles when he was fourteen. And that was where Christian Hewitt became Christian Taylor. It was almost as if they'd wanted to disappear.

Tessa's father had marked the print-out with a big, bold question mark. She knew what he wanted to know. Not just "*why?*" but "*how?*" How could a single mother, working as a school teacher, afford to move countries to start a new life in middle-class suburbia in California?

They'd cut all ties to Los Pajaros. There was no mention of his being born or raised there in any of his official biographies. She

34

rubbed her forehead.

The only new information Tessa had for her father was that Christian wasn't wearing the ring now. She couldn't have missed it if she tried. His bare chest glistened with a sheen of sweat as he and Dominic danced around each other, moving slower as they tired.

"Enough," Christian said, breathing hard.

"You're getting soft." But Dominic's laugh was just as breathy. "Are you letting this 'being a movie star' thing get to your head?"

"Never!"

They sheathed their swords and Christian turned to her. "I'm going to take a shower, then we can head back to my hotel."

Tessa nodded and glanced at her watch. She needed to check in with her father. And Anna. And she needed to call Stefan. What time was it in New York anyway?

While the two men hit the showers, she made the most urgent call of all, to her dress designer. "I'm so sorry, Anton. Something's come up. Is there any way we can re-schedule for later?"

She was going to have to put the wedding together in what little down-time her new job offered. This was one of those moments in life where the presence of a mother would have been good. Someone who could choose floral arrangements and discuss menus, and all the other stuff she still had to tick off her to-do list. For the first time in her life, she was going to have to leave the details to other people.

Anton wouldn't let her go without an explanation. She could practically hear him drooling down the phone at the mention of Christian's name. "You change your mind, love, and I'll take the job!"

She smiled.

Christian emerged from the adjacent bathroom, his short hair still damp. "It's a miracle: she smiles!"

She ended the call, her smile turning to a frown. "What are you wearing?"

"The usual." He looked down at the old jeans and baggy

35

sweatshirt he now wore. "Is there something wrong with my clothes?"

"They're fine if you're planning to be mistaken for a homeless person." She'd thought Hollywood actors were obsessed with looking good.

Christian grinned. "You sound just like my stylist."

She switched back to professional mode. "Gerry arranged for your car to meet you at the front entrance."

"Tell him not to bother. You know where I stay. You can take me."

She pursed her lips. She remembered way too vividly how he filled the space in her little car. But she'd promised her father she'd stick with this until she could get the intel he needed. The sooner she found out what they needed to know, the better. And where better to start asking questions than alone in her car?

Christian matched her pace as she strode out to the car park, texting his driver as she walked.

"Where's the fire?" he asked, practically jogging to keep up. "Or are you just eager to get rid of me so you can get to your hot date?"

That was a little closer to the truth. She'd love to get rid of him. The quicker she could get this job over and done with, the happier she'd be.

She slowed her pace. "How did you know about the Tortuga curse?"

She tried not to seem as if she was holding her breath. If he lied outright about having grown up in the islands, her work was going to be much tougher.

They reached her car, and Christian moved around to the driver's door and held it open for her to climb in. His manners surprised her. Or maybe he was just avoiding her question.

He only answered when they were buckled inside. "I lived on the island of Arelat in the Los Pajaros islands until I was fourteen."

She let go the breath she'd been holding. "The curse doesn't bother you? You'll be filming there in a few weeks."

"I've been away from the islands long enough not to believe

that old claptrap any more. But on Los Pajaros, the belief is still alive and well."

"Why did you leave?"

He fiddled with the radio channels and Tessa gritted her teeth. Even Stefan knew better than to touch her pre-programmed settings.

Christian finally settled on a rock station, as far from her favourite classical station as one could get.

"This is a sweet ride. I bet she can do nought to hundred in four seconds."

"I wouldn't know."

Christian rolled his eyes. "Will you let me drive her sometime?"

"No."

He leaned back with his elbow on the window frame, his gaze fixed on her. "Tell me about yourself."

She kept her eyes firmly on the road. "There's not much to tell." She didn't need to look to know he grinned at her. But she looked anyway. His eyes, an unexpectedly bright blue, so unusual against his dark skin, were mesmerising. With an effort, she forced her attention back to the road ahead.

"Okay, let me guess then." Taking her silence as assent, he pushed on. "You've grown up with wealth and privilege. You've never wanted for anything in your life."

Wrong. Living in a big house and not having to worry about bills didn't mean there weren't things she wanted and couldn't have. Christian may not have had the same kind of wealth she had growing up but he had the one thing she'd wanted more than anything in the world.

And right now what she wanted more than anything was to see his ring, find out his secrets, and get back to her own life. Her neat, organised, quiet life where her pre-programmed stations were inviolate and a man's gaze didn't have the power to burn her.

Christian studied her. "You've lived your whole life here in Westerwald, and I'm going to bet you haven't travelled much

37

beyond these borders either."

"I love my home," she said, immediately on the defensive. "I don't need to go anywhere else." He'd touched a raw spot.

"You've never seen a different view of the world. You've spent your whole life in your neat, white world, being a big fish in a very small pond. You're too scared to leave. Am I right?"

The raw spot grew even more tender. "Now who's being judgie? Are you trying to get me back for last night? I apologised for everything I said. In my defence, I thought I was being car-jacked."

"Tell me about these escaped convicts you're so afraid of."

Another subject she didn't want to dwell on. But perhaps if she shared a few confidences, Christian would be willing to open up further too. "My father was a judge, and he convicted the two drug dealers for murder. They had a parole hearing last week and somehow on the way to court they managed to escape. My father's afraid they'll try to get revenge on him through me."

"No shit! So you thought it would be a good idea to come work for me? Thanks a lot." But he smiled. Having seen him wield a sword, she wasn't surprised he was unafraid. She had no doubt he'd be able to take good care of himself in a fight.

"I didn't really take the threat seriously – until you jumped into my car. Besides, I'm pretty sure they're long gone by now. Would you hang around in Westerwald if you had a bounty on your head?"

He laughed. "Last night I *felt* like I had a bounty on my head, and I was more than ready to get out of town." He sobered up. "From now on we travel with my car. The driver's also a trained bodyguard."

She sighed. Exactly what she didn't want. "You're as bad as my father. I'm not going to change the way I live my life for some vague danger. Then the bad guys *will* have won."

Christian said nothing, and she flicked a glance his way. She didn't like the way he looked at her. As if he was seeing her in a whole new light. Not unlike a hungry person eyeing a tasty meal.

She didn't like the idea of him giving her too much thought

at all.

"And your mother – what does she do?" he asked.

She shifted gears. "She's dead," she said at last.

"I'm sorry. Mine died recently too. Do you miss her?"

You couldn't miss what you couldn't remember. Tessa went back to being all business. "Your call time on set tomorrow is seven o'clock. I'll be ready and waiting with your driver at six thirty. Would you like me to give you a wake-up call?"

"Join me for breakfast."

Though the word "breakfast" was a misnomer, since he'd told her his idea of breakfast was espresso.

She floundered. Were meals part of the deal? She really should have checked.

"Or are you planning on sharing breakfast with your hot date?" he teased.

She set her jaw. "I'll meet you at six in the hotel's dining room."

"I usually breakfast in my suite."

"The dining room or not at all."

"Yes ma'am!"

She turned into the tree-lined boulevard that housed The Grand Hotel. It lived up to its name, a grand eighteenth-century mansion converted into a hotel, with a park-like garden at the rear. It was private, exclusive and she couldn't picture Christian, who was all vibrant energy, against the quiet, solemn, old-world interiors.

She pulled into the forecourt and kept the engine running. A valet leapt forward to open the door, but Christian waved him away.

"Is there anything else you need from me?" she asked.

When he didn't answer, she looked across at him. There was a decidedly dangerous twinkle in his eyes that stopped her heart. She'd seen that look a hundred times and it couldn't be from any movie. Why did he seem so familiar?

"Yes. I had a mishap with a dress shirt last night. Could you please arrange a replacement?" He opened his door and climbed out, then leaned back in to look at her. "Enjoy your date, but don't stay up too late. We work pretty long hours in the movie business and you don't want to burn yourself out."

She nodded and he closed the door. He remained at the hotel's front entrance until she disappeared from sight. Only then did her gaze leave the rear-view mirror.

"What do you mean you have a job?"

She hadn't been sure Stefan was listening but now she knew she had his undivided attention. "It's just a temporary thing, to help out my father."

This was her ace. Stefan admired her father, though his respect was tempered with a healthy dose of fear.

She flipped her mobile to her other ear and reached for her wine glass. She'd never needed a drink as much as she did tonight. It had certainly been a rollercoaster twenty-four hours, and the crash course Anna had given her in how to be a PA had left her with a nagging headache.

"Are you working with him in Intelligence?"

Trust Stefan to find that impressive. She sighed. "Not exactly. I'm hand-holding a visiting celebrity."

"Anyone I know?" There was a moment's pause and she could easily picture Stefan on the other side of the line running through the list of visiting dignitaries – US state senators, ambassadors…

She sighed. "I doubt it. He's an actor called Christian Taylor."

Stefan whistled.

"You've heard of him?"

"Of course I've heard of him. Who hasn't? That film where he single-handedly saves an entire city from terrorists was awesome."

*Awesome*? She frowned. "I didn't know you liked action movies."

She worried her lip, pleased she hadn't Skyped and he couldn't see her face. Maybe knowing someone all your life didn't mean you really knew them. And their courtship had been something of a whirlwind…

She shook her head, shaking off the niggling feeling that

something wasn't quite right. She was just tired, and there was still so much to do. When the wedding was over, this terrifying feeling of being suffocated would go away. She sipped her wine.

Stefan laughed into the silence. "I don't work all the time. And spending as much time away from home as I do, sometimes the only way to relax is to tune in to a mindless movie."

Mindless. Her point exactly. "What was the name of that film?" she asked.

"I can't remember. Does it matter? I'll check the internet for you…" and that was Stefan, always willing to make the extra effort.

"It doesn't matter." She'd made her point. That was the thing with a movie. A couple of years later and the viewers could barely remember its name.

What Stefan did was much longer-lasting. As a policy consultant for Westerwald's foreign affairs ministry, he had the power to shape the future, to affect people's lives. Just as her father did, as the Archduke did. This was the world she was raised to be a part of. The world where what people did mattered.

Not the frippery world of make-believe in which people believed in their own importance and chased shallow dreams. And when those dreams couldn't deliver, they invariably ended up dead. Or worse.

"He has a terrible reputation," Stefan said.

"Who does?" Tessa asked, trying to back-pedal through her scattered thoughts.

"Christian Taylor. Apparently he's something of a magnet for women."

She shrugged. "I guess I can see the attraction."

"Should I be worried?" though Stefan didn't sound in the least worried. Another of the things she loved about him. His faith in her. And she trusted him. He was steady, dependable, rock-solid. They were going to make a good team.

"I don't know. Should I be worried about what you're up to in the Big Apple?" she teased back.

"Never." There was a smile in his voice. "It's just back-to-back meetings. I can't wait to get home. And I promise when I return I'll have something from Tiffany's for you. It can be your *something new* for the wedding."

She smiled. If there was one thing she knew about Stefan it was that when he made a promise, he stuck with it. He was noble down to the core. He would never let her down. He would never abandon her.

"I look forward to it," she said. "Take care."

# Chapter 4

Christian was so not a morning person. It usually took a cold shower and two espressos before he could even think straight. So it was a surprise when his alarm sounded and he opened his eyes without swearing.

For the entire decade and a half he'd been in the movie business, even when he'd still loved what he did, every morning had been a battle to get up and ready for set.

It was getting harder these days. What had Teresa said to him the night they met? *When you've seen one action movie, you've seen them all.* Her words had cut deeper than Dominic's sword blade because he'd begun to feel the same.

All the movies he'd made had begun to merge together into an indistinguishable mass. He needed a new challenge. He just didn't know yet what it was.

He rolled his legs off the bed and sat up. Maybe the fact that he'd gone to sleep stone-cold sober made the difference. He and Dominic had gone out clubbing, but his heart hadn't been in it. He'd left the club before midnight. Alone. Something else his heart hadn't been into.

He must be getting old.

He stood up and padded over to the windows, flinging open the heavy curtains. Beneath him, the gardens lay dark and silent.

This city had more green space than any European city he'd visited before.

He looked up. The sky was still dark but clear, with the crisp, wintry feel he so loved about Europe. And he could see stars. That was the one thing missing in LA – the kind of stars you had to look up to see.

The night sky was the only thing he remembered fondly about Los Pajaros – that vast, empty sky with the entire Milky Way on display. How many times had he looked up at that sky and wished for another life? He'd got it, too.

He hadn't been home to the Caribbean since he'd left as an angry kid. Had it changed as much as he had? In four short weeks he would find out.

He turned away from the window and headed to the bathroom, resisting the urge to dive back into the warmth and comfort of the vast hotel bed.

Once he'd showered, he dressed in jeans and a rumpled sweat-shirt, stuck a beanie on his head, grabbed his coat, and headed downstairs.

He was early.

Teresa was earlier still.

She sat at one of the tables in the elegant dining room, sipping tea from a porcelain cup. There were no other hotel guests in sight.

And on the table before her stood the double espresso he'd instructed her to have ready and waiting. He should have been pleased. But instead, the unusually good mood he'd woken with evaporated at the sight of her.

She looked as immaculate and poised as ever, her hair neatly pinned back and her make-up flawless. This morning she wore a grey, calf-length skirt, heeled boots, a turtleneck sweater that didn't need a label to have *designer* written all over it, with a cashmere scarf artfully knotted around her throat.

One elegant eyebrow arched as she took in the crumpled sweat-shirt and beanie.

She made him feel rough and uncouth, as if he was still just some island boy carrying suitcases and fetching drinks for the rich out-of-towners. A girl like her wouldn't have given him the time of day then.

These days he didn't give girls like her the time of day.

Why the hell had he said "yes" to hiring her? He should have insisted on the kind of woman he preferred – confident, sassy. The kind of woman who wasn't afraid to show a little skin or live on the wild side. At least then he might have had a little fun alongside his espresso.

The repressed virginal types just brought out his dark side. He wanted to muss up her hair and wipe the satisfaction off her face. He wanted to see her hungry for something she couldn't have.

Which wasn't a good way to start the day.

He slid into the seat across the table from her and tasted the espresso. Exactly the way he liked it.

"Good morning," she said brightly. "I have your new shirt." She patted the wrapped parcel on the table beside her. The stores would have been closed by the time she left the hotel yesterday. How in all that was holy had she managed to go shopping between then and now?

And not just any shirt.

He looked closer at the brown-paper package wrapped in black ribbon with the name of the designer on the attached card. Anton Martens, one of Westerwald's most famous exports, designer to the rich and famous.

Christian flipped the card over. There was even a personal message from Anton himself hand written on the back.

No assistant he'd ever had would have been able to pull that off overnight.

Tessa sipped her tea. "I've spoken to Robbie, the Second Assistant Director. He says they're ahead of schedule this morning and would like you to join them as soon as possible. Your driver will be out front in ten minutes."

45

"You'd make a good boot-camp drill sergeant," he grumbled.

Teresa arched an elegant eyebrow. "Your thanks are overwhelming. Are you always this pleasant in the mornings?"

"No, I'm usually grumpier."

"I'll remember that." She sipped her tea and silence fell.

He downed his first espresso and Teresa waved for the waiter to bring another. With caffeine in his bloodstream, he felt a little less like a barbarian. Not that the urge to throw her over his shoulder and carry her up to his room abated any.

The waiter also delivered a platter of croissants with preserves, cold meats and local cheese, but Christian couldn't stomach food this early.

"You hungry?" He asked.

She shook her head. "I already ate. You should eat something. Coffee is not a breakfast."

"Wanna bet?"

Silence fell again. The caffeine worked its way through his system, and he started to feel a little less off balance. A little more rational.

"You're early. Does that mean your date wasn't a great success?"

"It was a lovely evening, thank you." And she smiled.

He leaned back in his seat and contemplated her. Smiling, she looked less stuck-up. Less like the brats he'd had to say "yes, sir" and "no, sir" to all that last summer in Los Pajaros.

"You should do that more often."

"Do what?" Her face smoothed out into the calm, unemotional mask he'd already learned was her default setting. She unconsciously tucked back a stray strand of hair behind her ear.

He reached across the table and worked it loose again. She froze at his touch. "You should smile more often."

He wouldn't have believed it possible if he hadn't seen it. She blushed as she turned her face away, revealing just how porcelain-thin her skin really was.

God, even her neck was perfect. For a wild moment he imagined

46

himself nipping that delicate skin at her throat with his teeth. His body pulled tight in response.

"I'll wait outside for the car to arrive." She began to rise, but he grabbed her hand.

"It won't be here for another few minutes and it's cold outside. Sit down." He grinned. "I won't bite, I promise."

She didn't look as if she believed him, but she sat back down and folded her hands demurely in her lap, eyes cast down. He had no illusions it was out of any kind of meekness. He'd seen enough to know Teresa Adler was neither meek nor shy.

She simply didn't want to look at him. Why? Other women had no problem looking. And looking. Could it be because of the colour of his skin, or because she thought he was beneath her? It couldn't be because she wasn't interested. That blush said she was *very* interested.

He wanted to reach out again and touch her, but resisted the temptation. It was growing obvious she didn't like to be touched. Yet that silky skin, the colour of fresh cream and just as soft, begged him to touch so much he ached with the desire.

He emptied his cup and put his shades on. "Let's go."

But walking was an effort.


Christian's car was a luxury grey sedan with darkened windows. She'd expected a stretch limousine, something showy and pretentious, so the understated elegance came as something of a surprise.

The driver stood waiting beside the car. He looked military, with his buzz cut and sharp eyes, though he wore an unremarkable suit beneath his massive overcoat. He held the door open for Christian, who climbed wordlessly into the back and turned to Tessa with a quick smile. "He'll be much friendlier once he's woken up. I'm Frank."

As they pulled off, she called Robbie on her mobile. "We're on our way. We'll be there in about twenty minutes, morning rush-hour traffic permitting."

"Text me when you're two minutes away," Robbie said.

This was ridiculous. Stefan didn't buzz his office with two-minute warnings. These film people really were angsty.

They drove in silence. She was sure Christian dozed behind his dark glasses. If she hadn't seen firsthand how much of a morning person he wasn't, she'd have thought it to be a pretentious Hollywood thing.

Except he hadn't looked sleepy in that moment he'd touched her. He'd looked as if he'd been stung, those mischievous blue eyes alight with interest. There'd been a startled intensity in his eyes, a focused look that unnerved her even more than his touch had.

It didn't bother her that he found her attractive. Many men openly admired her. What bothered her was the nervous flip her stomach had made.

She paged through the morning papers that had been provided ready in the car, and when they were mere minutes away from the palace she texted Robbie.

A military guard opened the massive palace gates as they approached, and Frank eased the car around the palace building to the gravelled forecourt, where at least half a dozen trucks were parked, their contents spilled out around them. Several large motor homes stood in a cordoned-off area to one side, and it was here they headed.

Frank pulled the car up beside the largest trailer before jumping out to survey the area. He opened the door for Tessa and she stepped out, Christian a pace behind, rubbing his bleary eyes as if he'd only just woken.

Robbie already awaited them, stamping his feet to keep warm in the icy wind that whipped about them. Of course the balmy weather had been too good to last. Tessa stuck her hands deep into her coat pockets. She'd left her gloves in her car back at the hotel.

"Good morning, Mr Taylor," Robbie said with a cheerful smile.

Christian grunted a return greeting as he climbed the stairs to the trailer. Behind his back Robbie rolled his eyes, and Tessa suppressed an uncharacteristic giggle. Robbie was a fresh-faced young Englishman, easy-going and easy to like.

"His costume stylist is already in there, then he'll be in the make-up trailer for quite a while. Come with me and take a look at the set."

Tessa cast a look towards the open trailer door. Christian had disappeared inside without a word so she shrugged and followed Robbie, who was already busy on his radio, letting the rest of his team know that "the eagle had landed". She rolled her own eyes.

Robbie walked her through the lot, pointing out the make-up trailer, the mobile production office, the portable toilets for the crew and non-featured cast. Then he led her through a side door and into the palace.

Organised chaos, that was the impression that struck her first.

She'd danced in the palace ballroom many times, especially when Archduke Christian, Fredrik's father, had been alive. Those parties had been legend, yet they'd never matched the spectacle before her now.

If she ignored the massive film lights scattered around the room, the great thick cables running along the walls, or the corrugated cardboard taped around the door frames to protect them from damage, she might have stepped back in time.

The ballroom, with its high ceiling decorated with an intricate frieze, thronged with people, all in magnificent period costume. Everywhere she looked there were massive hooped skirts, tall feathered head-dresses, and every colour of the rainbow. And that was just the women. There was more satin and silk on display than at a wedding fair.

Film crew darted between the extras, fiddling with equipment, arranging impressive displays of imported flowers, adjusting the performers' clothes, or moving people like chess pieces on a board, their modern clothing incongruous amongst the period costumes.

Tessa wondered what time the crew must have started work to get this all ready on time, especially the elaborate wigs and make-up.

Robbie introduced her to a few people, then left her on one side of the ballroom as he was called away. She hovered by a wall, trying to keep out of everyone's way.

Most of the activity centred around the camera, mounted on tracks that ran half the length of the room. She watched, intrigued, as rehearsals began.

Dancers swirled around the camera, parting as a young man of Christian's height and colouring, dressed in sombre dark clothes, made his entrance and strode across the floor towards the camera, a stark figure amidst all the bright colour and movement.

Again and again they repeated the move, with Christian's stand-in blocking his moves. The young man may have borne him a more than passing resemblance, but he didn't move with Christian's lightness, or have his mesmerising appeal. She had no problem dragging her gaze away from him.

"Hello, chica!"

She looked around to see Lee and smiled. He leaned up against the wall beside her. "I was hoping to catch you here. I had a few ideas after our dinner last night and started some sketches. Want to see them?"

"Of course."

"All good things come to those who wait." He smirked. "I'll show them to you over lunch."

She smacked him on the arm. "Tease."

"Speaking of which, how has Mr Taylor been so far?"

Infuriating. Unsettling. Occasionally charming. She couldn't pin down how he made her feel. One minute all intense, those seductive blue eyes making her feel like prey in the hunter's sights, the next minute prickly and combative.

"He's fine," she said.

"He shared any confidences yet?"

*If only.* But since she didn't know how much Lee knew, she simply shook her head. He leaned closer, dropping his voice. "You know that the quickest way to get him to reveal whatever you want to know is to seduce him? You're sure to catch him unwary in the throes of passion."

Her entire body stiffened in horror. "I couldn't do that!" Even if she wasn't engaged, it was unthinkable.

"Pity."

She followed Lee's gaze across the room to where Christian had just entered, flanked by Robbie, Christian's stylist, his make-up artiste, and the man Tessa had already gathered was the director. She wasn't the only one who turned to look. A flutter swept around the room. Christian seemed oblivious. With those looks, he'd no doubt had people falling at his feet his entire life. Add the athletic build and the attitude, and he was very hard to ignore.

Lee laid a dramatic hand over his heart and sighed. "If I were in your shoes, I'd so do him. He's even sexier in person than up on the big screen."

She didn't dispute that. She'd never met a man who made her skin prickle with awareness like Christian did.

Christian was joined by a young woman Tessa vaguely recognised, and this time it certainly wasn't from any late-night crime report. She was a brunette, at least a head shorter than Tessa, with an exotic Mediterranean colouring, slender yet with curves in all the right places, and a cleavage that needed no accentuation. Especially in her heavily embroidered Baroque ball gown.

Scarlet. It suited her.

Tessa pursed her lips as Christian bent to kiss the woman's cheek and whisper in her ear. The woman blushed and giggled.

"Nina Alexander, Christian's leading lady," Lee said. "She's not half bad for an actress who it's rumoured will be an Oscar contender this year. Almost as down-to-earth as Christian and she has a wicked sense of humour. The crew are laying odds she's going to make him wait until the end of the movie before he gets lucky, though."

"What are the odds he doesn't get lucky at all?"

51

Lee laughed. "Nil. As long as she's not married, she's fair game. And there isn't a woman who can say no to him if he sets his sights on her."

*Want to bet?*

Across the room, Nina laughed at something Christian said. He definitely seemed in a better mood now. Tessa bit her lip. "I hope the poor woman isn't looking for a relationship. Christian's attention span seems to be limited to about a week." Or so said the page and a half of her father's report that had been devoted to his love life.

Lee nudged her. "That's why you'd be so good for him. What you want from him is unique. It's not like you want to marry the man." He rubbed his stubble thoughtfully. "Might even be good for you."

"I don't mess around," she said stiffly.

The dimple appeared in his cheek. "Not even a last little fling before you settle down to marriage?"

They'd gotten to know each other well enough over dinner last night for Tessa to be pretty sure that that Lee was only teasing. In spite of the fact he never took anything seriously, she could understand why he and Kenzie were such good friends. And why he and Anna had hit it off so well last night.

He was a good listener. And he'd become even more excited about her wedding than the know-it-all wedding-planner she'd hired and fired. Certainly more excited than she felt.

There were days she wished they could just elope and get married on a tropical island somewhere. But Europe's entire aristocracy expected to be present at the wedding of the last heiress of the noble House of Arelat, the family that had given its name to the island where Christian was born, and noses would be out of joint if she didn't deliver.

"Well, if you change your mind, it won't be hard. We men are such suckers for a pretty face, and you're definitely a pretty face. And with Christian's reputation... "

As if he'd heard his name, Christian looked up and his gaze connected with hers, clear across the crowded ballroom, knocking the wind out of her.

He raised an eyebrow and grinned, a look so cocky and sure of his own appeal, that she had to turn away. Even if she were capable of seducing anyone, she wouldn't give Christian the satisfaction. And she would not let him get any more under her skin than he already was.

A man like Christian Taylor could not be trusted. People like him, who courted fame and adoration, always after the quick thrill of the moment, destroyed everything they touched. She was not about to be destroyed a second time.

Now what had put that look in her eye? Christian only listened to the director with half an ear as he stared across the ballroom at Teresa. The dislike in her usually unruffled demeanour startled him. What had he done to upset her? God, he hated mornings.

It definitely wasn't the pretty boy next to her causing her to frown, because she laughed as he made some comment.

Christian's gut clenched.

"You got that?" the director asked. "You're spurned and angry and about to take revenge on everyone in the room who ever slighted you."

Which was about right. Christian's hands fisted.

There were two reasons he'd signed on for this movie. The first lay beyond his control and he wouldn't be entirely surprised if he had to leave Westerwald without achieving it.

But the second lay firmly within his grasp. The chance to visit both the land of the father who hadn't wanted to own him, and the island that had been his childhood home. The chance to return not as the outcast child but as the victor.

He was here to show them all the man he'd become, starting with that prissy little PA who turned her back on him as if he was beneath her notice.

He took the starting position he was indicated and breathed deeply, focusing on the role at hand.

They walked through the rehearsal a couple of times, following the movements the director had already blocked out with his stand-in. He only gave half his energy to these run-throughs, saving his best for when the cameras actually rolled.

"Final checks," the AD called. The make-up and wardrobe stylists fluttered around him like agitated butterflies before hurrying away out of shot. Then "Quiet! Roll sound," the AD called.

Another voice called back, an indistinct affirmation.

"Roll camera."

"Camera speed," piped up the first camera assistant.

"Mark it."

The second camera assistant banged the clapperboard and leapt out of the way.

"And... action!"

The dancers moved around him, their movements eerie without music to accompany them. Their feet stamped, their costumes rustled, but the room had that strange sound film sets had during filming, the sound of a hundred people holding their breaths, trying not to make any noise that might be picked up by the microphones.

The AD waved his arm and on cue Christian stepped forward through the wide doorway and began to stride towards camera.

It was a big, emotionally charged shot with which to start the day. It should have been hard. It should have required more preparation and more focus. It should have required him to dig deep into his emotions. But he didn't need any of that.

Just having Teresa in the room, watching him from the sidelines, was all the preparation he needed. He didn't need to look to know she was there, to know that she watched him. He was aware of her every movement in his peripheral vision.

Her presence sparked a sensation he'd never felt before, an uncomfortable prickle beneath his skin. Rather like that very first

54

night in her car, when she'd questioned his worth to the world. Only now the itch seemed ten times worse.

The dancers parted for him. Waiting for him before the camera stood his co-star, Nina. A luscious little thing with dark, sensual eyes and full red lips. When they'd first met, at some party back in LA, he'd been determined to sleep with her. This movie had seemed like a good opportunity to accomplish that too.

Three birds, one stone.

Only now the thought of bedding her held no appeal. Unwanted, unsummoned, an image intruded of long pale, naked legs and white-blonde hair spread across his pillow.

"What are you doing here?" Nina asked in a scandalised stage whisper.

"I'm here to see you."

She toyed with her gold mask, using it to screen her face. "What if someone sees us together? You'll ruin me."

"We are two people passing the time at a ball. How could that possibly ruin you?"

Nina lowered the mask so he could see her eyes. Though the camera was focused on him for this shot rather than her, her expression held all her character's emotions. She was certainly a consummate professional. "Because of who you are."

He prowled around her, a slow, threatening glide, and the camera moved with him in a long slow arc. His voice was low, only just loud enough for the microphone carefully concealed in his clothing. "And what am I, Celeste? Your plaything, your rebellion, or your lover?"

Her eyes flashed angry darts at him. "You're an outsider. You don't belong here."

He laughed, low and dangerous. "You weren't saying that when I was between your lovely, naked thighs last night."

"Hush! What if someone hears you?"

"So what?" He stopped his prowl, stood poised at her shoulder to whisper in her ear. "I'm good enough to bed but not good enough to stand by your side in polite company?"

Nina's voice shook, but it was nowhere near as convincing as Teresa's had been the first night they met. "Do you even care about anyone other than yourself?"

Even with the screenwriter's words in his mouth, the answer was still the same as the one he'd had for Teresa. "No, I don't. Because no one else has given me a damned thing unless they wanted something from me in return."

He stroked his fingers down Nina's neck. Her skin was smooth and warm. He wondered what Teresa's skin would feel like. Probably cold as ice.

"Even you want something from me, Celeste, though you won't admit it. But you know what?" His voice hardened. "You're going to have to get down on your knees and beg me for it."

Nina shook her head. "I won't."

Though he spoke his words for the microphone, and the brunette standing before him, he directed every line at the cold-eyed blonde who watched from across the room. He released all the pent-up rage she'd stirred in him when they first met. "Oh yes, you will."

The actress stared at him wide-eyed. One beat. Two beats.

"Cut!" cried the director, jumping up from his seat behind the monitor. "That was incredible! I'm blown away, Christian. Do you think you can do that again?"

Christian nodded.

Nina's eyes were still wide, her mouth parted just a little now. "God, you're good," she said.

"Thanks." He bent to her ear, his voice a whisper he hoped even the sound man wouldn't pick up. "You ever want to find out how good, I'm in the penthouse suite at our hotel."

"In your dreams." But there was an extra sashay in her hips as she turned and walked away, and the coy look she cast him over her shoulder spoke volumes. Christian grinned. Nina was definitely his kind of woman, and a man had to keep his options open, after all.

"Back to the top," the AD shouted out to the room, and there was a mad bustle as everyone returned to their starting places amidst the AD calling out instructions for tweaks to the lights, a slower zoom in by the camera and "why the hell is there a wristwatch on that extra?"

# Chapter 5

If she'd thought Christian was grumpy that first morning, it was nothing on his mood the rest of the week. Until he'd had his second espresso, he could barely manage a grunted greeting.

And every day he got grumpier.

Teresa took it in her stride. She made sure his espresso was ready, that the car was out front, that his script sides were on hand, and she avoided conversation. She sipped her tea, read the morning papers and enjoyed the peace and quiet while it lasted.

"Didn't you sleep well last night?" she asked on the fifth morning as Frank drove them to the palace. The sun wasn't quite up yet, the sky lightening with a smudge of pink in the east. Though the morning rush hour had yet to start, she felt wired and ready to go. It was good to have a reason to get out of bed in the morning, even if that reason was something as trivial as making a movie.

Christian scowled back in answer.

As soon as they arrived on set he was hustled into his trailer, dressed by his wardrobe stylist, then handed over to the make-up artistes who had their own special truck, ready rigged with basins, mirrors and bright lights.

It was warm inside the trailer, crowded and noisy with voices and music from the make-up artistes' MP3 player. Since it was still too early to run Christian's errands, Tessa sat quietly in a corner and read the script as his make-up artiste Marie readied him for the cameras.

With Christian's hair trimmed so short, she couldn't figure out what took so long.

"They're getting rid of my excesses," Christian said, catching her eye in the mirror as Marie massaged moisturiser into his skin. He held her gaze a second too long, so that the blood in her veins began to fizz and bubble until she forced herself to look away.

"You really should sleep more and drink more water," Marie chided. "All that partying is damaging your skin."

"It's the film lights that damage my skin."

Marie giggled and glanced at Tessa who'd reached the last page and closed the script.

"If you want something else to read, there's a pile of magazines under the basins. They're mostly local rags, but I love all the pictures of the who's who of Europe." She sighed. "We don't have any Dukes or Counts or Princes in the States."

"And thank heavens for that." Christian's expression shifted from amused to bitter in a heartbeat. "Bunch of inbred brats."

"Why do you say that?" Tessa asked, keeping her voice level.

"I met my fair share of them when I was a kid working for my uncle's fishing-charter business. Self-indulgent and self-absorbed, the lot of them."

It was the first time he'd mentioned his childhood on Los Pajaros. She should have pushed, widened the crack, but she was side-tracked by the sting. He'd said it like a barb, as if he'd known she was one of them. And resented it.

She returned to her seat and opened the magazine, paging blindly past countless faces she recognised. Her social circle was certainly incestuous. Everyone knew everyone. And yes, there were parties and social events, so many they seemed to blur together these days, but in that respect her life in Westerwald wasn't much different from Christian's life in Hollywood.

Except for one big difference. The people she knew were no

more self-indulgent than she was. With privilege came responsibility and duty, and no one knew that better than the descendants of lines that had served their nations for hundreds of years.

Besides, who was Christian to lecture her about self-indulgence? He partied as if there was no tomorrow. Frank had told her at what ungodly hour he'd finally brought Christian and Dominic home from some nightclub in the early hours of this morning.

"What's so engrossing?" Christian asked, swinging away from the bank of mirrors and holding out his hand to her for the magazine.

She'd stared at the same page for a full minute without paying the slightest attention to it. She looked now and blood rushed to her face.

Christian beckoned with his fingers. "It can't be that bad. Let's see it."

She stuffed the magazine behind her back.

He beckoned again. "You know if you don't hand it over I'll have to come and get it?"

She had no doubt he'd do it too. Reluctantly she handed over the magazine. But not before she closed it. Christian took it and flicked through the pages.

And unerringly found the page she'd wanted to hide.

"Hey, that's you!" Marie peered over Christian's shoulder. "Who's the hunk you're with?"

Tessa's blush deepened.

"It's Prince Fredrik," Christian said. He laid the magazine down in his lap and contemplated her. "It says your engagement announcement is imminent."

"It's an old magazine and we were never engaged." They'd discussed marriage but Fredrik had never got around to proposing. Fate in the form of a blood test had intervened.

"A prince, huh?" Christian still looked at her strangely.

Unable to bear the hard scrutiny, she rose and wandered across to the shelves of cosmetic products lined up beside the basins.

60

"Not anymore."

"I met him at the welcome drinks party," he said. "He was there with your friend." He said it like a question.

"He and I... we separated by mutual agreement and there are no hard feelings. I'm happy that he and Kenzie are together now." And for the first time she meant it. If Rik could overcome being disinherited and find happiness, then she could overcome losing the safety net he'd provided.

"So how did you hook up with a prince?" Nina asked from the make-up station at the far end of the trailer, where her stylist was busy creating an extravagant up-do with a wig and thousands of pins, a process that took over an hour every day.

*Hook up.* Such an American expression. It had never been like that for Teresa and Rik. Or even for her and Stefan. But she didn't think this Hollywood actress, nice as she was, would comprehend relationships based on mutual understanding, on a common background, on shared ideals.

Tessa shrugged. "This is a small country. We grew up together."

Christian studied her with narrowed eyes. "Los Pajaros is a pretty small place too, but I didn't even attend the same school as the mayor's kids, let alone play with them."

She didn't like that look. It was worse than the constant prickle. It was even worse than when he'd tried to flirt with her.

"You're from Los Pajaros?" Nina asked, her already-big eyes growing rounder.

Christian's jaw tensed, a sign so subtle that no one else seemed to notice. Tessa did.

"Robbie wanted you to come to set as soon as you're ready. Shall I let him know you're on your way?" she asked.

If she'd hoped for gratitude for rescuing him from an awkward conversation, she was disappointed. He nodded and rose from the seat, removing the protective napkins tucked into his collar, then waved for her to precede him out the door.

"Don't go!" Nina called. "This is just getting interesting. Stay and tell me all about your prince."

Tessa cast Christian a beseeching look but he was far less magnanimous. "Yes, stay Baroness. You can tell her all about how you went from dating a prince to slumming it here as my PA."

Damn. He'd read the fine print in the article too.

By the time he stepped in front of the cameras each day, Christian turned into the Energizer bunny and there was no stopping him.

Especially when Dominic was around. They were like two little boys, egging each other on. Tessa learned to tell where they were on set by the sound of laughter.

Their pranks had become legendary. One of her tasks was to provide a steady supply of whoopee cushions and fake turds – and then there was the day she had to scour every pharmacy and supermarket across town for a very specific brand of condom that didn't appear to exist. She was sure the errands were designed for her maximum embarrassment.

At least she found a ready supply of fake blood in the make-up trailer and saved herself a trip when Christian decided to prank the director into thinking Dominic had wounded him during rehearsal.

But that was by no means her least-favourite task. That honour went to screening Christian's calls. While he was on set she kept his mobile, answered his calls and took messages. The press phone calls were a pain, but easy to deal with. She simply said "no" and "no comment" unless they were on the approved list.

The requests for charitable donations, memorabilia and signed autographs to auction, and the "please endorse my product" calls, were equally easy to deal with.

The incessant phone calls from women were not.

The worst of them was Christian's publicist. The poor woman was clearly desperate to talk to him. He was equally determined not to. Instead, Pippa turned to Tessa as her confidante, pouring out her heart and the minute details of their affair.

Having never been the confiding type, it was all Tessa could do to stop herself from telling the woman to get over herself. If there was one thing she'd learned in this first week, it was that Christian wasn't the type to stick around. He was the proverbial social butterfly, darting from one pretty flower to the next.

All a woman needed to do to make him run in the opposite direction was to expect him to return her calls.

The quicker his publicist learned that, the quicker her heart would heal. Or her ego. Tessa couldn't work out which had been hurt more.

"Who was that?" Christian poked his head out the door of his trailer's bedroom.

"Pippa. Again. Just Jared posted a picture of you leaving a restaurant with Nina and she wanted to know how serious it was."

He grinned. "What did you tell her?"

"I told her you were probably more serious about the Brazilian model whose name you couldn't remember that your pimp set you up with last night."

"You should be kinder to yourself." He laughed and ducked out of sight, which was just as well since the hand holding his brand-new iPhone itched to throw it at him.

Making the call to set him up with some woman he'd seen on page three of the morning papers had definitely been one of the lower points of her week.

Five minutes later Robbie knocked on the door to escort Christian back to set. Tessa sank down on the sofa in the trailer's living room. The sudden silence boomed loud.

After five days in his presence, twelve hours a day, she still didn't know much more about Christian than the way he liked his shirts pressed or how much he loved sweet seedless grapes. From her spot in the corner of the make-up trailer, she'd heard all his old "war stories" – adventures he'd had on various movie sets – and she'd learned way more than she wanted to about his love life. But nothing her father would consider useful.

63

Even the gossip she picked up on set wasn't of any use. Most of it was as contradictory as his interviews had been. At this rate, she'd be a married woman before she learned what they needed to know.

She dialled her father's private mobile number.

"Anything new to report?" He sounded eager.

"Nothing new." She definitely didn't feel eager. This job should have been over for her by now. "I haven't seen the ring once. I'm not even sure he has it. And aside from the fact that he was very close to his mother, he's never once mentioned her living here in Westerwald."

"It's been a week already. You need to get closer to him."

No shit, as Christian would say. She rubbed her temple. "I can't do that! I'm his employee." Not to mention she was about to marry someone else. Something she shouldn't need to remind her own father.

"I'm not suggesting you sleep with him." Victor sounded exasperated. "Just be friendly enough to get into his room and go through his things."

She wasn't so sure they could do friendly, and the thought of going to his room...

With Christian, everything had a sexual undertone. The spark of mischief in his eyes, his voice. And there was the way he looked at her sometimes; that intent look that made her burn hot and cold.

But as patently obvious as his interest was, she wasn't expecting an invitation to his room any time soon. Since he'd discovered who she was, and the title that went with it, Christian had made it equally obvious he didn't want to be interested.

She completely understood where he was coming from. She didn't want to be attracted to him either.

But that was a conversation she was so not having with her father. "I'll do what I can, but I'm not making any promises."

"That's all I ask. I know you can be very resourceful when you want to be."

Which was about as much of a compliment as she could expect. She sighed. "Yes, Father."

She stuck her phone back into the leather messenger bag she'd taken to carrying and headed back to set.

This morning they were filming an action sequence in the palace's entrance vestibule, a vast space with Carrara marble flooring and a magnificent staircase that circled up to the private royal apartments above. The front doors stood wide to provide access for the film crew. With the resulting chill in the air they might as well have been outdoors. Teresa pulled her North Face parka closer around her, and dug her gloved fingers into her pockets.

Most of the film crew looked like Michelin men inside their jackets, but Christian wore nothing more than a dressing gown at the top of the stairs. Hot as it was beneath the film lights, he had to be feeling the bite in the air.

As the AD called for final checks, he removed the gown to allow the make-up artiste a chance to touch up the shadows painted on his torso to emphasise his abs.

"Not that he needs it," Lee said, appearing beside her.

She jumped. Exactly what she'd been thinking.

"You can stop drooling now," she bit back.

"Down girl!" Lee laughed quietly beside her. "No need to go all possessive over him."

He was right. She did feel possessive. In spite of the stupid tasks Christian set her, she felt responsible for him. If he wasn't such a jerk whenever she was near, and aside from the way the mere sound of his voice could raise goosebumps on her arms, she might even like him. Everyone else did.

"What are you doing here?" she asked. Lee very seldom came to set. His team usually worked ahead of the main crew, preparing the next day's locations.

"We're on our lunch break and I thought I'd drop by and get an eyeful." He sighed. "Seems I timed it perfectly! Would you like

65

an apple turn-over from the craft table? They're fresh from the oven." Lee held out a beautifully crafted piece of pastry on a napkin.

She shook her head. "Thanks, but I don't like cooked fruit."

"Goodie, more for me." He grinned and popped the pastry in his mouth.

The food on set was good. Cappuccinos, fresh fruit and pastries on tap at the craft station, and hot meals prepared in the mobile kitchen every day. If Christian didn't keep her running for twelve hours of every day, she might not fit into her wedding dress.

"Have you made any progress yet?" Lee whispered as the AD called "Action!"

"Not you too?" She whispered back. "Zero progress. Christian doesn't trust me. I think perhaps I'm the wrong person for this job."

Lee rubbed his chin and contemplated Christian as he leapt down the stairs chased by a half dozen uniformed guards. Another group of guards emerged at the bottom of the stairs. He ducked between them and headed past the camera for the doors.

"Cut and re-set," the AD called.

Christian glanced their way, searching for her. When he spotted Teresa he crooked a finger at her. With an apologetic shrug to Lee, she followed the summons. But not before she caught Lee's low chuckle. "You're the perfect person for the job. You just need to work it."

He would get along great with her father.


The film caterers cooked in a mobile kitchen but the meals were served in what had once been the servants' hall. It was a vast, draughty room, though definitely warmer than eating outdoors, where the food was cold before it even reached the plate. A cloud of richly scented warmth hit Teresa as she and Lee entered the room.

"Like an army, we march on our stomachs," he said, grabbing a tray and joining the buffet queue.

"Would you like to go ahead, Ms Adler?" The person ahead of them in the queue asked. He was one of the set runners, fresh out of film school and one of the few locals employed on the production.

She shook her head and smiled. "I can queue like everyone else."

Lee's eyebrow arched. *"Do you get that often?"* he mouthed at her.

She shrugged. Didn't everybody?

She watched in envy as Lee loaded up his plate full of rich boeuf bourguignon and Parisienne potatoes, and a generous helping of cheesecake on the side, while she settled for a much more modest bowl of lamb tagine and salad.

"What do you men do with everything you eat?" she asked enviously.

"Who exactly do you mean by *we men*? I can't speak for anyone else, but me, I just have good genes."

She'd been thinking of Christian, but she didn't think good genes alone would account for the sculpted abs. He looked like a man who worked out, though she couldn't figure out when he found the time. Unless he never slept, which would certainly account for his morning moods.

Robbie waved them over to join him at his table. "So you've survived your first week?" he asked Teresa with a cheerful grin as she took the seat across from him.

She shrugged. Survival was a relative thing. Some of Christian's more bizarre demands made the political sharks she'd met seem like pussy cats. Though she was beginning to suspect his diva behaviour was purely for her benefit.

"Film people are nothing like I expected," she said instead.

"Oh?" Robbie raised his eyebrows.

"Everyone's so friendly and unpretentious. And you're all very accepting." Tolerant was the word she'd wanted to use, but that would be like admitting the people she mixed with were intolerant of anyone different from themselves.

What had Christian said about the narrow world she lived in?

She brushed away the thought. Her social circle might be small, and filled with people exactly like her, but she would have been much more useful at today's ladies' luncheon at the club to discuss

67

the next charity fundraiser than fetching and carrying all day for Christian.

"In this last week I've met film crew of every nationality, from all sorts of backgrounds, and none of that matters here. No one here cares where you've come from, only what you're doing right now," she said.

Robbie nodded. "I guess we're all so focused on the jobs we're here to do that all the other bullshit gets checked at the door."

Lee rested his elbows on the table and leaned forward as if sharing a juicy secret. "Did you know that the hunky assistant grip used to be a stockbroker before he burned out and started this as a new career?" He laid a hand over his chest. "Buff and brainy. Be still my beating heart... and speaking of buff and brainy... "

Tessa followed Lee's gaze to where Christian and Dominic had entered the room and joined the lunch queue.

"Which one?" she teased, and Lee sent his gaze heavenward, praying for patience. He'd already made it clear he was a card-carrying member of the Christian Taylor fan club.

"It's such a treat working with him," Robbie said around a mouthful of tagine, "Christian's one of the truly great actors."

Not him too.

Seeing her scepticism, Robbie waved his fork in the air as he explained. "Most actors, when you walk them to set, they don't talk to you. They're already in that zone where they're preparing to get into character. Christian stays himself right up until that moment he walks on set. Then it's like he flicks a switch and he becomes someone else. That's a rare talent."

Where she came from, that wasn't called talent. Sociopaths could also be charming and duplicitous.

Robbie's fervour mounted. "He's wasted in these action and special-effects movies. I'd love to see him do something with real meat in it."

"I'll remember to tell him that," Teresa said.

Robbie completely missed the dryness of her tone. His face lit up. "Would you? A friend of mine's written a script I think he'd be perfect for. It's a little different from his usual stuff, though. Could you get him to take a look?"

She doubted Christian would follow any advice she gave, but she bit back the comment. "No promises, but I'll give it a try."

She seemed to be saying that a lot today.


"Who *is* that guy?" Christian scowled at the flustered catering assistant attempting to dole more salad onto his plate.

"What guy?" Dom asked, craning his neck to look.

"The pretty boy next to my assistant." He really didn't intend the *my* to sound quite so possessive. But it did. His scowl deepened.

"That's Lee. One of the art directors. Apparently he's an accomplished set designer too. Talented young man."

Christian grabbed a napkin, knife and fork from the dispenser at the end of the buffet and made a beeline across the room, leaving Dom to catch up.

"May I have a seat?" He pulled out the vacant chair beside Teresa and smiled at the group around the table.

"Of course." The blonde hunk with the ill-concealed biceps on the other side of Teresa smiled and gave Christian the once-over. "Any time!"

Christian relaxed. Pretty Boy was no competition.

"I'm Christian." He leaned forward to offer his hand to Lee. His elbow brushed Teresa's arm and she shifted away. Or attempted to. There was nowhere for her to go. "And you're Lee, the set designer."

Lee preened as he shook Christian's outstretched hand. "Strictly speaking, I'm only one of the art directors."

"But very talented. I've heard good things about you."

Dom, in the process of sitting down across the table, choked on a laugh.

"Oh damn, is that the time?" Robbie pushed out his chair and rose. "We're back on set in five, everyone," he called to the room at large. Then he turned back to Christian. "We're moving the camera to the top of the stairs. We're going to be at least an hour, so take your time."

Christian nodded, and Robbie excused himself to head back to work.

"So how do you two know each other?" Christian asked, waving his fork from Teresa to Lee.

"We met through Kenzie."

It took him a moment to place the name. The freckle-faced redhead who'd brought Teresa to the wardrobe room. "The new girlfriend of Teresa's ex-boyfriend. How cosy."

Lee pushed his empty plate away and rubbed his stomach. His phone, on the table beside him, beeped a text message and he glanced at it. "Damn. I'd love to stay and chat, but I've got places to go and people to see." He rose and grinned at Christian, flashing his dimples.

Christian smiled back. "It's been a pleasure. We should do this again soon."

Lee winked, patted a hand on Teresa's shoulder in farewell, and headed off.

Teresa rounded on him. "Do you have to flirt with everyone?"

"That wasn't flirting." He held her gaze and smiled, then ran a finger over the back of her hand, where it lay on her lap. She shivered. "This is flirting."

The colour rose up beneath her pale porcelain skin, a wash of rose-pink staining her throat and her cheeks. But it took barely a heartbeat for her to regroup. Her eyes narrowed, turning to chips of burning blue ice, and he removed his hand.

She rose from her seat, all smooth grace and repressed emotion. "I'll be re-stocking your trailer fridge if you need me." Then she turned on her heel and walked away.

Damn. Any other woman would have been willing to sacrifice her firstborn after he gave them The Look. But not Teresa. She was so tightly wound, nothing he did could penetrate the armour. What would it take to get under her skin, to make her *feel*?

70

Her over-organised little life needed a good shake-up almost as much as she needed the volcano to blow. Almost as much as *he* needed the volcano to blow.

Dom's laughter brought him back to the present. "You're losing your touch, dude!"

Christian threw his napkin at him, but it didn't help. Dom was still laughing.

# Chapter 6

The next day Christian was due to wrap by mid-afternoon so his publicist had filled his rare spare hours with press interviews.

Not only did the first journalist arrive early but filming ran late, an-all-too frequent occurrence on film shoots. Tessa gave the young woman and her cameraman a guided tour of the set and made small-talk until Christian was ready. She breathed a sigh of relief that they represented a British TV breakfast show and didn't have a clue who she was.

She took them to the craft station, offered them tea and biscuits, and mentally ran through the brief Pippa had given her.

1. *Four interviews, each one to be half an hour only, including setting up lights and cameras. Not a second more.*
2. *They're there to talk about his last movie. No spoilers of the new one allowed.*
3. *No questions about his personal life. They ask any of the questions on the attached list, the interview is over.*

Tessa had memorised the list of banned topics. Christian's family and his childhood (great, that took care of everything she needed to know), his love life, his love life some more, and that incident with the fan in Houston. Tessa didn't think she wanted to know the story behind that one. Whatever it was, it certainly hadn't made it into her father's intelligence report.

"Does he have a girlfriend?" the reporter asked, taking the cup of tea Tessa offered her. She was very pretty, with auburn streaks in her lushly curling dark hair.

"Christian doesn't have girlfriends, he has dates."

"What's he like to work for?"

"Milk or lemon with your tea?"

After the third question the reporter gave up.

At four o'clock on the dot, Tessa knocked on the door of Christian's trailer. "May we come in?"

"Yeah, come on in."

The brunette reporter's lips curled in an eager smile as she heard his voice. Tessa couldn't blame her. Christian's voice was deep and sexy as hell at the best of times, but when he added that come-hither tone…

Tessa swung the door open and held it wide for the cameraman to get his gear inside. The door opened straight into a compact kitchenette. To the left was the living-room area, the bedroom on the right. The door to the bedroom was closed and there was no sign of Christian.

"Make yourself at home," he called, his voice muted by the bedroom door.

The cameraman set up his camera for the best angle, and the reporter arranged herself provocatively before it. Spacious as the trailer was, once all their gear was in, there wasn't much space left, so Tessa ducked into the kitchenette and tried to make herself inconspicuous.

What character would Christian choose to play for the interview – smooth and charming, playful and teasing, or intense and brooding? He did all of them so well.

The bedroom door opened behind her back. From the reporter's gasp and the way her eyes dilated at sight of him, Tessa guessed Christian was in the mood for fun.

She was right. He strode past her and she could appreciate the other woman's gasp. If she hadn't been as self-controlled as she was, she would have gasped too.

He'd clearly stepped straight out of the shower. His short, spiky hair glistened with droplets and he wore nothing but jeans, slung low on his hips. The trailer wasn't exactly cold, but it was cold enough. His nipples were as hard as his abs.

He looked like a god – and he knew it.

Tessa swallowed, mouth dry, throat choked. She'd never considered herself a woman of wild sexual appetites – she was above all that – but if he'd asked her in that moment, she doubted she'd be able to say "no".

Luckily he wasn't even looking at her.

"Hi, I'm Christian." He held out his hand to the reporter, who took it gingerly. She looked dazed. Tessa hoped she found her tongue again before their half hour was up.

He smiled at the woman, holding her gaze. "Should I put a shirt on for the interview?"

It was the cameraman who finally answered. "If you're not too cold, it'll suit the part," he said gruffly.

Christian sat where the cameraman showed him and smiled at the camera, that smouldering public smile Tessa was learning to distinguish from his far more natural impish one.

She crossed her arms over her chest, leaned back against the refrigerator, which was about as far out of his line of sight as she could get, and tried to pull herself together. Sensible, unemotional, unaffected Teresa still had to be inside her somewhere.

"What would you like to ask first?" Christian prompted the reporter.

The young woman cleared her throat, glanced at her clipboard and asked the first question.

The to-and-fro of question and answer was mildly interesting. Christian's answers were about as shallow as a petrie dish, but he added enough banter – and flirtation – to keep the reporter eating out of the palm of his hand.

"In your last movie you played a Roman gladiator. What sort

of training did you do for the role?"

"I trained for six hours a day with a master swordsman. It was gruelling but it was so worth it. Do you want me to show you a few moves?"

The interviewer declined with a giggle, and Tessa sighed. No wonder Christian's ego had been punctured the night they met if this simpering was what he was used to.

"Tell us how you got your break in acting."

"I was at a party in Hollywood and this guy comes up to me and says 'How would you like to be an actor?' I thought he was pranking me, but it turns out he was Steven Spielberg."

"Who is your role model?"

"Working with Steven was just such an incredible experience that I'd have to say he's my idol."

"What is your favourite holiday destination?"

"I really like sunshine and warmth, so without a doubt it has to be the Bahamas."

"Time's up," Tessa announced brightly as the minute hand on her watch clicked over onto the half hour.

The next journalist was already waiting, under the watch of a not-so-patient Robbie. He bounced from foot to foot. "I have real work to be doing," he whispered to Tessa.

"Lucky you," she whispered back.


Fun though it was to watch Teresa work so hard *not* to ogle him, while she was out of the trailer Christian slipped on a shirt.

This next interview was for a French magazine and they would use pre-approved photos supplied by his publicist, so there were no cameras. Even if there were, he'd suffered enough for his art. He had the heating cranked to the max, but the trailer was still bloody cold.

Not that the shirt made much difference to his next interview. The next reporter Teresa ushered in was just as speechless at the sight of him. The novelty had worn thin years ago.

He suppressed a sigh and switched on the charm, but being charming took more effort than usual. The woman's heavy perfume made his nose itch. He'd grown used to Teresa's softer, understated scent.

"How did you prepare for your role as a gladiator?" she asked.

"I did an army boot camp for three weeks before filming began. It was one of the toughest roles I've ever prepared for, but it was an incredible experience. I really learned a lot about myself in those three weeks."

"You were a stunt man before you became an actor. How did you make the leap into acting?"

"I was training a lead actor for his role as a professional boxer. He got arrested for driving drunk just before filming started and was sent to rehab, so the director offered me the role."

Over the woman's shoulder he glimpsed Teresa in the kitchenette. Though he resented what she represented, beside these brassy reporters, with their heavy make-up and too-trendy clothes, her style appeared all the more elegant and effortless. He could almost admire her, if only things were different...

"Who is your greatest role model?"

"Nelson Mandela. If I can be just half the man he was, I'll be happy."

He caught Teresa's eye-roll and his mouth quirked in response.

"What is your favourite holiday destination?"

"I really like the cold, so I'd have to say my ideal holiday would be spent skiing. I have a holiday home in Colorado."

When the half hour was over and the reporter showed no sign of letting up, Tessa quietly and firmly ejected her from the trailer. Christian grinned. "That's Germanic precision for you. Who's next?"

The third interviewer – another woman – was from a fashion magazine, and all she wanted to know was where Christian bought his clothes. He had no idea. He recommended she interview his personal stylist. Or she could have interviewed Teresa. She clearly knew how to shop. He hadn't yet seen her wear the same outfit twice.

The fourth was a minor celebrity in her own right, hostess of a local television talk show. Or so Frank had reliably informed him. From the confident way Susanne introduced herself, holding eye contact rather than descending into a gibbering mess, Christian rather thought this interview had potential.

"What training did you do for your last movie?"

Teresa's lips twitched.

"I spent a week with a Roman history professor, who taught me how to use all the weapons of that period. It was fascinating. Ask me anything you want to know about the gladius sword."

Susanne tittered. "Tell me how you got into acting."

Or maybe not. Same questions, same glib answers.

He suppressed a sigh. He'd learned long ago that the media and his fans wanted facts as much as they wanted to know the real him. Which was not at all. They wanted the fantasy of Christian Taylor. They wanted to be entertained, wooed. As long as he gave them what they wanted, they forgave him his outrageous lies. He charmed, he seduced, he smouldered, and they loved him for it.

"I fell completely head over heels in love with this girl who was an actress. She asked me to go with her to an audition one day, to help feed her lines. She was so pissed off that I got a part in the movie and she didn't that she never spoke to me again. She broke my heart."

Susanne sighed, though it sounded more like "aaaw". "If you could be anyone, who would you be?"

Christian looked straight past her to Tessa. "I'd like to have been Albert Schweitzer, for all the humanitarian work he did. I really want to make a difference in the world."

Her expression flickered, caught half way between disapproval and amusement. What would it take to tip the scales? Beneath that prim and proper exterior lay a woman with hidden depths. What would it take to get her to reveal them?

"What is your favourite holiday destination?"

"I'm a bit of a city slicker, so I think for me it's got to be a toss-up between New York or London. I'm all 'bright lights, big city.'"

"You grew up without a father. How did that affect who you are as a person today?"

Tessa stiffened imperceptibly. He smiled for the camera pointed in his face, though it took a little more effort. "Of course it had an impact. But I was blessed with a mother who more than made up for any lack."

Susanne looked down at her notes. "Did coming from a mixed-race background hinder you in any way, or did it spur you on to achieve what you have?"

He gave his scripted answer, the one he'd given a million reporters before her. Forget potential, this interview had descended deep into dull territory. Sometimes he wondered why the reporters even bothered. They could just as easily dig a story out the archives and stick a new picture on it.

But he smiled and held Susanne's gaze until she blushed. She batted her long and very obviously fake eyelashes. "There's a rumour that you weren't born in the States as your official biography states, but that you grew up in the Caribbean. Is that true?"

His smile no longer reached his eyes. Who he'd been before he became Christian Taylor wasn't something he wanted out there for all to see. But if he shut her down, he'd only make her scent blood. She was a reporter after all.

In the moment he hesitated, Teresa spoke. "This interview is over."

"Our time isn't up yet," Susanne said.

"Christian has other appointments."

The reporter pouted. "But that wasn't on the list of no-go questions."

Susanne looked to him for support, but she was looking in the wrong place. Christian shrugged, as if it was out of his hands. *I owe you one, Teresa.*

"Do you know who I am?" Susanne shook back her golden-blonde curls and sent Teresa a look filled with all the superciliousness of someone addressing a menial servant.

Teresa pushed herself away from the counter, her school-marm face on, and for a moment Christian felt sorry for Ms *I'm-a-Celebrity-get-me-out-of-here*. "I'll give you to the count of three. After that I call Simon Beck and we'll see if he knows who you are."

Both reporter and cameraman were out the trailer by the count of two, though the look of pure venom Susanne cast behind her as she exited would have made arsenic curdle.

Christian whistled as Teresa closed the door firmly behind them. "Remind me never to get on your bad side!"

She smiled, softening. "You do. Frequently."

He lazed back on the sofa, an arm slung casually across the back. "Who's Simon Beck?"

"Chief executive of Westerwald's national broadcaster."

"Geez. The way you said his name, it sounded like you have a direct line to him."

"I do." She averted her gaze. "He's my godfather."

"Handy connection." A knot he hadn't known was there clenched in his gut. Of course all these aristocrats knew one another. She probably knew all the rich Westerwald tourists he'd served as a kid, people who hadn't even seen him except to remark on how odd it was to see a boy of mixed race on Los Pajaros. As if he weren't there, as if he couldn't hear. As if he didn't already know.

He knew how it felt to be treated as a servant. He doubted Teresa had ever been spoken to like that before, yet she hadn't blinked at Susanne's lack of courtesy. And to her credit, in the time he'd known her Teresa hadn't once addressed anyone the way Susanne had spoken to her. Teresa's manners were more than skin deep and she noticed people. Perhaps she even noticed too much.

He rolled the tension from his shoulders and rose. She probably also knew all the gossip of Westerwald's upper echelons of society.

Which made her more dangerous than any reporter.

He crossed to the kitchenette, opening the fridge for a bottle of water. Teresa turned away, straightening the items on the spotless kitchen counter. "Is that how it always is? The same questions over and over again? Don't they have the imagination to come up with anything original?"

"There are a few rare interviewers with imagination. Ellen is always a hoot."

He unscrewed the lid and leaned his hip against the kitchen counter beside her, instantly aware of the static hum between their bodies. For once he didn't move away, didn't send her off on some stupid errand just to create a space between them. "If you were the one asking the questions, what would you ask?"

The corner of her mouth kicked up into a smile. "Before or after you kick me out?"

"What if I said I wouldn't kick you out?"

She held his gaze for a moment. God, but she had the most beautiful eyes he'd ever seen, bluer than any sea or sky, with tiny silver flecks that could turn her gaze to ice in a heartbeat.

"Ask me anything," he teased, at his most persuasive.

"Do you know who your father is?"

"Anything else."

She smiled, a slow, playful smile that did something to him he had never experienced before. It took his breath away.

"Why do you flirt with them all? Surely you know it raises their expectations?"

"Does it raise yours?"

She pursed her lips, and the smile was gone. "What's in it for you?"

It gave him grim satisfaction that she hadn't answered. "It gets me fans." He reached into his jeans pocket and pulled out the four business cards that had been slipped to him. One with a heart scrawled on it, another with a handwritten mobile number, the last with a lipstick mark in scarlet, the exact shade worn by

Susanne. "And I'll never be lonely. But that question was way too easy. Try something harder."

Her gaze dropped to the cards in his hands. He fanned them out on the counter and set his hand a fraction of an inch away from hers, deliberately provoking her. He only wished he was still shirtless. The effect of bare male chest on her was priceless, almost as if she'd never seen one before.

But since stripping off would be too obvious, he settled for the next best thing. He leaned closer, invading her space. With any other woman, the lean-in would have been as natural as breathing. With Teresa, the temperature seemed to go up a few degrees and her breath stuttered. She leaned away, but in the tiny kitchenette there was no place for her to go.

Her long eyelashes fluttered and slowly her gaze lifted to meet his.

Though she stood straight, though her expression remained cool and self-possessed, up this close she couldn't conceal what she was feeling.

He'd shaken her composure at last. As she shook his.

"Your time's nearly up. You get one more question."

Her gaze didn't waver. "Who are you really, Christian Taylor?"

*I am whoever you want me to be.* The flippant answer hovered on his tongue, but he held it back. He was tired of trying to be all people to everyone. For just this one moment, he wanted to be honest with someone. He thought for a long moment before he answered.

"I'm a chancer. I'll take every opportunity that's offered to me and I'll do anything if it benefits me."

He'd admitted as much the night they met. Then he'd said it to provoke her. Now he said it because he meant it.

This time there was no accusation in her expression, no judgment. She let out a sigh, as if disappointed in him. "Why?"

"Because I'm never going back to the boy I was."

She didn't push for more. She didn't need to. Her gaze pierced right through him, through all the defensive layers, the layers of deception he'd lived with for so long that even he didn't know where the truth ended and the lies began. She saw straight through him to the hurt and bullied little boy who had brought nothing but heartache to everyone he loved.

But he wasn't the first one to look away.

"You have a date tonight. I'll call for Frank to bring the car around."

To hell with his date. She'd laid him bare to his core, and now she expected him to entertain and amuse some starlet he had no interest in?

"Cancel it."

Her eyes widened, but she didn't argue. She slipped away from him, though she had to brush against him to get past, and pulled her phone from the bag.

He didn't listen as she made the calls for his car and to the starlet's agent to cancel dinner.

What the hell had just happened here?

Thank heavens tomorrow was the film unit's day off. Because he needed time away from Teresa to regroup. He needed to get his head back in the game.

# Chapter 7

"You're quiet today," Anna said, as they left Anton's bridal boutique, the flagship store in his design empire.

Tessa shrugged and climbed into the back of the sedan idling at the kerb. Her father's car, provided less for her convenience than for his.

"Are you missing Stefan?"

Tessa started. Far from missing Stefan, she'd barely thought of him these last few days. She hadn't even called. But then, neither had he. Since he'd left New York for Montreal, she wasn't even sure what the time difference was between them now.

She looked at the bare finger on her left hand. She still hadn't collected her ring from the jeweller's. Something Stefan didn't need to know.

And she still hadn't mentioned her wedding to Christian. Something *he* didn't need to know.

Tessa rubbed the sudden ache in the centre of her forehead and Anna cast her another of the sidelong glances she'd been doing all morning.

"What?" Tessa asked, irritated. "Have I grown horns?"

Anna chuckled. "No, but there is something different about you."

"I'm just tired."

"I've worked for you for three years. I know the way you look when you're tired, and that's not it. You look…edgy. Kind of restless. Are you getting cold feet?"

"Good heavens, no!" What a preposterous thought. Scions of the House of Arelat didn't get cold feet. They made calculated, rational decisions and then stood by them. All but two, and look what had happened to them. Clara Adler had run off with her lover and died an ignoble early death and the other… well, her mother had never been an Adler by birth, only by marriage.

"Are you sure Stefan is the right man for you?"

There was something in Anna's voice, a hesitance, that made Tessa turn and look at her. "Of course I'm sure. There isn't a man more suited to me than Stefan. Why do you ask?"

Anna blushed. "I'm sorry. It's not my place to ask."

Tessa frowned. Of course it was Anna's place. She was more than just an assistant. She was also the closest friend Teresa had. The one person who saw behind the carefully composed image to the person underneath, a person with weaknesses and frailties just like anyone else.

Apart from Anna, the only person who saw her shortcomings was her father, the master at whose knee she'd studied. He was impossible to deceive.

And then there was Christian.

She rubbed her forehead again.

He seemed to have developed an uncanny knack for seeing through her too. Except that he didn't accept her as she was. He used the insight to goad her, to get under her skin.

Like that dig yesterday about being willing to do absolutely anything if it benefited him. He'd meant it… and yet, he hadn't. Hard as he tried to conceal it beneath all the attitude, she'd seen it there in his eyes – Christian had an honourable streak.

"You're doing it again," Anna commented.

"Doing what?"

"Rubbing your forehead. Something's worrying you."

"Of course something's worrying me. I've been summoned

to lunch so I can give a report and I have no new facts to give."

"Then don't give facts. Give your impressions."

Tessa stared at her assistant as if she'd grown two heads. "Impressions?"

"Yes, you know… listen to your gut instincts. I know you never pay the least attention to them, but you have really good instincts about people. You should trust them."

Tessa shook her head. Anna was normally such a rational person. What had gotten into her today? Instincts were as unreliable as following one's impulses. Her father would want facts, not feelings.

The car pulled up outside the gabled brick façade of her father's club. Tessa waited for the valet to step forward and open the car door before she turned to Anna. "Have fun, and please don't let Lee go overboard with hearts."

She climbed out and watched as the car pulled back into the flow of traffic on the wide boulevard. She wished she were going with them. She had no doubt that Lee and Anna would have more fun selecting the décor for her wedding than she would have lunching with her father.


The day off flashed by in a blur. Since he'd ditched his date, Christian hit the town with Dom instead. They'd been mobbed in one nightclub and only escaped thanks to the intervention of Frank and a couple of especially burly bouncers. After that, they'd gone to a far more exclusive and dull-as-ditchwater club, where at least the whiskey had been good, even if the only woman worth flirting with had been the barmaid.

Dom had taken her home.

By the time Christian had gotten over his hangover, half the day was gone and he hadn't known what to do with himself. Dom was still ensconced with the barmaid – at least Christian hoped it was still the same woman – and unavailable, so he'd pulled on a cap and scarf in an attempt to disguise himself and gone out for a walk.

In an effort to clear his head and escape the confines of the hotel, it didn't work.

He found himself heading in the direction of the palace, the only place in town he knew. So he'd turned back and sought sanctuary instead in an old-fashioned movie house.

*To Catch a Thief* was showing.

It had been one of his mother's favourites. After they'd moved to California, in those early days when they'd been cut off from everyone and everything they'd ever known, growing into their new identities, she'd often sat awake late into the night and watched old movies. Sometimes he'd crawl onto the couch beside her and fall asleep tucked into her side.

He'd forgotten how much like Teresa Grace Kelly was in the movie. Imperious, entitled, with a simmering passion beneath her frosty exterior.

So much for clearing his head.

He sat now in the back of the car, cradling his head against another almighty hangover as they headed back to set and back to work.

At least he was only scheduled in two scenes today, which would have been a bonus if he'd been able to sleep in. But no, fate was not so kind. His call time on set was six o'clock. The sky was still dark, the streets slick with black ice. Even with snow tyres, the car slid ominously every time it cornered.

"Remind me again why we're shooting this movie in the bloody middle of winter," he moaned to Dominic, who'd cadged a lift with them.

"Because your dance card is already full and this was the only gap left in your crazy schedule. You're the one who wanted to do this damned movie," Dom reminded him. "I had a long, lazy holiday in sunny Acapulco planned before you decided to take this trip down memory lane."

Christian glared warningly at him, flicking a glance at Teresa in the front seat beside Frank. Dom only shrugged.

"She won't run to the papers," Dom mouthed back at him.

Christian bloody hoped not. The last thing he needed right now were press hounds prying into his past. Any day now, one journalist more intrepid than the others might realise Christian Taylor was a fabrication, with no corresponding birth certificate.

The car turned into the wide, tree-lined boulevard that led to the palace gates, which swung ponderously open at their approach. As always, their arrival was anticipated. Security hardly seemed a necessary precaution for the film shoot these days. The weather had turned bitter enough to discourage even the most determined of fans.

Teresa turned to him. "You have a long break in the middle of the day. Should I make a reservation for you somewhere for lunch?"

Christian shook his head and the world tilted for a moment. He could barely think about breakfast without his stomach roiling, let alone lunch. He sighed and rubbed a hand over his face. "I'm never touching another whiskey again in my life."

"Yeah, if I had a dime for every time I heard you say that, I'd be a wealthy man," Dom retorted.

"You are a wealthy man."

Dom laughed.

Inside his trailer, Christian downed his third espresso of the morning and changed into the costume his stylist had laid ready. Then he stood in front of the long mirror in the trailer's bedroom. He breathed deeply, set his shoulders back, lifted his chin, and put the smouldering trademark smile in place.

Christian Taylor, Movie Star.

*Now* he was ready to face the rest of the world.

He opened the door. In the living-room section, Teresa sat on the couch, legs tucked beneath her. She hummed something lilting and vaguely familiar as she read the *Financial Times*. Her hair was pulled back into its usual neat bun, but a tendril had escaped and curled down the curve of her neck.

His driving force for more years than he could remember had

been the quest for adoration and respect, but in this moment he wanted something new, something different.

He knew the bookies ran odds on who he'd bed next and how soon, but none had ever taken a bet on when he'd settle down in domestic bliss. Christian wouldn't take those odds either. But for half a moment he savoured the scene before him. The two coffee cups on the table, a beautiful woman who looked as if she belonged in his space.

He clamped down on the ridiculous notion as Teresa set down her paper and looked up at him. "You look tired."

His smile slipped. "Don't give me that 'you shouldn't stay out all hours' speech. I know, okay?"

She arched an eyebrow. "I didn't say a thing." Then she grinned, flashing a rare glimpse of impishness. "I don't need to. Marie's waiting in the make-up trailer for you and I know she'll have a lot to say."

*Women!*

It was well after dark that night when Frank pulled up the car beside Christian's trailer. Teresa stifled a yawn as she climbed into the back. Christian slid in beside her, looking far more wide awake than he had any reason to be. He was in almost every scene, worked twelve-hour days, and all he'd done was party away his rest day.

Not that she had rested either. Between the grilling from her father and the hundred and one wedding-related errands, she'd actually looked forward to returning to work so she could recover from the day off.

But being on set was no sinecure for Christian as it was for her. His energy output during the day was staggering. Even when the cameras weren't rolling, he still seemed to be playing a part, cracking jokes, making conversation with everyone from the boomswinger and set runners to the visiting studio executives.

Everyone loved him, but at what cost?

She knew the effort is took to maintain an image, but at least she was able to switch it off in the glorious solitude of her home.

As Frank shut the car door and moved to the driver's side, she asked the same question she asked every night. "Is there anything else you need?"

She braced herself for whatever stupid request Christian would come up with tonight. The white Piedmont truffles had been easy to come by. A DVD copy of some obscure Canadian musical had kept both her and Anna on the phone half the night – though the look on Christian's face when she'd handed it over the next morning had been worth the effort.

"Frank tells me *The Playhouse* is a popular restaurant. Make the reservation for eight thirty."

It *was* popular. Reservations-made-three-months-in-advance popular. But Tessa didn't bat an eyelid. "For how many?"

"Just you and me."

She pressed her lips together. "That would not be appropriate."

"Nonsense. Your job is to keep me happy and tonight I don't want to eat alone. So tonight you keep me company."

When she still didn't answer, he arched an eyebrow. "Do you have other plans, or have you changed your mind about this job? I did make it clear it was twenty-four-seven."

She smiled sweetly. "I'm just surprised you don't have a date tonight. I'll meet you at the hotel at eight."

At least this meant she'd have the opportunity to talk to Christian without someone calling for him to be someplace else. But Anna *did* have a date tonight, so she'd have to take up Lee's offer of help with more than just the décor. He would have to take her place at the meetings with the wedding photographers she'd set up for this evening.

She'd arranged some of the biggest parties this town had seen, and here she was leaving a virtual stranger to plan her wedding. She would have laughed at the absurdity of it if she hadn't been secretly relieved. She was tired of people asking where the groom was.

And tonight she would show Lee that she could work it.

Every morning, Teresa had beaten Christian to breakfast and been ready and waiting when he emerged. So her surprise at finding him waiting for her for once gave him a buzz.

Not that she ever showed much break in her composure, but a week in her company and he'd learned to read the signs. The way her lips pursed in disapproval, the tightening of her jaw when she wanted to say something impolite but couldn't, the small tug at the corner of her mouth when she wanted to laugh but didn't.

There was a powder keg beneath that flawless façade, he was sure of it. And if she didn't release a little of that emotion soon, it was going to blow sky-high.

"You shouldn't be hanging around at the front door," she reproved as the doorman held open the passenger door of her sports car for him. "You might start another riot."

"Yeah, but I knew you'd be here to rescue me again. May I drive?"

She shook her head, and with a grin he got in and closed the door. She put the car in gear and took off. "So how much of this city have you seen?"

"Apart from the palace and getting lost the night we met? Not much."

"We'll take the scenic route, then."

He'd visited Paris a few times. Neustadt was a quarter the size, but it had the same tree-lined boulevards and the same gracefully proportioned buildings. Against the velvet sky the city lights stood out, a rainbow of shimmering colours reflected in the dark river and off the streets, where a thin layer of snow had begun to settle.

"This city is bleak in winter," she said, in full tour-guide mode. "But it's magical in the spring when the cherry trees blossom, and in the summer when the shops stay open late, the sidewalk cafés are full and the river boats are more frequent."

"I can see why my mother loved it here," he said, looking out the window at the light drifts of snow settling on the icy road and turning the cityscape into a sparkling wonderland. He was begin-ning to understand why she'd believed this place to be magical.

"She visited Neustadt?" Teresa kept her eyes on the road, driving cautiously.

He relaxed in his seat and watched her. "My mother studied at the university here on a scholarship, then spent a year working at the palace before she returned to Los Pajaros."

"What did she do?"

"A doctorate in politics and industrial relations, then she got a job as an intern with some sort of think-tank that was trying to bring the unions and employers together."

Until she'd fallen pregnant with him, been dumped and uncer-emoniously thrown out of the country. He shrugged. "She met my father here in Neustadt. I was conceived here."

"How did they meet?"

"I have no idea." He turned away from the window he'd been staring sightlessly out of and faced Teresa. "She never spoke of him. All I know is that he was from Westerwald."

"Not even a name?"

"Least of all a name." Christian sighed. "There's a part of me that hoped by coming here I'd found out who he was. Whether he's alive or dead. But of course that's not going to happen. It's worse than searching for a needle in a haystack because I have nothing to go on."

Teresa slid the car into a narrow parking bay in front of the restaurant and cut the engine. "Maybe I can help."

"How do you figure that?"

"My father works with the government. He has access to infor-mation you wouldn't be able to get on your own."

He processed that for a moment. "He would need some place to start."

"He often says that putting a case together is like connecting the dots. On its own, each piece of evidence is nothing more than a dot, but when you connect them you start to see patterns. We can make a list of anything and everything you remember your mother telling you about her time here. Then perhaps we can start to connect the dots."

Well that should at least take them until their drinks arrived. He shrugged. Why not? This was ancient history and couldn't hurt him, unlike other more recent events. And since she'd signed a non-disclosure agreement along with her employment contract, what harm could come from talking about his past?

# Chapter 8

"It's a pleasure to see you again, Ms Adler."

The *maître d'hôtel* bowed to her and she smiled. "Good evening, Philip."

"Your request for privacy was noted, so instead of your usual table we've seated you in the Royal Box. Please follow me."

She ignored the curious sideways look Christian sent her.

Since the main floor of the restaurant was known as the place to see and be seen in this town, Teresa was immensely relieved when they were led down a wide, completely empty, corridor and through a private door to their table.

The building had once been a theatre and their table was above the main floor. It was used for private functions, and obscured from sight by an elaborate carved wooden screen. They could see without being seen.

She wasn't sure whether she'd taken the precaution for the sake of her celebrity guest or herself. Stefan knew she'd taken this job but most of their acquaintances didn't, and she wasn't in the mood to explain why she was out at a romantic dinner for two with a man who wasn't her fiancé.

And it *was* romantic. Candlelight, rose petals strewn across the starched white-linen table cloth, the soft serenade of strings in the background.

Christian ordered a bottle of one of Westerwald's finest vintages, and the *maitre d'* bowed himself out of the room. It was just the two of them. For a room that was large enough to seat ten comfortably, it suddenly felt very small.

"I'm impressed." Christian lazed back in his chair. "I was told it was impossible to get a booking here."

"It is. But you knew that and you asked anyway. Are you always this demanding of your assistants?"

"No, just you." He grinned, all impish charm. "You said you could get a table in any restaurant. I wanted to see if you'd told me the truth."

She stiffened. "I always tell the truth." Though she'd learned at the feet of the master the many ways to skirt the truth.

She contemplated Christian across the table. He'd made it clear he didn't like aristocrats, and by extension he didn't like her. He needled her at every point. Yet, he'd invited her out to dinner alone tonight. What game was he playing?

She reached into her purse for her moleskin notebook and pen. Hopefully having a task to focus on would make this evening fly faster and stop her from dwelling on other less-comfortable thoughts.

Like how fine he looked tonight. He'd practically disrobed in the coat room, and now he wore nothing more than dark trousers and a dark jacket over a crisp white shirt open at the neck.

She cleared her throat. "Did your mother mention anything about the work she did in the palace?"

"What's the hurry? We have all evening."

Not if she could help it. The box was far too cosy, far too intimate. She couldn't wait to get this evening over with, to get away from that clear blue gaze that seemed so familiar and yet so disquieting at the same time.

Their waiter arrived with the wine, and they placed their food orders. Tessa took a sip, the velvety-red burgundy steadying her nerves. Since she wasn't easily unnerved, this constant state of agitation around Christian was beginning to wear her thin.

After a week in his presence the discomfort level had at least dropped to a low-level simmer. With a little luck, by the time the next two weeks were up he would no longer have any effect on her at all.

With even better luck, her job would be done long before then. Tonight would be good.

"My parents might have worked together." Christian swirled the wine around in his glass and stared into it. "I thought perhaps they met at the palace, though I suppose he might just as easily have been a visitor. As I've realised while filming there, the palace is more of a corporate HQ than a royal residence. There are a lot of people coming and going all the time."

In her head she scrolled through the list of questions her father had made her memorise. His people had already interviewed as many of his mother's former colleagues as they could find, and none had known a thing about Connie Hewitt's personal life. Or if they knew, they weren't telling.

"When did your parents meet?"

"In the spring the year before I was born. Their affair lasted through the summer. By Christmas she was home in Los Pajaros, in disgrace. No job, no husband. Just me a few months later."

"How did her family take it?"

He shrugged and set the wine glass down. "Her father was already dead. Her younger brother, my uncle, was now the head of the family. Though he'd benefited from the money she sent home for his education, he said she brought dishonour on the family and refused to acknowledge her. The only person who stood by her was my grandmother."

*She sent money home? How much?* Teresa scribbled in her notebook.

"Are you still in touch with any of your family?"

He shook his head. "My grandmother died a few months before we left Los Pajaros, and my uncle… we never spoke to him again

95

after we moved to the States."

"You said you worked for him as a kid."

His lips tightened and he took a long draft from his glass before he answered. "He made a deathbed promise to my grandmother that he'd look after us. So he gave me a job. It didn't work out."

There was a whole lot more to it than that. She didn't need the elevated tension around the table to tell her that. It was in the hard, uncompromising look in his eyes.

She changed the subject. The secrets she needed to uncover didn't lie in the islands.

"What sort of things did your parents do together?"

"Aside from the obvious?" Christian laughed, but it sounded forced. He closed his eyes as he tried to remember. "They spent a weekend at some castle upriver. It was surrounded by vineyards."

That was no help. There were at least eight castles along the river where it ran through the hills. More than half had been converted into hotels and all of them were surrounded by vineyards. But she made a note in her notebook anyway.

"Did she mention any of her colleagues? Anyone she was particularly close to, or anyone she was afraid of?"

Christian frowned, and she couldn't blame him. It was an odd question. But her father needed to know not only what his mother had stolen from the palace, but who she'd done it for. *Why* was of no importance to him, unless it could help determine who had bullied, blackmailed or seduced her into doing it.

"Not that I know of. She had a mentor she spoke of once, an older man who'd been one of her industrial relations professors in university. I think it was he who got her the position at the palace."

She jotted down a note. "Do you know his name?"

"Alexander Wolff."

Her breath caught. Stefan's father. It wasn't possible he and Connie could have… no, that would make Stefan and Christian… She downed half her glass of wine before she added the name to her notebook.

96

"But he wasn't my father."

She looked up. "What makes you so sure?"

"Because I asked my mother and she said 'no'."

"And you believe everything she told you?"

"She never lied to me. Unless you count the one about Santa Claus, but every parent lies about Santa, don't they?"

No, they didn't. Her father could be economical with the truth when it served him, but he'd never been one for sugar-coating things either. The Santa gifts under the tree had stopped the day her mother left home. Two weeks before Christmas.

More wine.

The waiter arrived with their first course, topped up their wine glasses, and withdrew. Tessa forced away her bitterness and concentrated on the food.

As they ate, Christian spoke about his mother, about the stories she'd told him of Westerwald. The history and the legends. Ice-skating in the winter, hiking in the forests in the summer. Student wine-tastings and late-night study sessions.

She'd had friends, that much was clear, but she'd never mentioned them, and she hadn't kept contact with a single person after she'd left Westerwald.

Most of what he told her was irrelevant to what she needed to know, but she let him talk. She had the feeling he never spoke about his past and she'd opened a floodgate.

By the time their main course arrived, she'd built a picture of the bright young woman who'd been set for a meteoric career until she'd met a man and succumbed to single motherhood.

It was an age-old story, but still there were things that didn't add up. Tessa kept her reservations to herself and made a mental note to ask her father to dig deeper.

During their desserts and coffee, Christian spoke of his child-hood in Los Pajaros, growing up rejected and alone. His bitterness coloured every memory.

There was so much about his life she would never understand.

She had never known how it felt not to belong or to be judged on the colour of her skin. Never having known anything but privilege, she would never know how hard he'd fought for his success.

But he had fought and succeeded. Those years had made him the man he was today. Strong, fearless, determined. And she admired him for it.

Christian attempted to empty the last dregs of the bottle of burgundy into her glass, but she covered it with her fingers. "I'm driving, I can't drink anymore."

She might be within the legal limit, but her head was fuzzy enough. Almost fuzzy enough to let her guard down, and that couldn't happen.

Christian grinned and removed her fingers, filling up her glass. "I'm sure your father the judge can bail us out if we get drunk. Or are you worried Daddy might think the big bad playboy American is leading his perfect little daughter off the rails?"

Though he meant it as a joke, he could have no idea how close he was to the truth. Her father had even less reason to trust fickle actors than she did. "It's not my father I'm worried about as much as the papers. *Christian Taylor in drunk-driving arrest* as a headline in the morning news will not please your publicist."

*Teresa Adler found drunk in company of Hollywood actor* would be more likely and infinitely worse. Though her father could be trusted to find a way to spin it in their favour, he would not be pleased either. The Arelat name could not be besmirched.

"At least it'll give Pippa something to do to earn that generous retainer I pay her," Christian said.

"Not to mention it would probably land me out of a job. Speaking of which, shouldn't you be learning lines, or something? Don't you actors ever need to prepare?"

He rolled his eyes. "I have an eidetic memory. Do you take everything so seriously?"

"Do you take *anything* seriously?"

"I'm being serious now." He took her hand across the table and refused to let it go when she pulled away. "Thank you for your help. Even if the trail is cold and I can't find out anything more about my father, you've shown me tonight that I knew a great deal more about my parents than I realised. In fact, I think we should celebrate. We need champagne."

He let go of her hand and she was almost disappointed. There was something magical in Christian's touch, something she'd never experienced before. As if the world had been painted in shades of grey until the moment he touched her. Then the room had suddenly lit up in technicolor.

She nursed her hand. This wine must be more potent than she realised. She'd definitely had enough. "No champagne," she said firmly.

"Yes, ma'am!" Christian leaned back in his chair. "It seems crazy now, but I thought perhaps my mother named me for my father and that would be a clue. It was only after I arrived here that I realised just how common the name Christian is in Westerwald."

"The previous Archduke was named Christian. A lot of our generation were named after him. In this next generation every second boy will most likely be called 'Max' after our new Archduke."

His gaze fixed on her. This was what made people love him. When he looked at you, he really looked. As if you were the only person in the world for him in that moment.

"How does Prince Fredrik fit into all this? I met him the night of the welcome drinks at the palace. He wasn't very friendly." He frowned. "He's Max's older brother, right? Shouldn't he be the new Archduke?"

She was the first to look away. She fiddled with the stem of her wine glass. "Fredrik was a bastard."

"He wasn't popular?"

"Not like that. He was… " Oh lord, there really was no way to say this without summoning that familiar pang, the regret for everything that had changed so irretrievably. "He was disinherited. It turned out he wasn't Archduke Christian's legitimate child."

"Seems there was a lot of that going around Westerwald at the time. Does *he* at least have any idea who his real father was?"

"I never asked," she replied at her driest.

Christian grinned, and she squirmed. There was mischief in his eyes, as if he saw way more than he should. She fought back the urge to blush and composed herself.

"Europe in the 80s was not so backward that your mother's career would have been over because she was pregnant. Why did she leave and go back to Los Pajaros, where being an unwed mother is about the worst thing one can be? Why didn't she stay and raise you here?"

His gaze hardened, all the mischief gone. "Would it have really been any different? I still wouldn't have belonged here, in your neat, white world."

She flinched at the word, though she knew he wasn't talking about race. He was talking about Westerwald's society. Tolerant, but only to a certain extent. Unlike their neighbours, this little nation remained frozen in a bubble, where the old hierarchies, the traditions, were still deeply entrenched. It was a society in which her father, Stefan, Max, could pursue a career, but in which she was expected to be nothing more than be an ornament. At least she was determined to be a useful ornament. Marriage to Stefan would enable her to do more than serve meals at the soup kitchen.

Like the snow-blanketed streets outside, Westerwald was a perfect, frozen world. But beneath that unblemished surface lay the cold, hard realities of stone, concrete, asphalt.

She and Rik had talked about changing things when he acceded as Archduke. Max and Phoenix were equally determined.

But the changes would be too late for someone like Christian.

She shook her head. "You might not have belonged, but you wouldn't have been bullied as you were. Your mother would have had a good job and a good income."

He leaned forward, his elbows on the table, and his eyes burned with that intense look he got sometimes that made her hot and shivery. She shivered now.

"My mother was forced out. Her work permit was rescinded and she was deported. I once heard her say she had to leave because her pregnancy was found out. It was such an odd thing to say that I've always remembered it. She had to leave *because she was found out*. By who – my father? By her boss?" He sighed, frustrated, and ran his hands through his hair. "Did my father have her deported to avoid the embarrassment of a mixed-race child?"

Tessa closed the notebook. She didn't need to write this down. She wouldn't forget.

*Because she was found out*. She had an uneasy feeling that it wasn't a pregnancy his mother had been talking about. But who had driven her out and why?

Her next question wasn't one on her father's list. It was also the toughest question to ask. "Do you think your father might have been married?"

Christian stared past her, through the screen to the vast space of the auditorium beyond. "I've considered it, but I don't think so. My mother wasn't that kind of person. I don't believe she would have had an affair with a married man."

Not knowingly, not intentionally. But even good people made mistakes.

"And you're sure your father knew about you?"

He pulled his focus back onto her. "He must have. I can't see my mother sneaking off without telling him he was going to be a father." He sighed and rubbed a hand over his face. "I always thought he dumped her when he found out she was pregnant, but I guess it's possible he didn't know."

He sprawled in his chair, the energy ebbing out of him. He looked tired, not in that still-half-asleep way he had in the mornings, but bone weary.

"It must take a lot of energy being you," she commented. It was the first thing she'd come to admire and respect in him this past week. She felt tired just keeping up her own façade. How much more difficult, then, for Christian, who not only had to live up to his movie-star image, but had to do it while wielding a sword or dodging punches or leaping down stairs? Or into moving cars.

His gaze met hers, and she looked straight into the face of honesty. This was the real Christian Taylor. Not the laugh-a-minute performer who kept the crew entertained on and off camera. Just a man trying to live up to the world's expectations.

And no one understood that as much as she did.

She toyed with the stem of her still-full wine glass and asked the last question on her father's list. "Why did you leave Los Pajaros and move to the States?"

The shutters came down. It was so instantaneous that she blinked. Then he smiled, and it was the glossy, charming smile that adorned a million magazine covers. "Why does everyone move to the States? In pursuit of the American Dream."

He was lying. As he lied to every reporter who interviewed him, even to the people he worked with. She should feel grateful he'd shared as much with her tonight as he had. She should, but all she felt was hurt.

"Shall we go?" She pushed her chair out from the table. "I'll get the bill on the way out."

He rose. "I invited you to dinner. It's on me."

She laughed softly. "I think I can stand you for it."

Besides, this dinner was worth every cent. He'd given her something new to tell her father. Not that it was of any use in tracking down how his mother came into possession of the Waldburg ring, but enough for her sixth sense to be screaming that there were secrets buried deep here. And where there was smoke, there was inevitably fire.

When they reached the coat room, the restaurant manager himself came to meet them. "I am so sorry," he said, rubbing his hands together in anxiety. "I have no idea how word got out, but there's a crowd waiting for you outside the entrance. Not just fans, but paparazzi too."

Tessa caught Christian's gaze. "The only way to the car is through them. We can wait and hope they give up, or we can go out there and face them." Already she could see Christian gearing himself up, pulling on his energy reserves so he could smile for the fans and make small-talk. She'd seen him do it on set with visitors, making time to speak to each person individually, to sign autographs and pose for pictures. But he was tired and he deserved one night just to be himself.

"There's a third option." She turned to the manager. "You have a back door?"

He nodded. "The staff entrance through the kitchen. It comes out into an alley. But any car turning in there is sure to be spotted by the crowd outside."

She pulled her phone out of her purse and hit speed dial. "Frank, we need help. Can you meet us on the Old Bridge in fifteen minutes?"

She nodded and put the phone away. "He can make it in twenty." She looked at Christian. "Two people leaving the staff entrance are less likely to attract attention than a car. Are you willing to risk it?"

He glanced towards the main entrance. They could hear the raised, shrill voices from there. "Risk is my middle name."

The manager led them down a narrow corridor that smelled of fried onions and garlic, then through a bustling, crowded kitchen.

"No one sees anything," the manager shouted in local dialect to the staff who'd stopped what they were doing to gawk. "Back to work!"

The noise and bustle resumed, and the manager let them out through a back door into the alley. In spite of the cold, the reek of decaying rubbish hung in the air.

"I am so sorry," the manager said again, before pulling the metal door closed behind them.

Christian looked at her and laughed. "Welcome to my glamorous life."

They walked to the end of the alley. Ahead of them, the river

103

glittered silver in the moonlight. Tessa peeked around the corner, towards the crowd huddled outside the restaurant's main entrance, heedless of the snow falling softly but steadily all around them. No one looked their way.

Her heart picked up its beat as adrenalin coursed through her. She'd never done anything like this before. The thrill was strangely invigorating.

"We turn right, then about a hundred metres further on the left there's a flight of stairs down to the walkway along the river. It'll most likely be deserted at this time of night," she whispered.

Christian nodded. Then they stepped out into the main road and turned right, walking at an unhurried pace. There was no cry of alert, no footsteps chasing after them. They found the stairs and descended to the level of the river. The walkway was indeed deserted.

Christian breathed out a sigh of relief. "Thank you."

She shrugged, trying to appear composed even as her pulse still raced with adrenalin. She prayed the falling snow would obscure their footprints.

"It's my job to keep you happy, isn't it?" No way was she going to admit that sneaking out had been fun.

Nevertheless, he laughed softly, sounding pleased, as if he'd won some sort of victory over her. "So where do we go now?"

"Frank will meet us on the bridge." She gestured to the shadowy stone arches ahead.

They walked slowly along the river's edge in silence, their breath creating wispy clouds in the frosty night air. From downriver music floated on the icy breeze that wrapped around them, a soft, romantic ballad. In spite of the cold, it was a perfect night, like something out of an old black-and-white movie.

When they reached the bridge, they climbed another flight of stone stairs. There was no sign of Frank yet, so they walked half way across to lean on the stone parapet and wait.

A near-empty taxi boat passed beneath them, gliding through

the darkness, and the cathedral bells began to peel in the distance, solemnly announcing midnight. She hadn't realised it was so late. The evening had flown by.

"This city *is* magical," Christian said, staring across the water to the illuminated façade of the magnificent Gothic cathedral. The cathedral where, on Valentine's Day, she'd be walking down the aisle.

Stefan was due back in a few days. How was she going to explain to him that she hadn't made time to collect his ring?

She could have sent Anna to collect the ring any time this last week. Should have. She didn't know why she hadn't.

Perhaps because if she had the ring she would have no excuse not to wear it. And if she wore it…

How was she going to explain to Christian that she had a fiancé who might want more than two minutes of her time? Or that in three weeks she was getting married? Why that even bothered her, she had no idea.

"This is a winter wonderland, and we have it all to ourselves." Christian's voice rang deep and resonant in the still night air, an actor's voice, trained to seduce.

He stood close enough that she could feel his solid warmth, and smell the musky scent of his aftershave. She wanted to lean into him, to bury herself in his warmth and his smell.

She commanded her body not to be seduced by either sound or scent, and looked out over the river. Anywhere but at him. "You should see this city before Christmas, with the market stalls lined up on the river bank and carol singers everywhere. Or in the summer, when there's music and dancing and beer." She smiled. "Lots of beer."

"I'll have to come back in the summer. I can see why you don't want to leave."

She breathed in deeply, relishing the sting of the icy air as it filled her lungs, crisp and clean. Perhaps it was all the wine she'd drunk. Or perhaps it was the way his warmth seemed to draw her in, but she wanted to be as honest with him as he had been with her tonight. "Yes I love it, but you were right."

"Of course I am. About what in particular?"

"I haven't left Westerwald because I'm afraid." Holidays in Greece or Spain didn't count. She'd never been away from her homeland for more than a few weeks.

But Stefan was a diplomat. He could be posted abroad for months or even years at a time. She wanted to go, she wanted to see the world, yet at the mere thought of leaving the frightened knot in her stomach stretched tight.

She'd never discussed her fear with Stefan. Or with Fredrik.

Christian leaned his elbow on the parapet beside her, moving even closer, into her personal space. She fought the urge to shift away.

"Afraid of what?"

Afraid that if she left she wouldn't come back. Afraid that without her security net, she'd crash and burn, as her mother had. "I can't leave my father."

"What does your father have to do with anything? You're a grown woman."

She drew in another deep breath of the steadying chill air. Its bite seared her throat. It was on a night much like this that her mother had left. It had been snowing and the ground was white. Tessa remembered padding out after her mother, dressed in nothing but her pyjamas, the ones with the pink rabbits on them, and her thick bed socks, crying to know where her mother was going.

Amalie had stood on the street corner, that same one where Christian had done his flying leap into her car a little over a week ago, and she'd blown Tessa a kiss. Then she'd picked up her suitcases and turned the corner, passing out of sight.

It was the only memory she had left of her mother and it wasn't a happy one.

It had only been the two of them ever since, the workaholic father and the lonely child. If she left, he would be truly alone.

And what would she have?

So she would create a new family, for the both of them, and she would never be lonely again. And one day, hopefully soon, when she had children of her own, she would cuddle them lots. She would make up for every hug she'd never had.

She shook her head. When she spoke again, her voice sounded oddly calm for the amount of emotion coursing through her. "My mother didn't die. She left us. This country was too small for her. *We* were too small for her. She had big dreams and she wanted to fly. So she flew. And she never came back."

"And in return you clipped your wings, too afraid to fly."

She didn't need Christian to state the obvious. Just as she'd never needed some therapist to tell her that she'd played it safe ever since. She stayed home and didn't make waves because she was afraid of the fall-out, of tarnishing the family name and her own reputation, of disappointing her father. Of losing what little security she had left. And what was wrong with wanting to avoid all that?

"My father needs me," she said.

"You can't live your life to please someone else. What is it you want to do with your life?"

Until recently, she'd had a very clear idea of what she wanted for her life. She'd had it all mapped out. The perfect husband, the perfect house, the perfect family. An extension of the life she lived now, all neatly tied up with a big fat bow.

She was mere weeks away from achieving everything she wanted. So why did it feel so hollow? Why did she wake in the night in a cold sweat, feeling trapped and wanting to break free? She didn't even know what she wanted to break free from or where she wanted to go.

Tessa dug her frozen hands into the pockets of her camel cashmere swing coat, but it didn't help. She'd left her gloves in the car. But the cold seemed to be coming from the inside out. She took her hands out of her pockets and blew on them.

"That's the difference between you and me," she said. "I don't think only about myself."

Christian took her hands in his. He wore no gloves either, but his hands radiated heat. "You're cold as ice." He massaged her numb fingers. Slowly life crept back into them.

And feeling. More feeling than she could cope with. She shut her eyes and blocked out the onslaught of emotion.

When she opened her eyes, she wished she hadn't. Christian's penetrating gaze was focused on her, and the understanding in their depths nearly undid her. Why did he have to look at her like that, as if he was trying to see inside her? Why couldn't he be like other people and keep his distance?

She knew what people called her behind her back. The Ice Queen. But didn't they know… ice was brittle. The slightest heat, the slightest pressure, and it cracked.

Her father was a strong man, a proud man, but they were so very much alike. Only she knew just how deep the scars of that long-ago winter's night ran. Only she knew that another crack like that and the ice that held them together would shatter.

"Where is your mother now?" Christian asked.

"Buried somewhere in California, I believe. Her dreams didn't quite turn out the way she hoped. She chased an illusion and when it failed her, she turned to drugs. She died of an overdose when I was fifteen."

That was what happened when you thought only about yourself. You earned disgrace and dishonour. Amalie had lost her family, her friends, her social position and her wealth – and for what? An acting career that had never materialised.

That was not a mistake Teresa would ever make. Dreams were an illusion. Honour and family loyalty were all that mattered.

"I'm sorry," Christian said.

She tossed her hair back. "I'm not. That's what happens when you chase your own immediate gratification. She got what she deserved."

She pulled her hands out of Christian's. They were no longer frozen. But without Christian's touch the numbness returned. She welcomed it.

It was better to be frozen than to feel.

# Chapter 9

"You look like hell. Anyone else tell you that yet today?" Dominic popped the top off a beer bottle and handed it to Christian.

It was after lunch and they were stretched out on the sofas in Christian's trailer waiting to be called to set for their big duel scene. Christian would do his own stunts, and Dom would stand in for the movie's arch villain, a classically trained British actor who fenced but baulked at their more rough-and-tumble style of sword-fighting.

"Only you. Everyone else tells me I'm gorgeous."

"It's my pleasure. That's what friends are for."

Christian swigged from the bottle. "I haven't been sleeping well lately." More accurately, he hadn't been sleeping at all.

Every time he closed his eyes, he dreamed of long pale legs wrapped around him, and the only way to take the edge off the thrum in his blood so he could sleep was to hit the gym.

He wasn't sure when this had changed from being a punishment for her to being a torment for him.

Perhaps it had been trusting her with more of himself than he'd shown anyone in years. Or that moment beside the river when he'd caught a glimpse of vulnerability beneath her perfect façade.

Or perhaps it had been every day since, when she'd acted as if that night had never happened. She'd gone back to being distant and professional. He'd gone back to being a pain-in-the-ass movie star.

"Can I ask you something – do you think I'm a good actor?"

Dominic opened another bottle for himself and took a long swig. "As long as I'm working on your pictures, you're the best."

"I'm being serious. The studio wants to sign me up for another project. Want to guess what it is?"

Dominic rubbed his chin as he pretended to think. "Blockbuster superhero movie part twenty-seven?"

"Bingo! As if that hasn't been done before." Christian sighed. "Don't you sometimes feel as if we're just making the same movie over and over again?"

His friend shrugged. "They *are* all the same, but what does it matter? The box office loves you, the studios love you. We're living well off these movies."

"But five years from now, the fans won't even remember the name of this movie."

"Five years from now *I* won't even remember the name of this movie."

"If you've seen one, you've seen them all?"

"Sure." Dominic set his feet up on the coffee table. "What's got into you?"

"Nothing."

"How long has it been since you got laid?"

So long Christian had to think hard to remember. Certainly not since he'd met Teresa, in spite of the dates he'd asked her to set up for him. He wasn't the kind of guy who could make love to one woman while thinking of another. And Teresa had taken to occupying way more time in his thoughts than he was willing to give.

Dominic laughed at his hesitation. "Good on Nina for making you work for it. You're getting way too used to clicking your fingers and having everyone come running."

"Not Nina." Christian clamped his mouth shut, but not before

111

Dom's eyebrows shot upwards.

"Ah, the Ice Queen?"

Christian scowled. He didn't want to feel this way about Teresa. She was one of Them.

Of course, he'd known it from the night they met. That air of superiority she wore like an invisible cloak, the lack of feeling. She belonged to that same set of upper-crust snobs who'd chased his mother out of Westerwald for no other reason than that she'd been an outsider, not one of them.

But even now it didn't take more than a thought to conjure up the vision of that white-blonde hair spread loose and tousled across his pillow and Teresa smiling up at him. Not her usual cool, controlled smile, but that secret one he'd glimpsed so briefly, a look simmering with heat and desire.

He shoved the image away and took a long swig. He needed the alcohol almost as much as Dom did. Most of the time he appreciated his old friend treating him as he always had rather than as a big star. Today wasn't one of those days.

Dom hadn't taken it easy on him because the cameras were rolling, and he'd inflicted more than a few aches and pains during their morning fight sequence. Several hours of gruelling action, for the sake of a few minutes of screen time.

Christian swore and shifted in his seat. Even with the adrenalin still pumping, he ached all over. "Besides, she's not my type."

"All women are your type."

"She never lets herself be real."

"Yeah, and you're a good one to talk!"

"She's one of those bloody aristocrats, looking down her nose at everyone, like some sort of princess."

If that magazine article was right, she'd been well on her way to being one too. She would have been perfect in the part. She already walked as if she owned the world, head high, shoulders back, not giving a damn what anyone thought of her.

"That's your mother's prejudice talking. You can take the boy out of Los Pajaros, but you can't take Los Pajaros out of the boy. Do you have any more excuses?" Dominic took a swig from his beer.

Christian glared at him, but Dominic only laughed. "Have you considered you're just mad cause she didn't fall into your lap, and you're not used to anyone saying no to you these days?"

Had he really become the ultimate cliché, wanting what he couldn't have? Christian shrugged. "She didn't say 'no' because I didn't ask."

"I never knew you to back down from a challenge." Dom leaned forward, elbows on his knees and a twinkle in his eyes. "So ask! Just think – once you've had her, you can go back to getting some sleep."

"It's not that simple. The woman must be made of marble. None of the usual tricks work on her." Either that or he really was losing his touch.

No matter what he did, Teresa remained aloof and out of reach. He'd tried charm. He'd tried arrogance. He'd tried ignoring her and playing hard to get. He'd even tried being friendly. But she still shied away from the slightest casual touch and lingering eye contact didn't work on her either. Teresa barely blinked.

Usually he would have given up by now. No woman was worth the effort, and especially one of her kind. Yet Teresa Adler seemed to have a hold on him. Every day he spent with her, the desire in him burned more fiercely.

With an irrational intensity, he wanted to knock her down from that pedestal she lived on. He wanted to devastate her perfectly coiffed hair and melt the glacier and watch her feel real emotions for just once in her life.

Dominic was right. No one said "no" to Christian Taylor. No one but this uptight Ice Princess, who was so tightly wound she really needed to get laid. And he was more than happy to oblige.

But she was immovable. Impassive. Unreachable.

Dominic swigged from his beer bottle and grinned. They'd known each other long enough that he could read Christian's moods. "Have I taught you nothing? Take the seduction into her corner. What is she interested in and what does she like to do?"

Christian had no idea. Normally on a date, he was the attentive one. Normally he let the woman do all the talking. But Teresa had turned him so inside out he'd spent the entire evening out with her talking about himself. Revealing himself. He had no clue what she liked to do.

"She volunteers for a charity," he offered up.

"Great. Then be charitable. Don't you have that photo op thing at the children's home tomorrow? Take her along with you." Dom stretched out on the sofa. "I'm sure she'd be worth the effort. Those ice queens are usually the hottest once you get them into bed." He grinned. "If you're not interested, I'll take a shot at defrosting her."

"Only if you don't plan to use your limbs again," Christian threatened.

There was a knock at the door and Christian stashed his beer bottle out of sight.

"Come in," he called.

The door opened and Teresa's head appeared, accompanied by a blast of glacial air. "They're ready for you on set." She cast a pointed look at the beer in Dominic's hand. "Should you be drinking that before a fight scene?"

Dominic set the beer can down, looking like the schoolboy who'd been caught smoking behind the bicycle shed. "No, ma'am!"

As she disappeared from sight, pulling the door closed behind her, Christian laughed. "What was that about taking your shot? Chicken!"

"Forget a princess, she's like a bloody school marm." Dominic rose and dusted off his creased trousers. The wardrobe ladies were not going to be impressed, though Christian was sure it wouldn't be for long. No one ever stayed cross with Dom for long.

"Yeah, and I remember too well your school-marm fantasies. But if I catch you so much as laying a finger on her…"

"Yeah, yeah, working limbs and all that." With a grimace, Dom bent and drew one long swig from the beer bottle before heading to the door.

No one knew better than Christian how much Dom needed something to take the edge off the pain these days, and a beer was far sight less harmful than the drugs most stunt men needed to get through each day. Dom often quipped that there were no old stunt men – and he was rapidly getting old.

Dom paused, his hand on the door handle. "Though if you're going to try seducing her, you might consider being a little nicer."

Christian pulled a face. "Nice" wasn't usually what women wanted from him.

Teresa waited for them outside the trailer. On the surface, she'd come a long way since the day they met. The tailored pants suit and pearls were gone, replaced by heeled boots, skinny jeans, figure-hugging sweater, and a fur-trimmed vest jacket.

It took all his effort to pull his gaze off those skinny jeans.

The icy breeze funnelling between the motor homes stung roses to her cheeks and whipped tendrils of hair loose from the knot at the back of her head. She looked younger and a little less untouchable.

And a whole lot more like the woman he saw in his dreams.

Dom was right. He needed the dreams to stop. He needed to get Teresa out of his head and into his bed.

The end of another long week and they'd earned their day off.

Tessa sank back against the car's plush leather upholstery. Her legs felt cramped, but she resisted the urge to stretch them out. She'd discovered Christian had a fascination for her legs, and his admiration didn't do her blood pressure any favours.

Her blood pressure was already sky-high. Christian had unsettled her today, even more than usual. On the surface, he'd still been the same wisecracking livewire on set, but there'd been no pranks and no foolish errands. Almost as if he'd been trying to be *nice* to her.

She shook her head and returned to running through her mental list of all the things she needed to do tomorrow. Her personal to-do list had grown to stupid proportions. She was almost glad Stefan had been forced to extend his business trip. She wouldn't have had time to see him anyway.

As soon as she saw Christian back to his hotel tonight, she was going home for a bath and that bottle of sauvignon blanc chilling in her fridge. And once she'd had at least eight hours' sleep, she'd crack that to-do list, starting with collecting her engagement ring from the jeweller's.

She pulled Christian's schedule from her messenger bag. "You're visiting the state children's home tomorrow morning for a photo op, then you have the rest of the day off. Should I make lunch arrangements for you? Perhaps a trip to one of the vineyards upriver? Most are closed for the season but they'll open for you."

"I already have plans for tomorrow."

She didn't like his smile. It was way too smug. Did it involve a woman? And did she really want to know?

"I'll meet you in the dining room at nine," he said, sounding way too casual.

"*What?*"

"You have something else planned?"

"It's the day off!"

His grin was wicked. "For the film crew. But if I have to work tomorrow, you do too."

If she hadn't been raised better, she'd have sworn. She was Christian's whenever he needed her. So far twenty-four-seven had only meant one dinner out and a few completely unnecessary late-night phone calls giving her instructions he could just as easily have given her the next morning.

She gritted her teeth and nodded politely. She'd signed a contract, so her only option was to quit, and she wasn't doing that until she got what she'd come for – a good look at Christian's ring.

She turned back to the window, though she didn't see much beyond it as she mentally readjusted her plans. She was going to have to ask Anna to fetch her engagement ring after all.

And tomorrow she'd have to figure out how to get what she wanted from Christian, because this needed to end. Now.

When the car pulled up beneath the hotel's portico and the doorman stepped forward, she mustered every ounce of sweetness she possessed. "I hope you don't have any plans for tonight. Your agent sent over a script you need to read. It's in your suite." She smiled. "And he needs to know if you're interested by first thing LA-time tomorrow."

The look on Christian's face mirrored how she felt exactly.


So much for his day off.

The room was still dark. Christian cursed and smacked his ringing iPhone off the nightstand. It hit the ground with an ominous thud. At least the alarm went silent.

Damn. And Teresa had only just arranged this new phone for him.

He pulled the pillow back over his head, but it didn't help. He was awake now. Awake and exhausted.

He groped over the edge of the bed for the phone. It still had signal and he had unread emails. He clicked the email icon. The message from his publicist he deleted without reading. He opened the one from his agent.

Damn! Damn! Damn!

This time, the phone didn't hit the carpet. It ricocheted off the opposite wall with a sickening crunch and this time he didn't care.

He burrowed down under the duvet. The rest of the world could just go to hell.

When he woke again, sunshine had crept through the gap in the curtains and left a streak of wan light across the bed. He rubbed his eyes. He had no idea what time it was or what had woken him, until a shadow crossed the ray of light.

"I thought I was going to have to call Frank to get you up."

Teresa stepped away from the light and his eyes focused on her.

Dressed in dark clothing, with her pale hair tied back, she merged with the shadows.

Triumph licked through him. He'd finally managed to get her into his room.

"How did you get in here?" he managed, lifting his head off the pillows.

"The front desk manager let me in."

Christian shook his head to clear the fog. As rational thought returned, so did his anger. The flicker of triumph dissipated. "I got an email from my agent."

"Oh?" She raised one perfectly sculpted eyebrow.

"He only needed a reply on that script by next week. He seemed really surprised I'd read it already."

"My bad. I must have mixed up my dates."

Like hell. She never got anything wrong.

Teresa smiled angelically. "Did you lose sleep over it?"

That and other things.

He flung back the duvet, enjoying a swift flash of satisfaction as Teresa realised he was naked beneath the bedding. With a sharp gasp she turned away.

He rose from the bed and padded across the carpet to where the hotel dressing gown lay over the back of an armchair. He took his time.

"Your new phone appears to be broken," she said. Her voice sounded strangled and he grinned. Victory Number One.

"Yeah, please could you arrange me another."

"Do you often lose your temper like that?"

"Only when I don't get enough sleep." Though he was well used to getting by on five or six hours of sleep a night, it wasn't the quantity of sleep he craved now but the quality.

He'd had another of those dreams last night. Geez, but this needed to end.

"What are you doing here anyway?"

Maybe he was still dreaming. Though if he were dreaming, he'd dress her in something a little more colourful. Perhaps something the colour of her eyes, rather than her usual palette of browns, greys and beiges.

Today it was all black, which was the closest she'd come to revealing her feelings about working on their day off. Though she'd clearly had other plans for today, she'd set them aside with barely a flicker of emotion. He'd much rather she'd pouted or sworn. At least then he'd have known she felt something. What would it take to make her feel?

"We're late. You don't want to disappoint the children, do you?"

At the thought of the hordes of children awaiting him at the photo op he very nearly turned around and dived back into bed. In his experience, children were cruel, obnoxious creatures, and making nice to them wasn't high on his list of priorities. As his publicist well knew.

He headed to the bathroom and turned on the shower, stepping under the spray only when the steam clouded the shower glass.

Why was Pippa still trying to punish him anyway? Hadn't she enjoyed their time together? She certainly hadn't complained at the time.

When he returned to the bedroom, a towel wrapped around his hips rather than wearing the dressing gown, Teresa had moved to the living room, leaving the door between the rooms barely ajar. She'd laid clothes ready on the bed for him and he suppressed a laugh.

He didn't bother closing the door before he dressed. It wasn't often he managed to ruffle her feathers, and he'd take any advantage he could get.

"I have espresso here for you," she called from the other room. "But it's getting cold and we need to hurry, so you'll have to drink it on the way."

He pulled a sweater on over his shirt and towel-dried his hair, then glanced into the full-length mirror. He usually put more effort in if he knew there'd be cameras waiting for him, but this morning he couldn't be bothered.

He swung the door open and headed straight for the tray on the dining table, grabbing the Styrofoam cup of coffee and completely ignoring the toast and bowl of fruit salad. Teresa still hadn't stopped trying to get him to eat breakfast every morning.

More awake now, he gave her the once-over. No designer chic today, but an-oversized sweater over leggings and fur-trimmed boots.

She tapped her foot impatiently. With her arms crossed over her chest, she was back in school-marm mode. Dom would have got a kick out of that look. But Dom, lucky bastard, was spending his day off skiing with some of the crew.

Christian sipped from the cup, the welcome caffeine shooting through his system. Now he was ready for the day's challenges, the first and foremost of which stood mere feet away.

"Lay on, MacDuff." *And damned be him who first cries "Hold! enough!"*


He'd expected the state children's home to be a brick-and-concrete monstrosity, bleak and uninviting. Instead, it was situated in the snow-clad foothills that surrounded the city, and the cluster of buildings looked more like an Alpine ski resort than an institution.

Surprisingly, there were no journalists huddled together in the cold, awaiting his arrival. What the hell had he got out of bed for?

Frank pulled the car up before the main office and kept the motor running as he dashed around to open the door for Christian. The fresh smell of pine and crisp, clean air hit him as he emerged from the cocoon of the car's interior.

The office door opened and a grey-haired woman hurried out to meet them. Christian put on his most charming smile. But the woman rushed straight past him. "Tessa! I didn't expect to see you here today."

"Hello, Marsha." Teresa turned to him. "This is Christian Taylor."

"Oh, of course." The woman finally seemed to notice him.

120

"Thank you so much for coming to meet the children today. They're so excited. They love your movies."

Behind her, Teresa rolled her eyes and he stifled a laugh. "I'm glad someone does," he said, to her rather than to the woman, who was now shepherding them indoors.

"Your photographer was freezing outside, so I invited him into the dining room."

*One* photographer? Pippa had definitely lost the plot.

"Would you like some hot chocolate before we start the tour?" Marsha asked.

Christian was on the point of refusing when Teresa caught his eye. "That would be lovely, thank you."

He was rewarded with Marsha's beaming smile.

"Tessa?" he whispered to Teresa as they followed the older woman down a long corridor.

"It's what my friends call me," she whispered back.

He grinned like a kid with a new toy. "Tessa."

At the end of the corridor a door opened into a large, bright dining hall with a high pine ceiling and tall windows. Three people sat at one of the long bench tables that looked as if they'd been sprung from the Hogwarts set.

The photographer – Christian gathered as much, since he was the one holding the camera – rose with a quick smile and a flash of recognition. "What are you doing here, Ms Adler?" he asked in local dialect.

"I'm accompanying Mr Taylor during his stay in Westerwald. Consider me his tour guide."

She introduced Christian to the photographer, his assistant, and the article writer, all by name and without a moment's hesitation, and they all shook hands.

Polite, friendly, as if she'd done this a thousand times before. As she no doubt had. She'd dated a prince, hadn't she?

Damn, but she was going to be a hard act to follow when he returned to California and had to hire a new assistant. Hopefully

121

the next one wouldn't deliberately keep him awake all night, though.

As they discussed the shots the photographer wanted – for a spread for *Vanity Fair*, so Pippa was temporarily forgiven – Marsha served them steaming mugs of thick, rich cocoa. Christian wasn't much of a chocolate fan, but it warmed him from the inside out, and he understood why Teresa insisted he drink it as soon as the tour began.

The home was spread across a couple of acres, complete with its own classrooms, library, gymnasium, handball courts and indoor swimming pool. The children were housed in smaller chalets, more like family units than a traditional orphanage.

And every single building had to be reached by trudging through snow. It wasn't deep, but it was soft and wet and neither he nor the journalists were dressed for it. Only Teresa in her fur-lined boots seemed unaffected.

One thing he was grateful for – he didn't have to face a horde of screaming children all at once. Their school day continued uninterrupted, as he was escorted into classrooms and gym classes, and introduced to small, manageable groups under the watchful eyes of their teachers. He shook an endless parade of hands, signed autographs until his hand cramped, and smiled for the cameras.

He smiled as he dealt with the fawning teachers and the diva photographer. He smiled as the teachers, and most of the children, greeted Teresa by name. He smiled as she sat quietly in the corner, talking to the children and admiring their artwork, looking as if she were having more fun than she'd had any time these last two weeks.

He'd wanted to impress her and instead he was the one impressed. And again she made him feel like that angry bastard child from Los Pajaros, wanting something he couldn't have.

Christian tried to focus on Marsha's non-stop chatter, but it was increasingly difficult to concentrate. His brand-name trainers were sodden and his feet so frozen he couldn't feel his toes.

Anyone who thought being a celebrity was all parties and premieres knew nothing. 4a.m. wake-up calls were easier than having to smile and look interested in complete strangers' lives for hours on end.

"Westerwald's first orphanage was founded after our terrible civil war," Marsha said, as she led them back across a vast quadrangle of snow towards the sanctuary of the main chalet. "But this site was gifted to us after our original building was bombed during the Second World War." She cast a warm smile over her shoulder at Teresa. "The land was originally part of the Adler hunting grounds. Their lodge is over there – through the trees."

He looked where Marsha pointed. A steep wooden roof was only just visible over the distant copse of snow-covered trees.

Now he had no problem concentrating. Teresa's family had their own hunting lodge?

She was so far out of his orbit, he was amazed her feet still touched the ground.

Back in the dining room, coffee and apple strudel awaited them. He cradled the mug and feeling slowly seeped back into his fingers. His feet took longer to defrost.

He chatted to the journalist about the charities he supported, about paying it forward, while Teresa sat quietly beside them with her poker face on.

At last the journalist turned to her. "Your family are major donors to the orphanage, aren't they, Ms Adler?"

"The original orphanage was founded by one of my ancestors."

Marsha did her beaming-smile thing again. "Tessa doesn't just support us financially. She volunteers here too. She runs a reading project for the younger children."

Which explained how so many of them knew her name.

"If we're done now… " Teresa said, her tone clipped. "Mr Taylor has other events to attend today."

With a backward wave to the journalist and photographer, who seemed loath to leave the cosy warmth of the chalet's dining

123

room, Christian allowed himself to be hustled out the door and back to his car.

"What other event am I supposed to be attending?" he asked, casting Teresa a cheeky grin as he climbed into the car.

"You could say thank you I got you out of there before they started in on your love life."

"Thank you." Though he wasn't entirely sure she'd wrapped up the questions for *his* benefit. "You don't like to talk about your charity work? Strange, since you couldn't stop talking about it the night we met."

The look she turned on him was frostier than usual. "I don't attend charity benefits or visit children's homes to preen in front of the cameras."

Touché.

"Even without the cameras present, it's bloody hard for me to do what you do," he said defensively. "Everyone wants their pound of flesh, their moment with the person they think I am. I can't do what you do."

"And what is that?"

He didn't like the look in Tessa's eyes. It was as if she was daring him.

"Just help out. Be myself."

"You want to bet?"

Now he really didn't like the look in her eyes. This was definitely a dare.

124

# Chapter 10

Teresa gave Frank an address Christian didn't recognise. As they descended back into the city bowl, the snow thinned, then disappeared.

"Where are we going? Is this the kind of place where I'm going to get mobbed and torn to pieces again?"

Not that he really cared where they were headed, as long as he had Teresa at his side. The longer she spent with him – *him*, not the person he was on set – the better his chances of seducing her. He hoped.

And the more time he spent with her, the more he wanted her. He'd wanted to knock her off her pedestal and instead she'd climbed down willingly. The way she'd been with those kids today…she hadn't been the Ice Queen with them.

She laughed. "I doubt it, but if you like we can ask Frank to keep the motor running, just in case."

He remained clueless as to their destination until Frank pulled up to the kerb outside the magnificent Gothic cathedral. Not the tourist entrance where the visitors entered, but a porter's gate to what had once been the monastery.

"You're taking me to church?"

Teresa shook her head and smiled the smile he was learning meant *be patient*. Not something he was particularly good at.

Several people hung around on the sidewalk, so Frank did his usual scan of the area before he opened the door for them. "All clear," he said gruffly, his eyes peeled and his expression fierce.

"You're welcome to come in too, once you've parked," Tessa said to him as she climbed out.

Christian followed her inside, past the porter's gate into a dimly lit hallway, where his eyes took a moment to adjust to the sudden gloom.

"This way," Teresa said. She reached out to take his arm, nothing more than a guiding touch, but in the gloom she misjudged the space between them and her hand made contact with his. He wrapped his fingers around hers.

For a split second she resisted the touch, then her grip softened in his, yielding and compliant.

Victory Number Two.

"This way," she said again, giving his fingers a gentle yank.

In that moment he'd have followed her anyway.

Their hands seemed to belong together, as natural as salt and pepper, as shampoo and conditioner.

He didn't want to let go.

But at the end of the unoccupied corridor a thick and rather ancient wooden door opened into a vast, kitchen lit by tall arched windows, and as they entered, Teresa pulled her hand out of his. The sunshine dimmed and the colour drained from the room.

A half dozen people worked at different stations. All heads turned as they entered, and one man, tall and rangy with a shock of white hair, hurried towards them.

"It's such a pleasure to see you here, Tessa," the man said. "We've missed you these last couple of weeks."

"Father Tomas, this is Christian Taylor. He's here to help out with preparing today's lunch for the soup kitchen."

Father Tomas shook his hand. "Wonderful! Are you any good at peeling carrots?"

When Christian left home he thought he'd peeled his last carrot.

126

These days his housekeeper bought them ready-peeled and ready-julienned. But for the next half hour, he peeled, chopped and diced vegetables, and it was the most fun he'd had in years.

Teresa stood beside him, elbow to elbow and they chatted as they worked. He'd never seen her as relaxed as she was now. Perhaps because they were on her turf this time.

Alongside them, other volunteers cut and buttered bread rolls, and stirred and seasoned the massive pots of bubbling vegetable soup. Even Frank joined them, removing his jacket and rolling up his sleeves to wash dishes.

Once the meal was prepared, they stood at the hatch into the former monk's refectory and served the soup into bowls for the waiting crowd that had swelled to a vast number.

Many of the people queuing before them knew Teresa's name. None seemed to know his. More astonishing, Teresa knew many of them. Not just their names, but their children's names, their circumstances.

And she treated every one of them as equals.

He had to give Teresa credit. Stuck-up aristocrat she might be, but she walked the walk.

She certainly treated them more warmly than she'd ever treated him. Who would have thought the Ice Queen would be better at dealing with people than he was?

While she talked, he kept his mouth closed and listened, and learned. He learned that she was respected. That she was generous, with both her time and her money.

That she would have made a great Archduchess.

He also learned that perhaps he did care after all.

Because now he'd met these people they were more than the recipients of an anonymous donation. Now he would lie awake in his vast, warm bed, with room service at the other end of the line, and wonder where these people he'd met slept at night in this bitter cold.

Posing for photographs was much easier than connecting with

real people.

She'd made her point.

The food line seemed never-ending, but at last everyone had been fed and the crowd thinned. Christian's face ached from smiling and his feet ached from standing. And Teresa did this three times a week?

He was now also starving. Teresa doled the last of the nutritious soup into bowls and at last they got to sit down and eat themselves. Frank joined Father Tomas and a few of the other volunteers, and Christian and Tessa found themselves alone at one end of a long refectory table.

He gave Frank a thumbs-up when he was sure she wouldn't notice.

"I win," Tessa said with an easy smile that melted though her haughty exterior. "You're doing real work and not a camera in sight. Thank you."

"I didn't have much choice, did I?" He mopped up the last of the soup from his bowl with the bread roll. "And I enjoyed it. It's very refreshing to be in a crowd of people and not one of them asking for an autograph."

Her shoulders stiffened and he gave himself a mental slap. Way to go for making this all about himself again. He never seemed to be able to say the right things when she was around. He tried again. "The food's also really good. Almost better than the food at The Playhouse."

"Food one cooks oneself always tastes better."

"You like to cook?"

She nodded. "I love cooking."

So that made two things he knew about her now. Charity and cooking.

He broke apart the last of the fresh-baked bread roll with his fingers. "I take back what I said the first time we met. You're not a princess and you are making a difference in the world. I think perhaps I needed to meet you. You challenge me in ways I need to be challenged."

He expected her to say "thank you" in her polite, perfectly enunciated voice. Instead she smiled that warm, melting smile again. "That works both ways. I didn't know it, but I needed to be challenged too. And you are definitely challenging."

He took that as a compliment.

She was silent a moment, and when she raised her gaze again he was surprised to see a flash of emotion in them. Worry. Doubt.

"What is it?" he asked.

She pinched her lips together, but this time the shutters didn't come down. She sighed. "Sometimes I feel like a ghost. It's as if I'm simply killing time, as if I have no real purpose." She straightened her shoulders. "Which is stupid. I help out here at the soup kitchen, and I teach reading and supervise homework at the children's home. I arrange parties and fundraisers and business dinners for my father and his business associates. I have a full and active life."

It sounded as if she was trying to convince herself.

"But you feel something is lacking," he prompted.

He understood the feeling well. He'd achieved every goal he'd set for himself and still he felt as if something was lacking. He felt hollow inside. "I only got into acting because I wanted more fame and money than being a stunt man could provide. But now that I have them, it's still not enough. I want more."

She stiffened.

"I want to make a mark, to do something meaningful with my life." To be the man his mother had believed he could be. She'd told him a hundred times that he was born for great things.

Teresa's expression softened, and he glimpsed another flash of emotion before her mask reasserted itself, calm and impenetrable as ever.

"I was wrong about you," she said. "You're not as shallow as I believed you were."

He was every bit as shallow. And as self-serving. But he suppressed the twinge of guilt and took her hand. "And you're

129

not the pampered princess I thought you were."

She didn't pull her hand away.

Victory Number Three.

They stepped out of the porter's lodge and Tessa gasped. Giant soft snowflakes whirled about them, melting as they hit the pavement. And stayed. She closed her eyes and lifted her face. The snowflakes settled on her nose and eyelashes.

"You like the snow?" Christian asked.

"I love it! It's so magical, so pure and clean."

"I like you like this."

She opened her eyes and frowned. "Like what?"

"Less uptight. Carefree. Smiling. I didn't think you even knew how to relax."

"I can't. Twenty-four-seven, remember?" But she did feel lighter and freer. More like herself and less like the Teresa Adler she showed the world.

Frank pulled the car up to the kerb and Christian climbed in. The blast of the car's heating hit her. But instead of diving into the warmth, as Christian had done, she savoured the swirling snowflakes a moment longer.

Snow's most magical attribute was that it made the world anew. It wiped away the traces of what had gone before, leaving the slate clean and ready for fresh footprints.

Reluctantly she slid into the too-hot, too-enclosed interior of the car. As always, Christian dominated the space, with his scent, with his energy, with his awareness.

They drove slowly through the quiet streets as the snow softly settled around them, smothering the greyness of the city in a blanket of bright, shimmering white.

In preparation for Valentine's Day, every shop window they passed seemed to be decorated in shades of pink and red. Fluffy toys, chocolates in bows...and more hearts than Tessa could stomach. She wasn't sure which she detested most – the crass commercialism or the excess of sentimentality.

Either way, the decorations felt like a warning. Half her time had already elapsed and she needed to fill in the final gaps in Christian's story and see his ring. She'd barely managed a quick glance around his suite before he'd woken this morning. It hadn't been in the closet with his clothes either.

The warning also felt like a death knell. She was no longer quite so keen for this assignment to be over. She hadn't had this much fun in years, not since she'd left university. Though even that could hardly be described as "fun" since she'd spent the entire four years working to be the top of her class.

And for what? So she could be the country's most underpaid party-planner?

At the hotel's entrance, Frank got out the car to open the door for them, and Tessa stepped out first. Snowflakes settled on the car's roof, on the ground, clung to the dark shoulders of Christian's coat.

She pulled on her gloves. "Robbie texted me that there are revised script pages waiting for you at reception. I'll check for them, and then is there anything more you need from me today?"

"Don't go just yet." Christian laid a hand on her arm. "Everyone else will still be out enjoying their day off and I don't feel like being alone. Please come inside for something warm to drink? You too, Frank."

Frank shook his head. "If you're not needing the car again, I'll be heading home."

Christian shook his head. "Have fun," he said, then he cocked an eyebrow at Tessa, no doubt fully expecting her to refuse too.

It was a request, not an instruction, but even though she still had that dratted seating plan to work on, she didn't feel like being alone this afternoon either. The big house had never felt as empty as it had since she'd started working on this job.

And she certainly didn't want to be alone while she felt this unsettled. Because then there would be no distraction from her thoughts.

She nodded.

At the reception desk she found the envelope waiting with the new script pages as well as a revised schedule for the next few days' shoot. Clearly the production team hadn't had a day off either. She handed the envelope to Christian, who barely glanced at it before rolling it up and stuffing it into his coat pocket.

He led her to the hotel library, a dignified room lined with tall windows overlooking the gardens, where a log fire blazed in the hearth. Teresa stripped off her jacket and gloves, unwound her scarf, and sat on one of the chintzy sofas while he ordered from the hovering waitress, cappuccino for himself and cocoa for Teresa. Then he sat beside her.

She suppressed a shiver. Not her usual tremble of unease, but a rather thrilling sensation. Not once in all the time she'd known him had Stefan made her feel like that. Which was a good thing. She didn't want this awkward sensation with the man she was going to spend the rest of her life with. Did she?

She and Stefan were comfortable together, and that was far more important for a happy marriage.

The waitress brought their steaming mugs and Tessa sipped carefully as she studied the schedule changes. "We'll be on location for the next few days, then we shoot the pirate-ship interiors at the studio." She frowned as she flicked to the next page. "Why would we need to start and end so late if we're shooting inside a studio?"

"To ease us into the night shoots at the end of the shoot." Christian grinned.

"What's so funny?"

"You said *we*. You've been bitten by the film bug."

She shook her head so vehemently that Christian laughed at her. "What do you have against the movie business?"

She paused a long moment before she answered. Her first answer was easy. *Because it's an industry of self-involved, self-important people.* But she bit back the words. That wasn't her real reason. "Because my mother abandoned me for it." The raw honesty

132

scalded her throat.

Christian's eyes rounded. "That was your mother's mistake, not the movies'. She made a choice, but that doesn't make the movie business the devil's work. It's a job like any other."

"Not quite like any other." The crew worked so hard, labouring long hours, because they were passionate about what they did. But they made sacrifices. They spent months away from home, away from their families. So many had failed marriages, estranged children and no fixed home to return to.

They also partied hard and drank too much. The downward spiral her mother had taken was only just a few steps away.

Some sacrifices weren't worth making.

Tessa leaned back against the invitingly soft cushions of the sofa. "The night we met you admitted to being a narcissist. I don't think you are at all."

He laughed. "Of course I am. I couldn't do what I do without having an above-average dose of self-interest. Though I don't usually go around admitting it. It wouldn't make me very popular. Can you imagine the Twitter fall-out?"

No, she couldn't. But she didn't understand this fascination with social media. Her friends had Twitter accounts and Facebook accounts and Instagram accounts. What for? So they could talk to each other online rather than in person? It was hard enough being the person she was supposed to be, without adding an online persona to manage too.

Yet Christian did it every day. He pretended to be someone else. Not just the characters he played, but the persona of the likeable, roguish, devil-may-care actor. She'd seen enough now to know he wasn't that person. He did care.

And he wasn't always likeable and charming.

She shook her head. "Have you ever considered just being the real you in public?"

"Have you ever considered being the real you in real life?"

Her eyes narrowed. But it was hard to be cross with him with

133

her limbs growing languid and the fire's lazy warmth stealing into her. As long as she'd been busy and on the move, she hadn't felt the effect of the long hours spent on set, but just sitting still, the tiredness crept in.

That feeling of being stretched thin all the time, of her emotions scraped raw and exposed, had also worn her out. She no longer had the energy to keep up her defences.

They lazed in comfortable silence, and Christian put no pressure on her to make conversation. Or maybe he was tired too. She had made him stay awake all night, after all.

"I'm sorry I made you stay up all night reading that script," she said, shame gnawing at her. It was unlike her to be so vengeful.

Christian shrugged and stretched.

"So are you interested in making the film?"

"It's not a bad script."

She smiled. "Your enthusiasm knows no bounds. What's wrong with it?"

"It's not what's wrong with the script. It's the third in this superhero franchise and surprisingly well written for what it is. The problem is with me. I'm bored."

She bit her lip, contemplating him. He seemed in a mellower mood today. Not so full of quick comebacks. Less likely to dismiss her.

"Robbie has a script he thinks you should look at. He says it's very different from what you usually do. Would you read it?"

He looked thoughtful. "I'll ask him about it tomorrow. What do I have to lose apart from another night's sleep?" He grinned, and his eyes crinkled at the corners.

She'd reached the bottom of the mug of cocoa, that ultra-sweet, ultra-thick layer that settled at the bottom, when she made the decision. "I have a list of names for you." She'd had it for two days. She just hadn't been sure until now if she would show it to him.

"A list of names?"

"People your mother associated with during her time in

134

Westerwald."

He sat up, at instant attention, as she dug the list out of her messenger bag. It wouldn't be of much value to Christian. It was just a list of names and addresses, with those who'd died marked with a star. Unless he knew more than he'd admitted.

Her father's intelligence people had already checked out everyone on the list, and narrowed it down to only three who had access to the palace's most closely guarded secrets.

One of those three had to be the traitor who'd stolen the ring from the palace vault, the ring she still hadn't seen. All of them belonged to the royal family's inner circle.

If Christian could help them narrow it down…

"How did you get this?" he asked.

Not a question she was willing to answer, so she asked one of her own instead. "Do any of these names mean anything to you?"

Christian flipped through the pages, running a finger down the list as if searching for something.

"What are you looking for?" she asked, working hard to keep her voice neutral.

He didn't look up. "There are a lot of titled names on this list."

"Your mother worked in the palace and in the higher levels of government. She was bound to meet a few."

What was with this hatred he had for aristocrats? Then something clicked. "Your father was titled, wasn't he?" she guessed.

Christian looked up, his expression guarded. "I overheard my mother and my grandmother arguing once. My grandmother said: *You should have known you were nothing more than his plaything. You didn't honestly think a man of his birth would have married you?*"

"You didn't tell me that before."

"Would it have made a difference?"

"Of course it would."

His jaw tightened, and she sighed, impatient. "Not because he might have been noble, but because it would have narrowed down the search. Was there anything else?"

135

Christian shrugged. The movement might have been intended to make it seem he didn't know, or didn't care, but Teresa could see straight through him.

"My mother said: *I would never have married him, even if he'd asked. It would have ruined him.*" He looked straight at her. "She believed herself inferior to him."

And that was where all his hurt came from. Teresa had learned enough during their dinner at The Playhouse to know how much Christian admired his mother. She'd been beautiful, fierce, clever, loving, yet she'd thought herself unworthy of the man who'd knocked her up and then walked away.

Tessa had never wanted to put her arms around someone and comfort them as much as she wanted to comfort Christian now. But she didn't know how. It was hard to give what she'd never received.

She blinked away the sheen that obscured her vision. "I'm sorry," she said.

Christian lifted his chin. "I don't need your pity."

"No, you don't." He'd used that hurt to drive his entire life. He'd become a star, the man every man wanted to be, the man every woman wanted.

"I won't let anyone make me feel inferior." He met her gaze, and held it, and she was the one to look away first.

"We're not all like that," she said. But she had to swallow before she could get the words out.

He looked down at the list in his hands. "I suppose I should contact a few of these people and see if anyone can tell me anything about her? One of them might even be my father."

Why was he so determined to face his father if he hated the very thought of him? To show him the man his unwanted son had become? Tessa frowned. "It's equally possible his name might not be on the list. Who knows how or where they met? And what are you going to do – ring up all the men and ask '*did you sleep with my mother thirty-seven years ago?*' You start making calls and it'll be all over the papers tomorrow. You'll have every hopeful with either stars or dollar signs in his eyes after you and another mob wherever you go. And you probably still won't find the one person you're looking for."

He sighed. "Good point. So what do I do now?"

"Nothing." She took the list from between his fingers. "You let me deal with it."

Though she had no idea how. Yet. "Do you have anything of your mother's, perhaps something from her time here?"

She held her breath as she waited for his answer. He paused. Then he shook his head.

She wished she could swear. If she could just see the ring...

Christian reached for the envelope stuck in his coat pocket. "If you're not in any hurry, could you run lines with me?"

"I thought you had a photographic memory?"

"I still need to read through the new pages." His azure eyes twinkled, the dark mood banished. He looked more like himself and she breathed an audible sigh of relief.

"Please?" he pleaded.

How could she resist that twinkle? She agreed.

Christian glanced through the script pages, printed on salmon-coloured paper to indicate that it was already the eighth rewrite, then handed them to her.

Tessa skimmed the scene. She knew now that movies were not shot in sequential order. She'd also read the entire script and knew the story. While the bulk of the movie took place in the Caribbean, it began and ended in Europe, climaxing in the dramatic duel they'd filmed the day before.

This scene, a quiet moment just before the climax, was scheduled to be filmed on the film unit's last night in Westerwald, in one of the palace's drawing rooms, which Lee was currently transforming into a stately bedroom.

It was the love scene.

When Lee had proudly walked her through his set yesterday,

she'd admired the magnificent antique canopied bed, still with its original oriental silk hangings. She hadn't imagined then that Nina and Christian would soon be naked together in that bed. She did now.

She blushed as Christian settled back on the sofa beside her.

"I know this is awkward," he said, "but trust me, it's a lot less awkward than me having to run through this scene with Dominic."

"I can imagine." She cleared her throat, held the pages between them where they could both see, and began: "Dance with me at the King's ball tomorrow."

"There was a time you didn't want to be seen dead in public with me."

"There was a time you would already have had me naked by now."

"A lot has changed."

"You're not going to make love to me?"

Christian laughed and she looked up.

"You're supposed to sound a little disappointed when you say that."

"I'm not the actress."

She didn't like Christian's grin. "Aren't you? Is there anyone who knows the real you?"

She looked back at the page and it took her a moment to find her place again. She could feel another blush starting to work its way up her neck. Or perhaps it wasn't a blush. Perhaps it was simply the fire's heat.

He carried on with his lines, unblinking, in a voice softer than before, and even more seductive than usual. "I fully intend to make love to you. But not before you tell me what's changed. The girl I used to know was too afraid to stand beside me where everyone could see. I've done much worse things since then. So what's changed?"

He leaned forward and brushed his fingers over her cheek, stroking back a strand of her hair and tucking it behind her ear.

The move wasn't scripted. She had no idea whether it was part of the scene or not. She only knew that she couldn't have moved away from his touch even if she'd wanted to.

Heat burned her skin where his fingers trailed, down over her jaw, her neck, to settle on her collarbone, against the very edge of her shirt's neckline.

She glanced down at the script. "I learned there are worse things a girl can lose than her reputation."

Christian raised an eyebrow. "Like what?"

"I lost my heart. It's hard loving someone who doesn't love you back."

"I have always loved you."

It was increasingly hard to tear her gaze away, to read the words on the page, with those piercing eyes holding her captive. "But not enough to stay and fight for me."

"And you didn't love me enough to acknowledge me publicly."

They faced each other, the emotion in the room cranking higher until the air around them crackled with the tension.

He laid his hand on her arm. She'd seen him do this again and again with one woman after another. She really should know better. She should pull away. She was a respectable woman, engaged to a very respectable man.

Only her body didn't seem able to move.

He ran his hand down over her arm, and even through the thick cashmere of her sweater, she shivered. Not the usual shiver when someone touched her. No uncomfortable squirm this. This felt like an electric charge building and building under her skin until she was sure her body would explode with the pressure.

"Tell me how I make you feel," he asked. This wasn't in the script.

She looked at the page in her hand, struggling to focus, flustered, breathless.

Hot, bothered, stretched thin. Doubtful. That was how he made her feel.

She hadn't doubted herself or her place in the world for a single moment until the night Christian had vaulted into her car. Now she could barely remember why she was here.

"So are you going to make love to me or not?" she read. Her voice sounded needy and desperate. What was wrong with her? Had the cocoa been spiked?

Following the stage directions, Christian leaned in even closer. His arm draped across the back of the sofa, a mere inch from her neck. In spite of the prickles rising up along the back of her neck, she didn't move away. She couldn't.

"Beg me," he said.

She swallowed. This time she didn't look down at the page. "I don't beg."

He leaned closer. His breath brushed her cheek. He was so close all she had to do was lean the tiniest distance and her body would press against his. Into his.

"Say that again." His voice was so low it thrummed across her skin.

"I don't beg," she repeated, her throat croaky. For the first time in her life, she wanted to beg for something. He hadn't even kissed her, and her entire body had turned to molten fire.

She glanced at the page. Not that she needed to. The words seemed to have seared themselves into her brain. "I'm stronger than you think."

He laughed and leaned back, away from her.

She almost wanted to cry with disappointment. It was easy to see how actors could get so carried away while filming. She certainly wouldn't blame Nina for getting a little swept away while filming this scene.

"Please," she said. She kept her eyes on the script, hoping, praying, that he wouldn't hear in her voice how close she was to begging.

"See, that wasn't so hard."

Steeling herself, she lifted her gaze to his. His usual teasing grin was gone, replaced by that intense look that turned her insides

140

more slushy than melting snow.

He leaned in close again. Would he really kiss her? Her entire body froze.

"What, you couldn't wait for me?"

Christian turned towards the intrusive voice. Tessa sank back against the sofa cushions, emotionally depleted.

Dominic.

Christian leaned back, away from her, but his arm remained slung on the back of the seat behind her.

"Geez, but it's warm in here! I hope I'm not interrupting anything." Dominic flung his coat on the edge of the sofa across from them and sprawled on it. He grinned like a naughty school boy and winked at Christian. "Not that I blame you. She's a much more attractive rehearsal partner. I wouldn't have waited either."

"Dom usually rehearses with me," Christian explained. "He doesn't make half as good a Celeste as you do."

She cleared her throat. "You were right about your memory being good. I don't think you need much more than that read-through. Shall I order another round of coffees?"

"Don't stir yourself. I'll do it." Dominic leapt up, all vigour and energy. She wondered how he was ever able to sit still long enough to read lines with Christian. "But forget the hot drinks, I think it's time for alcohol."

She managed a smile. "I'd love a sherry."

"Sherry it is. No need to ask what you want, you uncouth lout. Beer, right?"

Christian nodded, but he didn't take his eyes off Teresa. When Dominic left the room, heading for the hotel bar, he laid his hand on Teresa's knee. "Thank you."

Words deserted her. His hand on her knee seemed to have short-circuited her brain.

"Are you okay?" he asked, frowning. "You look stressed."

Of course she was stressed. She had a wedding to plan, an absent bridegroom, a job she didn't need and shouldn't want, and

141

a top-secret assignment that wasn't going as well as she'd hoped. And a moment ago she'd nearly kissed him without a moment's thought.

"I'm fine." She moved her knee so his hand fell away. "It's late and it's been a long week. Please give Dominic my apologies, but I have to go."

She rose and reached for her coat. Christian rose too, took the coat from her nerveless fingers, and helped her into it. His fingers brushed her neck as he straightened the collar, sending a most unacceptable tremor through her.

*Not now*, she instructed her body. *Not him*. Her body didn't seem to want to listen.

The buttons of her coat also seemed to have developed a mind of their own, slithering into the wrong holes.

"Let me," Christian said with a soft laugh. He buttoned up her coat and tied the belt while she tried her damndest not to blush. Again. Especially since her mind had decided to indulge in a little flight of fantasy that he was undoing her coat rather than buttoning her up.

She grabbed at her bag, scarf and gloves. "I *really* have to go. I'll see you in the morning."

If she could have run out of the hotel without losing her dignity, she would have. She was pretty sure she heard Christian snigger behind her as she left.

Damn him!

So much for not going all fangirl on him. He'd seduced her, as easily as he seduced every woman he met and she'd fallen for it like one of his blindly doting fans.

Fury at herself fuelled her all the way to her car.

# Chapter 11

One step forward, two steps back.

Just when he thought she'd begun to thaw, Teresa clammed back up again. It was as if these past weeks hadn't happened and they were back in her car that first night they met, Tessa cold and haughty, Christian annoyed and irritable. And very, very horny.

Outside the trailer, the snow still swirled down in thick drifts. No longer pretty, just wet and cold and inconvenient. Between the trailers and the trucks it had turned to sludge, trampled by booted feet and the wheels of the carts used to ferry the film equipment.

The trailer door blew open, banging against a kitchen cabinet as a gust of sharp wind took it. Tessa stepped inside. Out of a crew of hundreds she alone seemed unaffected by the cold. Her face glowed, her eyes shone. She looked happy. God, but she was mesmerizingly beautiful when she allowed emotion to leak through.

Then she saw him and she dimmed the glow, hiding it from him. He scowled. He hated when she did that. Hadn't they already shared so much? She knew him better than anyone alive. Didn't he deserve the same?

"The journalists have started to arrive for the press conference. Robbie will radio when they're ready for you." She shut the door behind her and removed her padded North Face jacket. "It's warm in here."

He set down the script Robbie had given him. "This isn't warm. You should try LA in July." Or Los Pajaros in February. He was starting to look forward to the next leg of this journey. Except...

He rubbed a hand across his face. Since when did he need a woman in his life to make it complete? Since never. He belonged to no one. He was footloose and fancy free, and that was exactly the way he liked it.

"So what do you normally do on a Sunday afternoon?" He asked, determined to change the subject and stamp out the direction his thoughts had started to take far too often.

The light in her eyes dimmed further. "Usually I have lunch at the country club."

"Who with?"

"Friends." She seemed on the verge of saying something more, but stopped herself.

He frowned. "Would you rather be there now?"

She shook her head. "Making small-talk with people I've known all my life sometimes feels like harder work than running up and down between your trailer and the studio. How do *you* usually spend your Sunday afternoons?"

"I work. And on those rare occasions I'm not working, I stay home. Run on the beach, read scripts, watch movies. Normal stuff." No fans, no paparazzi. His beach house was as close to heaven on earth as he could imagine.

So why did he spend so little time there? It wasn't as if he needed to make three movies a year. He could afford to take it easier these days. So why didn't he?

Because the house seemed empty these days. Too quiet.

The radio at Tessa's hip crackled and Robbie's tinny voice sounded. "Teresa, go for Robbie."

She unhooked the radio from her belt and pressed the talk button. "Teresa here. Are you ready for us?"

"Any time you are," Robbie answered.

Christian hoisted himself off the sofa. The press conference had been the brainwave of one of the executive producers trying to milk his stars for every bit of free press he could get. Usually Christian hated the distraction of the media while he was in production, but today he welcomed it.

Better than going back to his sterile hotel room. Better than being apart from Teresa. Better than being with her, so close he could touch her without being able to. The wall she'd raised between them since that afternoon in the hotel library seemed higher and more impenetrable than ever.

It was driving him so crazy he was sure he was going to explode any day now.

"We're on our way." She re-hooked the radio on her belt and retrieved her jacket.

Christian jogged down the steps and waited for her as she locked the trailer door and pocketed the key.

They walked together across the car park towards the studio buildings. The press conference had been set up in the canteen, adjacent to the warehouse space where they were filming the pirate-ship interiors.

The room was packed. Photographers and reporters jostled against one another. It must be a slow news day in Westerwald.

On a dais knocked together by the set-builders, stood the production's phalanx of producers, the key cast members, the unit publicist, and the film's official behind-the-scenes photographer. A seat remained free for Christian. At the door, he handed Tessa his coat, then strode forward.

*Game on.*

At sight of him the noise levels in the room boomed. He knew, they all knew, that he was the one they were here to see. He stepped up onto the dais and took his seat, and the unit publicist waved her hands to quieten the crowd.

The speeches that followed were dull. Christian tuned them out and focused instead on his audience. A few faces he recognised. Those he didn't were no doubt from the European presses. Over

145

their heads he looked for Teresa, unobtrusively pressed up against the back wall. One of the reporters, looking just as bored as he felt, followed his glance. The reporter nudged his neighbour. A few more heads started to crane.

Christian repressed an urge to pout like a petulant child. Just how small was this bloody country? Did Teresa know every damned person in it? Did everyone know her?

She didn't appear to notice the whispers, but he had no doubt she was just as aware as he was. She missed nothing.

When the prepared speeches were done, the Q&A began. The journalists sat up in their seats, awake and eager now. Christian wished he felt the same. He'd done this so many times he could practically sleep-walk through these events.

There were questions for the producers, more for Nina, most for him.

*What is your role in* The Pirate's Revenge?

"I play the pirate out for revenge."

In his peripheral vision, Teresa's eyes narrowed in disapproval. Okay, so he wasn't being his usual cooperative self. He made more of an effort. "I play the bastard son of a king who becomes a pirate in order to exact revenge on the aristocrats, who once said he'd amount to nothing."

*How does it feel to play a character so different from yourself?*

This character was far closer to his own than any other he'd played, but he gave an answer that fitted his whitewashed official back story.

*And your character comes in to save the day?*

"Of course – and don't forget the bit about getting to kiss the pretty girl."

Laughter.

*What do you think of Westerwald so far?*

"The road between my hotel and the palace, where we're shooting is very interesting."

More laughter.

*Do you plan to stay in Westerwald a little after you've finished shooting?*

"I'd love to, but I have a premiere in Paris, and then I head to Los Pajaros to work on the next leg of this film."

*How does it feel to be called Sexiest Man Alive by GQ?*

"Pretty damned good, but I don't think they used my best pictures." He struck a pose and his audience laughed, soaking it up.

*What was it like kissing Jennifer Lawrence?*

"Even better than being called GQ's Sexiest Man Alive."

*What made you choose this current project?*

"The script says I get to kiss Nina Alexander."

Titters from the audience. Reminded of her presence, the reporters turned to Nina.

*Are the rumours about the two of you true?*

She laughed. "Which rumours are those? The ones that we're dating, that we're sleeping together, or the one that I'm pregnant with Christian's love child?"

Good girl. He knew he liked her.

One of the reporters in the front row turned in his seat to face the back of the room.

*Ms Adler, is it true that there will be three crowned heads of state attending your wedding next week?*

Christian kept the smile plastered on his face, but it took a huge effort.

As all heads in the room turned to her, Teresa smiled, calm and composed as ever. "At our last count it'll be four. As you can imagine, the seating plan is a nightmare."

More laughter.

*Your engagement has been very short. Are you trying to get in there before the royal weddings in the summer?*

Her expression was as neutral as ever but her mouth had the pinched look that suggested she was reigning in a strong emotion.

The reporter had said weddings. Plural.

Christian might not know much about this country, but he

147

knew enough. Westerwald had only two princes. And one of them was Teresa's ex.

He clapped his hands, recalling the journalists' attention to the front of the room. "Enough talk about us. I'd like to thank our amazing team of producers who put this movie together. Let's give them a round of applause."

His audience was forced to clap in acknowledgement.

"I'd also like to thank the Archduke, who has so kindly let us use his palace as a film location."

More applause, more genuine this time.

The unit publicist rose to wrap up the proceedings. Christian kept his expression interested and his gaze off Tessa, but she was impossible to ignore. The air in the room seemed to pulse between them.

She was getting *married*? Next *week*?

No wonder she'd been so good at keeping him at arm's length. And no wonder she'd seemed so reluctant to reveal her interest in him. It wasn't for any of the reasons he'd once thought – not because of the colour of his skin, or because he was shallow, or because he made his living in Hollywood.

But she *was* interested.

At last he allowed his gaze to find her. She didn't have that glowing look of a bride-to-be. And she hadn't mentioned her fiancé once in all the time he'd known her. Most women couldn't shut up when they were in love and about to be married.

Why hadn't she told him? What game was she playing?

The storm of emotion wracking her body threatened to erupt. Teresa crossed her arms over her chest with the effort to hold it in.

Why hadn't she told him when she'd had the chance? She'd been on the verge of telling him earlier. She should have. It would have been better than this, in a room full of strangers.

And that look in his eyes… for the most fleeting of moments before he'd shut it down, she'd seen more than just surprise in his

148

eyes. She thought she'd seen disappointment, and anger.

A hand touched her arm and she jumped.

"Frank has the car waiting. We need to get Christian out of here before the press pins him down," Robbie said.

She nodded and headed back towards the door to wait for Christian. He moved through the crowd, smiling, exchanging a word here or there with the journalists, who pushed forward to get to him. The unit publicist remained at his side, shepherding him through the crowd.

But even though he smiled and laughed, the tension in him seemed obvious to her.

He closed the distance between them and made it to the door, pausing beside her. Anger radiated off him in waves. "What else don't I know about you, Teresa?"

But he didn't wait for her answer. He pushed past her through the door.

"Well, he's a ball of fun today. I wonder what got into him?" Robbie asked, watching Christian's retreating back.

She rather suspected she knew.

He'd been thwarted. He'd tried to seduce her and he'd failed. Just once in his life the big-time movie star hadn't been able to get what he wanted with a snap of his fingers.

And now he knew he never would.

She should have felt something like triumph. Instead, she felt hollow inside.

She turned to follow him out the door, but Robbie's hand tightened on her arm. "A few of us are meeting up for drinks at the Landmark Café tonight. Why don't you and your fiancé join us?"

Tears burned her eyes. She blinked them away. "Thank you for the invitation."

Beyond the door, the car waited. Frank revved the engine and she jumped in the back beside Christian.

He looked out the darkened window and avoided all eye contact. She did the same. The city rushed by in a blur.

She broke the silence when they were mere blocks away from the hotel. "Are you angry that I'm getting married?"

She was sure she saw a flash of something in the depths of his eyes before the shutters came down. "Why on earth would that make me angry? It's not like there's anything between us. Is there?"

It was that first morning in the hotel dining room all over again, that intense, probing look that rendered her breathless and speechless.

She shook her head.

"You're not wearing a ring."

She looked down at her hands, clasped neatly in her lap. "It was at the jeweller's for an insurance appraisal."

"For nearly three weeks?"

She had to clear the lump in her throat before she could speak. "I haven't had time to collect it."

"I'm sorry I've kept you from such an important errand. I won't need any hand-holding tomorrow, so you can get Frank to take you."

She cleared her throat. "Thank you, but my assistant took care of it."

He said nothing and she glanced up. She didn't like the hard, speculative look in his eyes. "My assistant has an assistant. Interesting."

She could think of nothing to say. She'd already said too much.

The car pulled up beneath the hotel portico. Neither of them moved.

"So why does a Baroness, who has her own assistant and can afford a designer wardrobe and a fancy sports car, need a job as my chaperone?"

She gave him the same sort of answer he'd given the reporters – glib and palpably untrue. "Because you're an esteemed guest of this nation, and it was felt you should have an assistant suitable to your position."

He held her gaze and her heartbeat raced. Would he call her

out on the lie?

Then he turned away, climbed out of the car, and she let out the breath she'd been holding. The door slammed shut behind him.

"When's the big day?" Frank asked.

"Valentine's Day."

In the rear-view mirror, Frank's eyes rounded. "That's just one week after filming ends," he said.

She nodded.

"What are you doing messing around here then? It's not as if you need the money."

She wished she knew. She sighed. "It's complicated."

"Try me."

"It started out as one thing and turned into something else."

# Chapter 12

Tessa knew all the best restaurants in Neustadt, the kind of places where money was no object, where clients could be impressed and business discussed. Bars were another matter. The closest she'd come to the city's nightlife was driving past it on the way to somewhere else. But even she had heard of the trendy Landmark Café.

The bar overhung the river at its widest point, a modern, glass box built into the side of the opulent *Beaux-Arts* Guildhall.

She hadn't planned on taking up Robbie's invitation tonight. Not until she'd stood in her palatial bedroom and the walls had begun to press in on her. That suffocating feeling had returned, stronger than ever before, and she'd had to get out.

The cab dropped her close to the entrance, but even so it took her an age to traverse the short distance across the ice-slickened pavement. Tonight she'd opted for heels. High heels. Red heels.

Her hand felt heavy with the ring back in place. As if weighted down. She was tempted to remove it but that would only invite questions. Everyone on the crew would know by now.

A queue stretched from the bar entrance, but at her approach the door swung open and the young doorman whistled and waved her in without question. At least she must have got the dress code right.

The space inside was bright with electric-blue light, the colour mirrored in the glass walls, the shining brushed-steel bar, and the reflections falling onto the smooth surface of the river beyond. The noise levels were higher than she was accustomed to, an overwhelming mix of voices, laughter, and loud music.

For an anxious moment her heart fluttered, then she spotted Robbie across the room, surrounded by a knot of people. She recognised a few of the cast and crew. Gerry, the unit production manager, Marie, the make-up artiste, Nina with her entourage. Dominic.

The flutter in Tessa's heart accelerated. Oh God. *He* wasn't here too, was he?

Robbie waved her over then ordered her one of the bar's signature cocktails, as electric blue as the light around them. She sipped it gingerly, the drink's cloying sweetness sliding down her throat like soda. Dominic offered her his seat as he rose with his phone in hand, mid-text. There was no sign of Christian. She breathed out and relaxed.

Their group swelled as more crew members joined them. Most came straight from set, dressed in their "uniform" of jeans or cargo pants matched with sloganned sweatshirts. Casual, relaxed, still on a natural high after a day on set.

She relaxed further. In such a large group she could fade quietly into the background, listen to their lively chatter without needing to make small-talk.

Parties had only ever been work for her. Introducing people, encouraging conversation, playing the hostess, living up to her family name. She could never drink too much, never be herself.

But tonight was different. Tonight she would let her hair down, figuratively if not literally, and she would drink and enjoy herself. No work allowed. She wanted to feel young and wild for just once in her life.

"You didn't bring your fiancé?" Robbie asked, replacing the empty glass in her hand with another. Since it would be impolite to refuse, she accepted the drink.

"He's in Canada," she replied. "He'll be back in a couple of days."

Over Robbie's shoulder, she spotted Dominic, still busy texting on his phone. The reed-thin brunette beside him had begun to pout.

Tessa had just finished her second cocktail when a voice she hadn't wanted to hear sent a tremor down her spine. A deep voice, a little husky. She pressed her eyes shut.

"Christian! There's a seat over here," someone called out.

She opened her eyes, and colour and light flooded back in. As it always did in Christian's energetic presence, the room shifted from shades of grey to iridescent colour. The light around them seemed impossibly brighter.

The entire group turned to him as he took the unoccupied seat across the circle from her, like flowers turning to the sun. Or more aptly, like worshippers beneath the throne of a demi-god.

She resisted the urge to roll her eyes just as Christian caught her gaze. He grinned, amused, and lifted his glass to her in silent salute.

He certainly wasn't angry now. He looked in the mood for mischief, and she wasn't sure which was worse.

Dominic picked up the tale he'd been regaling the group with before Christian's interruption: "So Chris and I choreographed a fight scene for this has-been actor. His star was on the wane, but he still thought he was something special. He came on set, throwing his prima donna weight around, and refused to do the fight scene as we'd planned it. He and Chris are trading fake punches and this guy starts messing around, trying to show off. He's not pulling his punches, but he's hardly managing to land one since Chris is always a step ahead. And the guy gets mad cause Chris is making him look like the fool he is. So he knees Chris right in the groin."

His audience groaned in sympathy. Christian sipped his drink, the only one unaffected by the story.

"Chris had the guy on his back, flat on the floor, his arm across the actor's windpipe, in less than a second." Dominic laughed. "The director laughed so hard he forgot to call 'cut.'" He took a swig of his beer.

"What happened next?" Nina leaned forward, all eagerness for the rest of the story, inadvertently giving both Dominic and Tessa a good view of her more-than-ample cleavage. Or maybe not so inadvertently.

"We were barely a week into filming and already the director was sick of the actor's antics, so he fired him. Something about his ego being a safety hazard. And he hired Christian to replace him. The rest, as they say, is history."

Tessa arched an eyebrow at Christian. Was this the real story then of how he got his break as an actor? He shrugged a shoulder and flashed her that roguish grin, the one that lit up his eyes, and for half a second she was sure she recognised why that look seemed so familiar. Then it was gone.

Dominic turned to her. "Is that your phone?"

Only then did she register the buzz from the vicinity of the Dior bag slung over the back of her chair. She reached into it just as the call cut off.

She scrolled to her missed calls. Stefan.

"Please excuse me." She rose, stepping away from the group as she dialled his number.

"Where are you?" Stefan's voice was barely audible over a shout of laughter from the other end of the bar.

She covered her other ear so she could hear Stefan better. "We have a late start tomorrow, so we're out having a drink tonight."

"Who's we?"

"A bunch of crew and cast."

"Is Christian Taylor there?" There was too much ambient noise for her to hear if there was any jealousy in his tone. She doubted it. They didn't have that kind of relationship.

"Of course."

"You were going to call me."

"Not until ten." She glanced at her watch. Heavens, how had it got so late?

"Can you go some place quieter?"

"Sure." She elbowed through the crowd to reach the doors at the back of the bar that led to a paved courtyard around a stone fountain. In the summer she was sure it would be packed. Now even the die-hard smokers had abandoned it. The fountain stood ghostly still, decorated with an intricate frieze of frozen icicles.

She'd left her jacket slung over the back of her chair.

"I've changed my flight." Stefan sounded grim.

"Are you coming home earlier?" She wrapped her arms around herself in a vain attempt to stave off the cold. Her jersey dress was not designed for outdoors in midwinter.

"I have to go to Paris on the weekend, then Stockholm for a couple of days."

A shiver of foreboding ran down her spine. Or maybe it was just the cold. "When will you be back?"

"The twelfth."

A whole week away. "But that's only two days before the wedding!"

"I know and I'm sorry. It can't be helped. This is an important trade agreement we're setting up and the negotiations are proving problematic. I can't abandon them now. I promise, I'll have this locked down before we get married and then I'm all yours."

Until after the honeymoon, then it would be back to the endless travelling. She'd lived her entire life with a workaholic. She knew the deal. She wiped a hand across her eyes. This was what she'd wanted, wasn't it? Of course it was. She liked that he had a life and interests of his own. She liked that he had an important role to play.

She just hadn't thought being in a relationship would feel so lonely.

"What about the wedding rehearsal?"

"Move it to the afternoon I get back."

She closed her eyes and counted to ten. This would mean moving the rehearsal dinner too. A new venue and a new caterer at the very least. Not to mention the hundreds of phone calls, to

156

the guests, to the press. And they'd need a new security plan for the visiting dignitaries.

She rubbed her forehead. "It'll be a lot of extra work to move everything."

"If you can't cope then quit that daft job. This is not like you, Teresa. You're usually so reasonable."

Yes, that was her. Always the reasonable one. The one who quietly stayed home and kept everyone happy while they went out to play. Her mother with her acting career. Her father and his career. Now Stefan and his job.

Tears burned her throat. She'd tried so hard not to turn into her mother. She'd been reasonable and accommodating. She'd done as she was told. She'd stayed close to home, played hostess at her father's parties, run his household while he worked, and worked, and worked.

And all she was doing was swapping her father's household for Stefan's.

She choked on the thought. With blinding clarity she understood how her mother had felt. Trapped.

She couldn't breathe. She tore at the scarf around her neck, needing air.

"Are you still there?"

"I'm here." But not for much longer. She needed to get back indoors. Her toes were already numb. These shoes were not designed for outdoors either.

Maybe this was what they called wedding jitters. She regained control. "I can't quit the job just yet. Besides, it's only a few more days." She sighed. "Don't worry about me. I'll be fine. I have Anna." And Lee. She pulled her shoulders straight. "I'm sorry. I know I'm not being very supportive. It's just a shock. Of course everything will be alright, and I'll see you on the twelfth."

"We'll talk soon, okay?"

She nodded, even though he couldn't see. "Take care." She ended the call and stared at the phone, as a voice from long ago

157

filtered through her thoughts.

*I'm tired of being so alone.*

Her mother had said the same thing as she'd walked out the door. Tessa shut down the thought just as a door behind her swung open. The raw emotion was not so easy to subdue.

*Take care.* Not *I love you.*

Christian pushed the door wider and stepped out into the courtyard. He'd heard enough of that conversation to get the gist.

Teresa looked unhappy, and he didn't blame her. What kind of man could keep away from such a gorgeous bride? Her fiancé had to be insane not to want to be with her at every possible moment.

Christian couldn't seem to keep away.

He kept his face expressionless as he stepped forward into the light. She'd spoken in local dialect and it didn't suit him to admit he'd understood every word.

"I brought your jacket." He held it out to her. "I thought you might be cold."

Especially in that dress.

Her only concession to the cold was a lightweight scarf wrapped around her neck. She wore a charcoal-grey wrap-around dress that clung to breast and hip, nude stockings and heels so high she almost looked him in the eye. Heels so damned sexy he almost didn't give a damn that she wore a great big flashy diamond on her left hand.

But she was as good as a married woman, and unlike Dominic he had rules about things like that. He didn't mess with other men's wives. Even if that man was out of town and no doubt living it up while his fiancée waited patiently at home for him.

"I am cold." She shivered as she slipped on her jacket. "Thanks."

He stepped closer to lift her pale hair out from under the fur-trim collar. Her eyes widened momentarily at the intimacy, but she didn't flinch back.

"Let's get you inside." He stepped back and headed indoors, into the darkened passage that led to the toilets. Once they were both inside, he shut the door behind them. Instantly, the temperature went up a few degrees. He took the phone from her lifeless hands, stuck it into her jacket pocket, and began to rub some life into her frozen fingers.

"You okay?"

"Yes." Pause. "No."

"What was that all about?" he asked.

"I should leave. I'll call a cab. I need to move the rehearsal dinner."

"Not right now, you don't. Besides, it's Sunday night. What you need to do is have another drink."

She shook her head.

"You're cold and it'll warm you up. Then I'll call Frank to take you home."

"Promise?"

"Promise." Only it wasn't a promise he intended to keep. Not until much later.

She was upset. She needed a drink for more than its warming qualities. And she really needed to loosen up and have a little fun. Heaven only knows her fiancé probably was, wherever he was.

Thank heavens Dominic had texted him to get his butt over here. Though to be more precise, Dom's message had read *Your Ice Queen is wearing red heels. If you don't take your chance tonight, I will.*

Christian hadn't been able to get there quickly enough. And if he was honest with himself, it had less to do with a chivalrous urge to protect Teresa from Dom's attentions than a desire to see her in these red heels. They'd been worth setting aside his anger for. Though the laps he'd done in the hotel's indoor pool had helped with that too.

He took her hand and dragged her back to the group in the bar. The music and laughter were even louder now. There'd been more arrivals and more chairs had been brought in for the newcomers, tightening the circle. When Christian returned to the group with two more of the lurid cocktails, he found himself squashed up against Tessa, his thigh pressed against hers. He slung his arm across the back of her chair.

She leaned back, trustingly, into his protection.

The victory was bitter-sweet. He rubbed the back of his neck. Wasn't that just his luck? She finally thawed, his seduction objective finally seemed possible – and she'd just shot straight from being a challenge to being forbidden.

He downed his drink and waved to the waiter for another.

When she'd finished her drink, sipping far more sedately than he had, Teresa didn't ask him to call for his car. And he didn't offer.

Another round, and the crowd began to thin. Dominic gave Christian a *'cheers, dude'* and a fist pump, and left with his arm around the pouty brunette.

"Hey, it's early yet!" Christian objected, as the last of the group rose to leave.

"We don't all have a late call tomorrow," Gerry said, downing the last of his Malibu and diet cola. "You guys get home safe now." He pinned Tessa with a stern look. "You'll make sure he gets to the studio on time tomorrow?"

"Of course."

Then it was just the two of them.

Her unruffled serenity might have fooled Gerry, but she didn't fool Christian.

Tessa's eyes were over-bright, her cheeks pink. But the biggest clue that the alcohol had done its work in loosening her up was the way her shoulders relaxed. She leaned back in her chair, against his arm, which lay once again across the back of it.

"Shall I call Frank?" he asked.

She shook her head. "It's the middle of the night. He's probably asleep."

"I'll ask the barman to call us a cab, then."

Her eyes followed the barman mixing drinks behind the counter. "I know it's not the sensible thing to do, but I don't want to leave

160

yet."

"I know the feeling. My home is a hotel room, remember?"

"Suite," she corrected, with a small smile. "And try a whole house of empty."

"You miss your fiancé?"

It was an obvious question and he expected an obvious answer, but Teresa didn't reply. Instead, she shook her head.

"You want to talk about it?"

Another head shake. "I'd like to do something I've never done before." The slur in her speech was so subtle he would have missed it if she hadn't spoken with such care.

"What's that?"

"I want to get drunk."

He choked on his drink. *She'd never been drunk before?*

The eyes that looked up at him were big and round. She looked so much younger, so vulnerable, now that the alcohol had stripped her of her airs. He liked this new Teresa. Innocent, with a hint of warmth beneath the uptight façade. It took all his willpower not to wrap her in a protective embrace.

He resisted the urge. Because once he got her close he wasn't sure he'd be able to let her go. Not after three weeks of wanting.

"I'll get us something to drink." He pulled away, rose, and moved to the bar counter to place the order. No more cocktails, just coffee. It wasn't often he got to be the responsible one. It was a good feeling. Perhaps he should try it more often.

*My Chemical Romance* played in the background, not so blaring now. Glancing around the room, he could see only couples cuddling in the darkened corners of the room.

When he returned with the coffees, Tessa had moved to one of those shadowy corners, to a recently vacated white-leather sofa, too upright and stylish to be comfortable, but she'd removed her shoes and sat with her legs curled beneath her.

He handed her a cup and she frowned as she took it. "Why won't you let me get drunk?"

Because he needed someone else to stay sober and sensible. He wasn't so noble that he could resist taking advantage if she chose tonight for the volcano to blow.

"You'll thank me in the morning, I promise."

She stared down into the depths of her coffee cup.

He blew on his coffee and eyed her over the cup's rim. "Do you want to tell me why you kept your engagement a secret?"

"It wasn't a secret. You just didn't need to know."

But she wouldn't look him in the eye.

He'd told her everything about himself. Or nearly everything. Her evasion hurt.

He placed his fingers beneath her chin and lifted her head so she was forced to look him in the eye. "Don't lie to me, Tess. Please, don't ever lie to me."

Her pupils dilated, swallowing the blue of her eyes. She moistened her lips.

"I don't know," she said. "I don't know why I didn't tell you."

He released her chin. "Tell me about this man you're going to marry."

She blinked, bringing herself back under firm control. Even tipsy, her strength of will was impressive. What would it take for her to truly let go and do something impulsive?

"Stefan's a diplomat. He works as a foreign policy consultant and he has a very bright future. My father says he'll be the youngest ambassador Westerwald's ever had."

"To be an ambassador means he'd have to live somewhere outside this country."

She nodded.

"And how do you feel about that?"

"Scared. Excited." She took a sip of her coffee, then lifted her gaze to his. A gaze stripped bare. "These last few weeks... I don't know what's wrong with me... I don't know what I want any more."

"Yes?" he prompted.

"I feel like I can't breathe." Her eyes were so wide and deep he

162

could drown in them, and the honesty in them took his breath away. "I suppose everyone feels this way when they're about to be married, but sometimes I feel like I want to run away. I want to go somewhere new, start over in a new life." She clapped a hand over her mouth. "I can't believe I said that out loud – and lightning didn't strike me down!"

He laughed. "Sometimes our dreams change. There's nothing wrong with that."

She eyed him, serious again. Perhaps she'd heard the bitterness in his laugh. "Have your dreams changed?"

He didn't talk about his feelings to anyone. Not even to Dominic. Yet he had to answer her with the same honesty he'd demanded.

"When I started in movies it was a means to an end. For Dom, stunt work was an extension of what he already did. He liked to take dares, to do what everyone else said was impossible. For me it was always different. I was the driven one. I wanted to be someone. To prove that I was better."

"Better than what?" she asked, homing in on his weakest point with unfailing accuracy.

"To be better than the world thought me. To be better than the kids who bullied me when I as a kid. Better than the father who abandoned us. I wanted to be rich and famous and for everyone to know my name."

"But now that you've got it, it's not what you thought it would be." Her voice was barely above a whisper.

He nodded. "It's not enough." He managed a grin. "Someone asked me not so long ago if anyone would remember my movies five or ten years from now. I've been wondering that myself. Is this going to be my legacy – a handful of forgettable action movies?"

"I'm sorry," she said. "I said some terrible things that night. I was wrong. You're a very talented actor."

He shrugged. "But I've always taken the easy way out. The easy roles, the easy money. I've never put myself on the line." Never let himself care. About anything or anyone.

Maybe it was time to change that.

He set down his coffee cup.

Unlike Tessa, who cared so much she had to build walls around her heart to protect herself from being overwhelmed. With every advantage in life, she could have taken the easy way out and lived her whole life in her ivory tower, surrounded by wealth and privilege. Instead, she took the time to know people, to care about them.

How had he ever thought her emotionless and uncaring? She cared more than anyone he'd ever met.

A tendril of hair had fallen loose from her usual neat twist. He caught it between his fingers, savouring its silky softness. "It's time for me to do what you do and give back to the world."

"But you do." Teresa leaned close. "What you did at the children's home – bringing attention to a charity that always needs more funding. That was you making a difference in the world."

He couldn't tell her now he'd only done it to impress her.

That was the difference between them. She was noble and honourable. He was still only just looking out for himself. He did nothing because it was the right thing to do, but because he could get something out of it. A conscience quieted, a publicist appeased, a woman seduced.

"I'm not the person you think I am," he said. She was so close that if he just leaned forward a little, he could kiss her. "I'm not your Prince Charming."

"I know you're not. But what if I don't want Prince Charming?"

He tucked the tendril of hair behind her ear and stroked a finger down her cheek to the edge of her jaw. Not cold at all. Warm and tempting as hell.

"That's the drink talking. You need a man worthy of you, not a bastard like me. You need your knight in shining armour."

Tears brimmed in her eyes, clinging to her lower lashes. Horrified, he brushed them away. Oh God! Tipsy he could cope with. He was more than halfway gone himself. But tears he couldn't deal with.

"You're the second man to tell me that," she said. "Fredrik told me the same thing the night he left. But I'm still alone."

"You're about to be married," he pointed out.

She turned her head away, and this time he could see the effort it cost her to pull herself together. When she looked back up at him, it was the cool, self-contained face he was so used to seeing, with all the warmth gone. "Please take me home now."

## Chapter 13

The cab dropped them in the same cul-de-sac where they first met. He hadn't had time that night to notice much, but as he stood now and looked up at the stone façade, Christian whistled.

Three storeys of elegant white stone, classically proportioned and topped by a slate roof containing dormer windows. The servants' quarters in a more elegant time, he was sure.

"Is this your place, or your soon-to-be hubby's?"

She entered a code into the key pad beside the wrought-iron pedestrian gate and pushed it open. "Neither. It's been in the Adler family for generations. I grew up here. But my father prefers the apartment he keeps close to his office."

He followed her up the neat flagstone path to the mansion's imposing front entrance, a pair of double doors between Grecian columns marked with a family crest. She unlocked the door and held it open for him.

"So you live here alone?"

Tessa shrugged. "I'm not alone. There's a housekeeper, a gardener, two maids."

"Is it just you and your father then – no siblings or wicked stepmothers?" He stepped into the hall, all marble floors and a staircase to match. "It looks like something out of Disney's *Cinderella*."

She grinned. "I promise I won't make you wash the floors."

"No, you have a housekeeper, a gardener and two maids for that."

She laughed. "Don't pretend like you don't have someone to do your laundry and wash your floors back in LA!"

He followed her into the living room. No, not just a living room. A *salon*. This was no shabby chic crumbling manor. There were no faded curtains or antique sofas, no inherited portraits of long-dead ancestors. The living rooms on either side of the hall looked as though they belonged in a style magazine. Neutral shades of grey and brown, accented by neat white trimmings, clean, modern lines. Uncluttered and practically unlived in.

It made his Malibu beach house seem positively homely by comparison.

She shut the door behind them and the sudden silence echoed. "Would you like something to drink? Tea or coffee? A mineral water? Or something stronger?"

"Definitely something stronger."

She crossed the room to an elegant antique cabinet inlaid with ormolu. "Whiskey, brandy or cognac?"

"Cognac."

Tessa removed a Venetian glass decanter from the cabinet, the kind of fancy decanter set-dressers usually placed on period film sets, and poured a generous shot into a delicate crystal snifter. He took the glass and sipped. The rich golden liquid slid down his throat.

"If your father's still alive, how did you come by your title? Isn't the usual way to inherit it after he dies?"

She turned away, fussing with putting the decanter back in its place. "The title of Baroness is from my mother's side. I'll become a Countess when my father dies." A small smile kicked up the corners of her mouth as she faced him again. "Countess Teresa Adler of Arelat."

He imagined Fate laughing maniacally, delighting in the huge disparity between them. The Countess of Arelat and the peasant boy of Arelat.

He swigged from the glass and her gaze followed the move. A hungry gaze, but what she was hungry for, he wasn't sure.

"Would you like some?" He held out the glass to her.

With barely a hesitation she took it from his hand and sipped, her gaze holding his as she eyed him over the rim of the glass. Then she handed it back and wiped her mouth.

He grinned. No way would she have done that if she were sober.

The air between them sparked, not the animosity of their first meetings as much as awareness. Or maybe it had always been this heightened state of awareness between them and he just hadn't realised it.

Her eyes darkened and her chest rose and fell with every breath. Then she cleared her throat. "Why did you leave Los Pajaros?"

It was obvious what she was trying to do. She wanted to put distance between them, to dampen this sizzle before it got out of hand.

It was the sensible thing to do.

If he were sensible, he would take her cue and escape before he revealed the secret he'd kept hidden for over twenty years. He'd seen her safely home. He should say goodnight now and head back to his hotel.

It would be the right thing to do.

Only he didn't always do the right thing. Or the sensible thing. And he hadn't asked the cab driver to wait.

He sipped the cognac and sat down on the nearest divan. "Why do you want to know?"

She sat beside him. "Because tonight we're not keeping any secrets. No more lies, remember?"

There was a reason he'd kept his past a secret. But right now, drowning in her eyes, he couldn't remember what it was.

He might still be able to walk in a straight line, but he'd entered that careless space where inhibitions loosened, where the gap between actions and repercussions became very wide indeed and he was likely to do something he'd regret in the morning. Like his publicist.

But this wasn't morning yet.

"I was only fourteen and in and out of trouble. Most of it not of my own making, I might add. My uncle took me on as his boat hand for the summer. He ran a fishing charter for rich tourists. Most of those tourists were so full of themselves they didn't even see me. Riff-raff like me didn't exist except to serve them. And those were the pleasant ones." He drew in a deep breath. "Then there were the kids who needed to prove how much better they were."

"What did they do?"

"When you're a snot-nosed kid who can get away with anything... whatever they wanted. Mostly it was just verbal. But there was one kid, full of himself because his father had some title." He dropped his gaze, not wanting her to see the bitterness, the old hatred that still burned.

"What did you do?" Her voice was so low that if the silence about them hadn't been so complete, he wouldn't have heard.

He lifted his chin and met her gaze. Defiant. Just as he'd been back then. "I gave back as good as I got. And unlike me, he was no street-fighter. I put him in hospital with a broken jaw and cracked ribs."

She frowned, as if struggling to trace a memory. Then her eyes widened. "Elijah."

Of course she knew him. Just as he'd suspected.

"He was a few years ahead of Stefan at the Academy." Her nose wrinkled in distaste. "He came back from his summer holiday with his jaw wired up."

Christian's chest froze. He couldn't breathe. But it wasn't anger or fear that immobilised him. He'd tamed the violence within him long ago. Dominic had taught him to redirect it.

But would Tessa understand that he wasn't that same angry child anymore? Or would she pull away, putting the distance between them that she'd so wanted? That they both needed.

He wouldn't blame her, but the thought of losing her friendship now, over this, was a wrench. Her aloofness he could bear, but her contempt…

"Elijah was a bully. He had it coming." She bit her lip and focused back on him. "But his father was head of the Bank of Westerwald, and in the same mould as his son. How did you get off without them pressing charges?"

"I didn't." He shrugged. "I don't know what happened, but the charges were dropped. My mother said the mayor arranged a pardon for me, though I can't think why. My uncle knew him, but he wanted nothing more to do with me after that. He said I was bad for business." Christian frowned. "Then my mother got the job in the States and within a month we moved. She said California was a fresh start for us both and we'd left the past behind, so we never spoke of it again."

And he hadn't spoken of it in twenty years. Not even to Dominic.

The fear of discovery had haunted him all these years, a weight around his neck. How close he'd come to reform school, to a permanent record. How much he'd wanted to kill Elijah. If his uncle hadn't intervened, he might have. And then there would have been no pardon.

He rubbed his hand over his eyes. The relief at having shared his terrible secret was incredible. But at what cost?

He risked a glance at Tessa. She wore that closed, impenetrable expression once again and his heart sank.

At what cost?

She took the crystal glass from his hand and downed the rest of the cognac. "Do you know that Elijah died?"

*What?* Shock rocketed through him. He hadn't been hurt that bad… he'd walked away… Christian was on his feet, without realising it.

Tessa set down the glass and jumped up too. "Not that! I didn't mean you!" She laid a hand on his arm, distress burning through her inscrutable expression. "He was running a drug factory out of his family's ski lodge and tried to cheat the dealers he was supplying. They killed him. They're the ones who escaped en route to court."

Her hand slid down his arm, until her fingers entwined with his. His heart beat erratically, a frantic, giddy pace, and he had no idea whether it was her news or her touch that caused it.

Who would have thought that the nobleman's heir who had everything would end up murdered, and the bastard outcast with nothing would end up a movie star?

Maybe Fate wasn't laughing after all.

She looked down at their intertwined hands, hers so pale against his darker one. Then she looked up at him, and the mix of emotions in her face scorched through him. Anxiety, sympathy, relief. And lust.

Now he knew what she was hungry for.

And she hadn't judged him. She hadn't mocked him. She hadn't pulled away.

He took both her hands in his. Unconsciously she licked her lips. Whether it was the alcohol in his veins or that sensual movement that set fire to his blood, he didn't know.

To hell with Sensible.

He let go of her hands and wove his fingers through her hair, loosening the knot at the back of her head. Pins scattered to the floor; something for the maids to gossip about in the morning. Her hair tumbled loose about her shoulders, long and straight and soft as silk between his fingers. On a sigh, she closed her eyes.

"Tessa. Tess." He wove a strand of her hair between his fingers. God, her hair was so pale against his skin, and it smelled of flowers. A light, innocent fragrance.

He stroked a finger down her cheek, to rest at the corner of her mouth, and her breath quickened.

"Look at me," he said. "I want to see what you're feeling."

"I don't feel. I think." But she obeyed. Her eyes opened. There was only one emotion left there for him to see. Burning, feverish desire.

171

The volcano unleashed.

"Tonight you're feeling."

She smiled up at him, eyes wide. With her barriers down and her inhibitions loosened, she was a different person. Softer, gentler, passionate. This was the woman in his dreams.

"I don't feel numb anymore." Cautiously, almost afraid, she reached out and laid a hand on his chest, right above his heart. His pulse kicked up at her light touch.

"I didn't even realise how numb I felt inside until I met you. Now I'm feeling all these feelings...what have you done to me?"

"I haven't done anything. It's all you. You've left your comfort zone." Taken a job she'd never done before, met people outside of that exclusive little clique she'd always lived in. She'd done what he was too afraid to do.

She nodded. "I was safe inside my bubble."

"And you don't feel safe now?" He stroked a hand down her hair and she sank her forehead against his chest.

"No, I don't feel safe with you," she mumbled into his sweater. "I haven't felt safe since the day I met you."

She wasn't referring to being outside her comfort zone or even the distant danger from escaped convicts. He knew, because he felt the same. She tilted his world on its axis. She challenged him, provoked him, made him want things he shouldn't want.

She was the one woman he should run from, the one woman he couldn't have, yet he wanted her with a greater ferocity than he'd ever felt before.

In the back of his head a small voice told him 'no', but the magnetic pull between them was too strong to resist.

He lifted her chin, forced her to look him in the eyes. "You don't look like a woman in love."

She tried to look away, but he held fast.

"What does a woman in love look like?"

"Radiant. And she doesn't look at other men."

"I don't look at other men."

172

He leaned in close. "You're not a very good liar, Tess."

Something flickered behind her eyes. A mix of amusement and bitterness. "You should know. You lie for a living."

"Yes, I'm a very good liar." He snaked an arm around her waist. "It's just one of the things I'm good at."

He bent his head to trail kisses down the nape of her neck.

"I can rise above this," she said. "I'm stronger than this."

But she didn't pull away. She stretched her neck, giving him better access.

"You're wrong," he whispered. "And I'm going to prove it to you."

Then he kissed her. A gentle meeting of lips, a tentative touch. But then the spark flared and he lost the last hold on Sensible.

Fire and ice. Instant reaction.

She placed her hands on his chest, palms flat as if to push him away. But she didn't. She kissed him back.

Her kiss caught him by surprise. Not the sting of burning ice, but furiously hot and bright, as if they stood in a darkened room and suddenly a spotlight had switched on.

Intense, illuminating.

His hands slid down her neck, over the soft swell of her breasts, to rest on her hips. He tugged her closer, hard against his body. She stretched into his touch.

The kiss lasted barely a moment, but it might have been a lifetime. When they broke apart, both breathless, both breathing heavily, the silence in the house was complete.

He could hear her heartbeat, was aware of every rise and fall of her chest.

He lifted her off her feet, laid her on the divan, and knelt over her, raining kisses down her neck to the tender spot at the base of her throat.

She arched against him, pressing herself into him. There was no way she could miss how much he wanted her. There was no way he could miss how much she wanted him. Not now that she'd finally let her immaculate self-control slip.

The release of all that pent-up passion was even greater than he'd imagined. She burned brighter, gave more, explored with her tongue and her hands.

He slid an arm beneath her back, raising her up into his kiss, and she twined her arms around his neck, holding him close. Another kiss that stretched time, another kiss that exploded something inside him. A kiss just as furious and mind-blowing as the first.

A kiss to lose himself in.

And then her hands slipped from around his neck, down to his chest. And she shoved. Hard.

He sprawled back, gasping for breath, stunned.

Tessa scrambled away, to the farthest end of the divan, and hugged her legs. "I can't do this! What am I thinking?"

"We weren't thinking," he answered, though he knew it was a rhetorical question. The wild, passionate woman of a moment ago was gone.

But she wasn't cold anymore. The Ice Queen look was gone too. In her eyes he read confusion and fear. And panic.

She swung her legs off the divan and rose, righting her dress, reknotting her scarf, patting down her hair, putting as much space between them as she could.

"This has got to be the stupidest thing I've ever done."

"We haven't done anything. Yet."

She shook her head. "You need to go. Now."

He didn't want to go. He wanted to take her back in his arms and carry on where they'd left off. He wanted to make love to her. He wanted to be burned.

But he scraped together the tattered remains of his willpower and rose too. "I'll call for a cab."

She shook her head. "That will take too long. You can take my car." She fumbled in her purse, pulled out the coveted set of keys and tossed them to him.

"You're not worried? I've been drinking."

She shook her head, not looking at him. "Not enough to be

over the limit."

No, it wasn't alcohol that had him intoxicated, though he still felt drunk on her kisses. He turned the keys over in his hand. This wasn't what he wanted, but he'd settle for a distant second prize. Not that he had much choice.

She led him through a cavernous, dimly lit modern kitchen, to a side door into the garage, careful to keep a distance between them, as if she were afraid that the slightest touch might be an incendiary spark.

Inside the garage it was dark, so dark he could sense the tension pulsing between them. She flicked a switch and light flooded the room. Harsh, electric light, not the dazzling golden illumination her kiss had awakened in him.

"Will you be able to find your way back to the hotel?"

In the cab he'd been too wrapped up in her, too aware of her close proximity, of her perfume, to pay much attention, but he nodded. He'd figure it out.

She opened the car door in a not-so-subtle hint that she wanted him gone. He climbed in and started the engine, opening the window as she pressed the remote to open the garage doors behind him. He leaned out the window and grabbed her arm.

"Are you sure about this, Tess? Because something that feels this good can't possibly be bad."

She pulled her arm away and stepped back, withdrawing completely from him.

"I'll see you tomorrow."

He backed out and she closed the door behind him.

Her entire body ached. Literally, her entire body.

Tessa groaned and rolled her face into the pillows. She wasn't sure which hurt more: her head or her chest. One felt tight and constricted. The other felt like it had exploded.

But she was awake now. Nauseous and awake.

She opened one eye. The room was murky. It had to be early

175

still. Really early. Why had she woken so early?

Since the film production was moving into night shoots tonight, she only had to meet Christian at midday.

She buried her head in the pillows but it didn't help. Her bladder was also about to explode. And she needed to take something for her head.

Moving very slowly, since every movement made her want to throw up, she eased herself off the bed and headed to the bathroom. When she opened the bathroom door, she did need to throw up.

Bright light streamed in from all sides. Brilliant, brain-cramping white sunlight.

She attended to one need, then the other, then finally splashed her face with water and met her reflection's gaze in the mirror.

Oh my…

So this was what a hangover looked like.

She managed to swallow a couple of pain-pills, then brush her teeth without throwing up again, and stumbled back to the bedroom. The room looked like an underwater cavern, gloomy, with an eerie pattern of light and shadow creeping up the walls.

She must have forgotten to open the curtains before she went to sleep last night. She never forgot to open the curtains. She liked waking to sunlight streaming in through the windows.

Not that she'd seen much of it lately, what with the early calls and having a job to go to. She moved to the windows and put her hand on the edge of the curtain. All it took was a glimpse of the pain-inducing light to make her twitch the drapes shut again.

It was too early to wake up. And if she opened those curtains she was likely to throw up again. She headed back to bed, pulling the covers right up over her head.

Tessa wasn't there when he got downstairs to the dining room the next morning, and he was already late. His chest stretched tight.

He was halfway through his first espresso when he gave in to the temptation and dialled her number. It went straight to voice mail.

He had no idea what to say, so he hung up.

The second espresso was a take-away cup in the back of the car. He slouched down in the back seat, which seemed starkly empty without Teresa beside him. Frank kept his gaze averted from the rear-view mirror, and Christian was grateful.

Had she simply overslept? Or had she decided, in the cold light of day, that she wanted nothing more to do with him after last night?

He rubbed his eyes. It had been a mistake, a terrible mistake. So why didn't it feel like a mistake? Why did it feel right to kiss Tessa and wrong to be here without her?

"Have you heard from her?" he asked Frank at last.

Frank shook his head.

"She drank rather a lot last night. Perhaps she's hung over."

Frank said nothing, and there was nothing more Christian could say.

# Chapter 14

Christian hefted the weight off his chest and held it aloft, grunting at the effort. Then he slowly lowered the weight back onto its rest. And again.

Sweat dripped from his brow, and his t-shirt clung damply to his torso. Perhaps a swim in the hotel's indoor pool would ease this tension inside him. Running on the treadmill hadn't. Bench-pressing weights hadn't.

Perhaps this was payback for every woman he'd seduced and walked away from. Or perhaps this was Fate kicking him in the groin just for the hell of it.

He'd set out to make Teresa's life miserable. He'd wanted to break her. And he'd failed spectacularly. She was as cold and unfeeling as ever. Instead, he was the one who was broken. He was the one unable to sleep.

He hefted the weight again, breathing deeply as he held it high off his chest.

Sunday night had changed everything for him. Tessa's kiss had flooded him with new hope, had given him something to aspire to. Forget the superhero movie. Forget the safe bets at the box office. He was going to sign up for Robbie's script, he'd even produce it if that's what it would take to make the movie happen. He was going to challenge himself and try new roles, and if the audiences didn't love him for it… then tough.

He'd had their love, he'd earned their money, and it wasn't enough.

He wanted something in his life to be proud of. And he wanted to try a real relationship. Perhaps not a lifelong commitment, since he had a tendency to bring nothing but pain to those he loved, but a relationship built on something more than exchanging phone numbers and bodily fluids. With someone he could talk to and enjoy being with; a woman who would inspire him and challenge him and awe him, as Tessa did.

It just wasn't going to be her.

She'd made that abundantly clear these last two days. She refused to talk to him, refused to be alone with him. Even refused to look at him.

The whispers around set were impossible to avoid. Which was how he'd discovered that much as though people loved him, they loved Tessa more.

There wasn't one person on the set who didn't think that whatever had gone down between them, it was his fault. The general verdict was that he'd made a move on an innocent, virginal, soon-to-be married woman and been slapped down for it. And they cheered Tessa for being the one to finally do it.

Even Dominic, the back-stabbing bastard.

Christian dropped the weight back on its rest. Hell, he'd earned the reputation, hadn't he? This was definitely payback.

But the worst wasn't that he deserved it. The worst was that the dreams had stopped. He'd lost her twice over. The real Teresa and the one in his head had both deserted him.

He raised the weight again, relishing the burn in his aching muscles.

The gymnasium door swung open and he turned his head slightly. It was well past midnight. Who else would be up at this hour?

"What are you doing here?" he panted. "I thought you'd gone out drinking."

Dominic stepped through the door. "And I thought you were dining with the studio money men after wrap tonight?"

Christian settled the weight back in its place and sat up, wiping his face with his towel. "I did. I'd rather have gone out drinking with you." Or out with Teresa.

He'd come close to inviting her along. Twice. She'd have charmed the executives' pants off. She'd have backed him up. But he couldn't face the torment of being with her and not being with her. Besides, she'd probably have known them all already. Been dandled on their knees as a kid, or something.

"They're still trying to persuade me to sign up for the super-hero movie."

"How many zeros did they add to the offer before you said yes?"

"I said no."

Dominic sat beside him on the bench. "Have you gone insane?"

Christian shook his head. "I've decided to do another movie. A dark drama with a bit of a twist. It's a very clever script and not a single stunt or special effect."

Dominic looked as if Christian had just floored him with a sucker punch. "That chick has messed with your head."

"It's not Teresa. It's me." Okay, it was all Tessa, but surely he could take a little credit for finally seeing the light?

"You seriously need to get laid. Since we're on night shoot tonight we still have a few hours to spare. Let's find a club, have a drink and find you a woman."

"I don't want to sleep with any other woman."

"Who said anything about sleeping?"

Christian rose from the bench and paced to the water cooler to pour himself a cup of ice-cold water. "I can't."

"Then you need to man up, dude. If you want her, go after her."

"I did. She said no. And she's a good person. She deserves her Prince Charming, and she's not stupid enough to give that up for

180

one night with me."

Dominic rolled his eyes. "What she deserves and what she wants are two very different things. Deep down, the good girls all want bad boys. Have you considered if you asked again she might say yes?"

"Yes. When hell freezes over."

Dominic threw his hands in the air. "Do you know nothing about women? Because the way she's been avoiding you these last couple of days, I'd say she's seriously tempted."

A large part of Dominic's success with women came from his knowing how they thought. He'd been the only boy in a family of five kids.

Christian, on the other hand, had no clue what made women tick. He'd never needed to. As long as there were women who liked him for his looks, his fame and his bank balance, he'd been assured of a good time.

But a woman like Teresa, who didn't care about the money or the name... what could he possibly offer a woman like her, who had everything?

But she didn't have everything, did she?

He stared past Dominic at the bare wall beyond. Beneath the composed façade, Tessa was a passionate woman who craved excitement and new adventures. She'd only just begun to discover that about herself. It was natural the discovery had frightened her.

And she didn't need a Prince Charming. She already had one of those. What she needed was someone who could let her explore her dark side before she lost the chance forever.

Was it possible Dominic might be right?

He needed more time. He couldn't just proposition her outright. He needed another opportunity like the one he'd had on Sunday night. He had to get her alone. But their time had run out. Two more days and the Westerwald shoot would be over. He'd be heading for that premiere in Paris and she'd be getting married. They'd go their separate ways and he'd never see her again.

His chest ached at the thought.

Dom was certainly right about one thing. He had to at least give it one last shot. He couldn't live with the regrets and the second-guessing and the *what ifs*.

Christian grinned. He felt a whole lot better now he'd made this resolution. "I think I could do with that drink now."

"The hotel bar's closed for the night."

"Then let's get it re-opened."


Tessa frowned as she pushed through the double doors into the long corridor leading to the artistes' dressing and green rooms. It was the second-to-last night of filming. Tomorrow night they'd be shooting at the palace. The bedroom scene.

Then this would all be over.

The wide corridor was cluttered with trolleys loaded with film equipment, and filled with people coming and going between the dressing rooms and the warehouse space housing Lee's pirate-ship set, or heading outdoors for a smoke break. They seemed oblivious to the tangled cables at their feet and the massive flight cases stacked against the walls. Many of them were dressed in pirate costume, but that no longer seemed odd to her.

A couple of sparks rolled passed with one of those massive film lights on wheels. She flattened herself against the wall to let them pass.

Muted music spilled from Christian's make-up room. Bouncy dance music, which meant Dominic was probably in there with him. Facing one would be bad enough, but both…

Like the coward she'd turned into these last few days, she turned away. She could find Robbie to take Christian the bottled water she'd been sent to fetch.

Her phone rang, and she snatched it out of her leather bag, checking the caller ID. "Hello, Father."

"I have good news and I have great news. Which do you want first?"

She smiled. Just what she needed. "Let's start with the good and work up to great."

"They caught the escaped convicts trying to get on a boat out of France. They're back behind bars."

A tension she hadn't even known she'd been carrying eased out of her. She wanted to laugh. Or cry. "If that was the good news, I can't imagine how fantastic the great news is going to be."

"I followed that lead you gave me."

The urge to laugh deserted her. She felt like such a traitor telling her father what Christian had told her in confidence.

She felt doubly traitorous that it had taken her more than twenty-four hours to even realise the significance of what he'd told her. She couldn't even blame her lapse on her hangover. She'd been so wrapped up in her own crisis that she'd let her father down, and Fredrik, and her nation.

Her eye had fallen so far off the ball it hadn't even occurred to her to wonder how Elijah's father had been persuaded to drop the charges against Christian. There had to be another hand at play here, someone who had way more influence than the mayor of a bunch of back-water Caribbean islands.

"What did you find out?" she asked, her mouth suddenly so dry she could hardly frame the words. *Please let Christian's mother not be implicated in anything terrible. Please let her be innocent of all this.*

"I told Elijah Senior his son's murderers were back in jail again, and this time they won't be seeing a parole board anytime soon. He was so grateful he was more than happy to tell me everything. He got a call from my predecessor in Intelligence asking him to drop the charges."

Her legs could no longer support her. She leaned against the wall of the corridor, needing its support, heedless of what people around her might think. "Why would the head of Intelligence be concerned with the welfare of one fourteen-year-old boy from Los Pajaros?"

"That's the question I intend to ask. You can leave this with me

183

now. We don't need the ring any more. Your job is done."

She covered her eyes. It was over.

"Teresa?" called a voice, and she looked up. Robbie threaded his way through the crowd, looking harried.

"I have to go. Thanks for the news." She hung up and placed the phone in her bag, just as Robbie reached her side.

"We're ready for Christian on set. Is Marie done with him yet?"

She swallowed. "I don't know. I went to the craft station to get him some water." She held up the water bottle that was her weak excuse for staying as far away from Christian as she could.

Further down the corridor a door banged open and Tessa glanced over her shoulder.

*Oh great.*

The crowd of people tripping over one another in the corridor parted like the Red Sea as Christian strolled through, oblivious to the gazes that followed him.

Was it too much to hope that he would walk straight on by?

Of course it was. Her heart hit her feet as he paused beside her.

"Hey," she said, faking a cheer she didn't feel. "Here's your water."

"Hey." His voice was low and sexy and suggestive as hell. He took the bottle, his fingers brushing against hers. She flicked a nervous glance at Robbie, who appeared way too aware of the undercurrents shimmering around them.

"May I have a moment with Tessa?" Christian asked.

Robbie nodded. "I'll let them know on set you'll be there shortly."

He hurried away, leaving them alone. Or as alone as anyone could be with twenty pairs of curious eyes watching them. She pressed herself back against the wall as a camera technician carrying a box of lenses rushed past.

She regretted it immediately. Christian stepped close, boxing her in against the wall.

"You okay?" He leaned in, resting his hand on the wall beside her head. "You look like you've had a shock."

184

This was the distinct disadvantage of someone being able to read you. She forced herself to smile. "I've just heard that the escaped convicts are back behind bars again."

"That's great news."

She nodded. Silence hung between them, as the background noise receded from her awareness.

"We haven't had a moment to talk these last few days," he said at last.

"And we don't now. You're needed on set and we're already behind schedule for the day."

"Screw the schedule." He leaned in closer. "Sunday night was... "

"...so stupid," she finished for him, while he still searched for the right word.

"Not where I was going."

She moistened her lips and his gaze followed the movement. The air between them seemed even more charged than before. And her rapid heart rate seemed to have affected the oxygen to her brain. She said the first thing that came into her head.

"I'm sorry I took advantage of you." She prayed he'd never find out how she'd betrayed his trust. He didn't give trust easily.

He frowned. "You didn't take advantage of me. I'm the one who kissed you, remember?"

"Yes, but I kissed you back. What is wrong with me? I'm not this person!"

"Yes you are. You're just... "

"I'm disgusting. I'm faithless. I've cheated on Stefan."

"That wasn't cheating, sweetheart. That was just a kiss. *This* would be cheating."

He pressed his thigh suggestively between her legs and she gasped. Her already desperately needy body responded and she had to clamp down on the surge of desire turning her bones to jelly.

"The problem isn't that I cheated on Stefan. The problem is that... "

"...it felt good." Christian leaned closer, so close their bodies

185

touched, shoulder to shoulder, hip to hip. Thigh to thigh.

"It felt good." She looked away. "But it can't ever happen again. Just two more days. We can be grownups about this for just two more days. Can't we?"

When he didn't answer she sneaked a look at him. He was frowning. He was going to give himself wrinkles if he kept doing that.

"So we just pretend it never happened?"

She nodded, relieved that he understood.

"Your fiancé is in Paris this weekend, right?"

Where was he going with this? She hoped he wasn't planning on taking advantage of Stefan's continued absence.

"Would you like to see him?"

"Of course I would." Even though she looked away again, she suspected he knew she lied. If she could put off the wedding and buy herself some time to think, she would. But she couldn't. The wedding was a little over a week away. It was too late to think.

Her throat closed with the all-too-familiar suffocating feeling.

"I'd like to ask you a favour, then."

She needed to clear her throat before she could speak. "What?"

"Come to Paris with me."

Taken by surprise, she met his gaze. And instantly regretted it as it scorched her.

"I have spare tickets for the premiere in Paris on Sunday night. We can fly in on Saturday, you can spend some time with your fiancé, watch the movie, and be back home on Monday."

"Why?" she managed. "Why me? There must be dozens of French actresses and models who will be more than happy to be your date for the night." And who'd be more than willing to provide more than just eye candy. She hadn't thought it would be possible to feel even more choked.

"It's not a date. Just a movie ticket, no strings."

"That's still a really bad idea."

"I'm asking you to watch one of my movies. Give me a chance,

186

Tess."

She closed her eyes but she couldn't block out the plea in his tone. He dropped his voice. "I'm sorry about what happened on Sunday night. But I don't want this to be the way things end between us. You've been a good friend and a phenomenal assistant. Let this be my way of saying thank you and I'm sorry." His voice dropped even lower. "I promise I won't do anything you don't want me to."

And there lay the problem. Because she *did* want him to.

She opened her eyes and lifted her chin. No way was she going to let him know how he affected her. No way.

"I'll think about it."

"Christian!" Robbie called down the corridor, more impatient than she'd ever seen him. "What's keeping you? We're on a schedule here!"

Christian stepped back with a grin. "I'm sorry for the way things ended between us the other night, but when it comes to kissing you, I'm never going to be sorry about that."

He turned on his heel and walked away. Tessa sagged back against the wall and let her breath out.

# Chapter 15

Anna ran her finger down the list. "Menus printed – check. Champagne on ice – check. Musicians rehearsed – check. Dress – check. Bridesmaid and page-boy outfits – check. I'll collect the men's suits from Anton's the day before if you can sign for the delivery from the florist."

"You do the florist. I'll collect from Anton." Lee stretched out on the divan. The same divan where she and Christian… Tessa hadn't been able to bring herself to sit on it since.

Anna scribbled a note on her list. "So that leaves only the cake."

"Yay – does that mean I get a cake-tasting session?" Lee asked.

"No need to taste. It'll be traditional fruit cake, with plain white fondant icing and decorated with real red roses. To be delivered by the bakery the day before. Someone needs to be here to make sure it gets positioned in the right place."

"But I thought Tessa hated cooked fruit?"

They both turned to her.

"What?" Tessa asked, starting guiltily.

"Are you paying any attention?" Lee scolded. "What's with the fruit cake? You don't like cooked fruit."

She shrugged. "It's traditional. It's expected."

"It's also traditional for the bride to be a virgin on her wedding night. Please, please tell me you're not still a virgin?" He ducked

188

away, laughing, as Anna smacked his arm. "Okay, just kidding. But you do know that traditions are meant to be broken?"

"That's rules, not traditions," Anna corrected.

"Potato, po-ta-to. I'll have my set-dressing team in here a few days before to set up, and the afternoon before the wedding my team coordinator will supervise where everything needs to go."

"You really shouldn't," Tessa protested. "Your crew have been working flat out. They deserve a few days off before they head to Los Pajaros."

Lee smiled. "They want to do it for you. Consider it a wedding gift from everyone on *The Pirate's Revenge*."

She blinked against the emotion welling up in her eyes. It must be wedding jitters making her so emotional these days. "Thank you."

Lee's smile turned into a grin, dimple flashing and all. "Besides, you're paying them all really good money for their time."

Tessa leaned forward and took Lee's hand. "I can't thank you enough. You've given up so much of your own time and put in so much effort. How did you do this in such a short time?"

"I told you, my best friend's ditched me. And since *I* at least have sworn off bad boys, and since there really don't seem to be any other kinds worth mentioning, I've got nothing better to do with my time. Besides, I enjoyed it. If I ever get bored of this movie lark, perhaps I'll become a wedding designer."

"I think I should take you out for a very big drink to thank you. What are you doing this weekend?"

Lee and Anna exchanged a look. Tessa's newly acquired gut instinct perked up. "What?" she asked.

"Dominic told Marie who told Robbie who told me that Christian has invited you to go to Paris this weekend."

"What is this – high school?"

Lee shrugged. "So are you going?"

"Of course not! It's a week before my wedding. I can't afford to go away!"

"I think we've just ascertained that everything that needs to be done for the wedding has been," Anna said gently.

"You can't possibly be encouraging me to go away for a weekend with a man who isn't my fiancé a week before my wedding!"

"It's not as if it's an illicit rendezvous," Anna said. Though she glanced at Lee again in that furtive way that was starting to drive Tessa nuts. "And I thought you wanted to see Stefan?"

Of course Tessa wanted to see Stefan. She needed to talk to him. He'd been away so long she'd grown confused. When she saw him again… maybe then these horrid doubts would scatter. Maybe then she'd find sense in the chaos of her emotions.

She toyed with the ring on her fourth finger.

"I like Stefan and all," Anna said. "It's just that…" She turned to Lee. "Help me out here."

He nodded. "When you speak about your husband-to-be, you don't light up. But when we mention Christian…"

"That's not attraction! That's anger, frustration, intense dislike…"

Lee smirked. "You could call it that too."

"You're wrong!" Teresa slid the ring firmly back onto her finger and rose to pace the room.

"We're just saying…" Anna took a deep breath and leapt. "Perhaps you might want to consider exploring your options before it's too late."

They were both mad. Certifiably, insanely mad.

So why did they both look so calm and rational sitting together on the divan, while she felt feverish and stifled? Tessa swallowed against the emotions strangling her. "It *is* too late. Three months too late. I accepted Stefan's proposal. The invitations have been sent out. I can't go back on that!"

"You don't have to." Anna rose and took her hands. "I just think… we both think… that you need to be a hundred per cent sure you're doing the right thing. Not for your father or for Stefan, but for you. If you can tell me absolutely without a doubt

190

that Christian means nothing to you and that you really want to marry Stefan, then great, don't go to Paris." Anna looked to Lee for support.

"*Chica*, if you have any doubts, then this is the weekend to address them. Talk to Stefan. Talk to Christian. Away from the wedding stress and away from the film crew. And if you have to, get Christian out of your system so that when you walk down the aisle next week you do it with conviction."

Great. She could walk down the aisle with conviction and a guilty conscience.

But maybe it didn't need to get to that. If there was one thing Stefan was good at, it was bringing order into chaos. Maybe just seeing him again would ease this awful tension inside her. And this weekend, alone, would be a better time to talk than waiting another whole week until he walked into the cathedral for their wedding rehearsal.

Lee's dimple flashed. "I knew she'd see sense." He stretched back on the divan, satisfied. "Go to Paris so you can decide once and for all whether you want traditional fruit cake – or decadent chocolate cake."

Rather than filming the bedroom scene in one of the palace's actual bedchambers, which were too small to fit a film crew, cameras and all the paraphernalia that went with them, the magnificent antique four-poster with its embroidered hangings had been moved to one of the drawing rooms. Black-out cloth hung over the windows to simulate night in the room as it was not yet dark outside.

It was the same room where, less than ten months ago, Fredrik had broken the news to her that would make headlines the world over the following morning. They'd sat in the deep window embrasure, with golden afternoon light falling through the lead-paned windows, the scent of spring flowers in the air, and they'd said goodbye.

And here she was again, preparing for another goodbye.

She stood behind the panel of monitors and watched the scene play out over the heads of the director and the producers, who sat on fold-up chairs with their headsets on, engrossed in the action.

Christian and Nina lay on the bed, bodies so close they touched. He wore nothing but snug-fitting black-leather trousers no real seventeenth-century pirate would have worn, and she wore a lacy nightdress that might have looked chaste had it not been practically see-through.

But this was hardly the intimate moment Teresa had envisioned. Even with the subdued mood lighting, it was hard to appear intimate with more than thirty onlookers and a microphone hanging overhead.

"You're not going to make love to me?" Nina pouted, sounding way more disappointed than Teresa had when she'd read the lines. Sounding way more like Teresa felt right now.

Christian's voice was low, but the seductive quality still managed to reach where Tessa stood. "I fully intend to make love to you. But not before you tell me what's changed. The girl I used to know was too afraid to stand beside me where everyone could see. I've done much worse things since. So what's changed?"

He brushed a finger over Nina's cheek and Tessa's heart raced. Her sensitive skin remembered the burn of his fingers over her cheek, down her neck.

When his hand rested on the very edge of Nina's neckline, her own breasts ached with need. She crossed her arms over her chest to hide her reaction.

"I learned there are worse things a girl can lose than her reputation." Nina whispered.

The room was so very still.

"Like what?" Christian asked.

When she'd read these lines, Tessa hadn't believed the words. There was nothing worse a woman could lose than her reputation. Her name, her reputation, was everything.

But now she understood. Now she knew how it felt to lose

her heart. To lose a piece of herself. It hurt so much she could hardly breathe.

And they hadn't even said goodbye yet.

But she didn't hurt enough to sacrifice everything else for what would never amount to anything more than an affair. Not enough to give up her home, her safety, her place in society.

Unlike losing her reputation, this pain was personal. It could be concealed.

She shook her head as Nina replied: "But you didn't love me enough to stay and fight for me."

"And you didn't love me enough to acknowledge me publicly."

A pin could have dropped in the room and she'd have heard it. The air crackled with tension. Or maybe the tension came from inside her. Tessa hugged herself closer, but it didn't help.

Christian ran his hand down Nina's arm, over her breast, over her hips, as the camera zoomed in. On the bank of monitors, Tessa got to see the intimate touch up close and personal.

A hand touched her arm and she jumped.

"Shhh." She turned to find Max, his finger on his lips in warning. Her eyes widened in delighted surprise and she smiled.

"And that's a cut," the director said, his words echoed louder by the assistant director. The director jumped up from his chair and moved to the bed to talk to Christian and Nina, and Tessa turned to Max.

"So you finally made it onto the shoot. I was wondering if we were ever going to see you here."

"We've been frantically busy with wedding arrangements and state affairs, but Phoenix threatened to kill me if we missed the entire film shoot." He wrapped an arm around his fiancée and pulled her close.

"Hi, Teresa." Phoenix's smile was warm and instantly engaging. Tessa couldn't help but respond with a smile. "Hello again."

They'd met at a number of official functions and she liked the soon-to-be Archduchess. And this time she felt nothing at that thought. It no longer hurt that this American cocktail waitress would have the role she'd once expected would be hers.

Tessa had finally moved on. To a whole new pain.

"This is a closed set – no visitors!" shouted the AD. The people at the monitors turned where he looked.

"This isn't a visitor," Tessa said, raising her voice so it would carry to the room. "This is Archduke Maximilian of Westerwald."

They were immediately swamped with attention, the cameras and action forgotten. Tessa was forced to make an endless round of introductions. She noticed that Phoenix repeated every name she heard, the same trick Tessa used when faced with an impossible number of names and faces to remember.

Yes, Phoenix would make the perfect Archduchess. Westerwald was in good hands.

Then it was Nina and Christian's turn to be presented.

Did Max have any idea yet that Christian might have the missing Waldburg ring? If he did, he showed no sign of it. He kissed Nina's cheek, exchanged a few pleasantries with her, then shook Christian's hand.

Max's eyes held the same friendly, mischievous look they always had.

Tessa started to choke.

"Are you okay?" Phoenix asked, patting her on the back.

Tessa nodded, but she couldn't breathe.

*Oh my God!*

All faces turned to her, but she could see only two. Two very different faces, two concerned expressions. Two pairs of identical eyes.

Now she knew why Christian had always seemed so familiar.

"Get her some water," Max called.

Christian was right beside her, his arm around her. He looked truly worried now. "What's wrong, Tess?" he asked, holding her tight.

She shook her head. "I'm fine." She pushed him away and

194

gratefully accepted the bottle of water thrust at her.

She gulped down the cool liquid and slowly began to breathe again.

"We're on a deadline, people!" The AD shouted. "It's nearly dark and we have night exterior scenes to get to."

Nina and Christian returned to the bed, the crew returned to their places, the cameras rolled. Only Tessa no longer watched the action. Her gaze moved from Christian on the bed to Max beside her. They even stood alike and moved alike. The same light, easy grace, the same cocky grin, the same laughter lines.

It wasn't possible.

But it was.

When Christian was conceived, Max and Fredrik's mother had still been working as a supermodel in New York. Her engagement to Prince Christian had only been announced in the late autumn.

Around the same time that Christian's mother, six months' pregnant with her illegitimate child, had been deported back to Los Pajaros.

Tessa turned away. She needed to sit. Her skin felt icy and clammy at the same time. She made her way soundlessly to the doors and out into the corridor. It was darker out here, away from the bright film lights. Film technicians sat on boxes and crates, whispering to one another. None paid her the least attention as she sank down to the floor and buried her head in her hands.

She couldn't go to her father with this yet. She had nothing but a gut instinct. She needed proof. She needed to see Christian's ring.

If she went to Paris with him this weekend she might be able to get one last shot at it.

What if she was wrong?

But if she was right, then Christian's mother hadn't stolen anything from the palace. She'd been given it.

Max and Phoenix stayed on set throughout the night. Though it was bitterly chilly outside, they stayed to watch the filming, met everyone on the crew – from the executive producers to the lowliest set runners. Tessa, firmly back in command of herself, stayed with them, introducing them to people, explaining the film-making process.

"You're really enjoying this," Max observed, as they sat down to a midnight supper in the old servants' hall, the last meal the film crew would eat together on European soil. "Perhaps you should consider a new career."

"It's not part of her big life plan," Christian pulled out the chair beside her. Instinctively, she shifted away, creating distance between them.

She didn't like the understanding look Phoenix sent her. Was her discomfort that obvious?

"I'm sure Stefan wouldn't mind you having a job," Max said. "After all, this is the twenty-first century. And he hasn't objected to you having *this* job, I gather?"

She shook her head. "He hasn't been here." She really didn't intend for that to sound as bitter as it did.

"How long has he been away?" Phoenix asked.

Tessa felt Christian's gaze on her; hot and unsettling as always.

"A month," she answered.

Phoenix glanced at her fiancé, her gaze softening. "I can't imagine being apart from Max for even a week. It must be so hard for you. Especially now, right before the wedding."

Tessa nodded, mute.

"When is he back?" Max asked.

"Next week." Tessa sipped at the warming soup before her. But it did nothing for the freeze that had overtaken her body. "Just in time for the wedding."

"You poor thing." Phoenix patted her hand.

"She has the opportunity of a romantic rendezvous in Paris with him this weekend," Christian prompted. "Perhaps you can persuade her to accept it. She won't listen to me."

His voice had taken on that soft, suggestive quality again.

Phoenix glanced between them and Tessa blushed.

"Not so romantic," she said. "We'd both be working. Stefan has meetings, and I'd be there to support Christian at his premiere."

Phoenix's eyes glittered. "I love premieres! It's one of the perks of marrying into royalty. We've offered to host the world premiere of *The Pirate's Revenge* right here in Westerwald." She turned to Christian. "You'll return for that, won't you?"

"I'm contracted to do a full promotional tour for the movie, but that doesn't mean I'll enjoy it." He looked straight at Tessa. "My date will be on another man's arm by then."

Tessa choked on her soup. She had to stop doing that.

The sun was just coming up as they left the palace for the last time. It was past eight o'clock and the morning rush hour was already in full swing. Since the thaw had set in, there was a crowd clustered at the gates; the usual mix of royal-spotters, celebrity-spotters and photographers. Tessa recognised a few of the faces from the days she'd dated Fredrik.

That seemed a lifetime ago now.

Frank's car inched through the crowd, the darkened windows subduing the incessant camera flashes. This was the last time they'd drive together through these gates. Unless she accepted Christian's invitation to Paris, this would be the last time they'd be confined together in the back seat of a car.

Three long weeks ago she'd prayed for this moment. Now that it was here, she didn't want it to end.

She cleared her throat. "If I go to Paris with you, I have a few conditions."

Christian raised an eyebrow.

"The existing booking is for one suite only. I want my own separate suite."

He nodded.

"On separate floors."

"If you insist."

"I'll be there as your assistant. Nothing else."

He didn't say anything, and she frowned.

He shrugged a shoulder. "Scout's honour."

She doubted he'd ever been a cub scout.

Why on earth had she agreed to this? She couldn't trust him to keep his word, nor could she trust herself.

But she had to do this. Forget what Lee and Anna thought, she had to do this for Westerwald.

She had a very good idea what temptation faced her in Paris. How was she going to manage to keep Christian at arm's length when it was just the two of them, alone in a foreign city, in a hotel? A place with beds.

But they wouldn't be alone. Dominic would be there. The film's producers and publicists and stars would all be there. And Stefan would be there. He was the reason her heartbeat quickened at the thought of Paris.

And she'd do some shopping. Nothing beat the Parisian shops.

Yes, that was it. Her excitement had nothing to do with Christian and everything to do with Paris.

Liar.

# Chapter 16

They flew to Paris on a private jet, just her and Christian and Dominic. Tessa wasn't sure whether Dominic's company was a help or a hindrance. She sat quietly in the corner, trying to concentrate on her novel, while the two men talked sports and drank beer, even though it was still well before noon.

As soon as they landed, Dominic made himself scarce and Tessa and Christian headed to the hotel, a discreetly luxurious establishment off the Rue du Faubourg St Honoré booked for them by the film's publicity team. The hotel overlooked a park-like garden, a Paris rarity.

"What do you have planned for the day?" Christian asked as they waited at the check-in desk. "Are you meeting your fiancé?"

He never used Stefan's name, she noticed.

"He has meetings until late. I'll meet him at the restaurant later this evening."

"He's not staying here?"

She shook her head. "He stays at the embassy."

"So why aren't you there with him?"

"We're not married yet. It wouldn't be appropriate."

She didn't like the look he gave her; one of those penetrating, see-all looks. "You're not still a virgin, are you?" he teased.

She pulled her shoulders up, indignation coursing through her.

"Of course not."

He grinned, eyes twinkling. "Just checking. Since your preference seems to run to the *gentlemanly*." His tone was only faintly mocking, but he was right. She and Fredrik had never… and Stefan…

"Our relationship isn't like that. It's not about sex. It's about companionship and mutual understanding." She felt an overwhelming urge to explain. Or to dig herself out of a hole. She wasn't sure which. "Sex is highly over-rated. I don't know what all the fuss is about." She was very proud of how cool and even her voice came out.

Christian's eyes glittered dangerously. "Then you haven't been doing it with the right person."

"That's what all you guys think." She dropped her voice to a deep tone: "*I'm such a stud that with me it'll be different.*"

He laughed and leaned closer, so that his breath tickled her cheek. Though he spoke softly there was no chance she could miss his next words. "Oh I guarantee with me it will be different."

She was no longer rolling her eyes. No, every ounce of energy left in her body was needed just to hold her legs up. She turned her head away so he couldn't read the temptation in her eyes. "Get over yourself, Stud."

He grinned as he stepped back. "Just as long as you recognise that."

He took the key card the blushing check-in girl handed him and headed for the lifts. Tessa leaned against the check-in counter and fought to get her breathing back under control.

What the hell was he doing to her? This wasn't her. Going all weak-kneed and flashing hot and cold. Perhaps she was coming down with something.

But she knew what she was coming down with. A very bad case of lust. And it wasn't for her fiancé.

"Your card, ma'am."

Tessa took the key card held out to her. She had a nasty suspicion it wasn't the first time the young woman had tried to give it to her.

The walk across the lobby to the lifts gave her a moment to recompose herself. She had a mission, and she needed to remember that. Her knees would have to wait until later to go weak. Preferably until she saw Stefan.

Christian still waited at the lifts.

"You have the list of stores your stylist wants you to visit?" she asked, back in professional assistant mode, even if only for the sake of the porters waiting beside them.

His nose wrinkled. "Do I really have to spend the afternoon shopping? Isn't that what I pay the stylist for?"

Tessa held out her hand and with a sigh he pulled a dog-eared printed email from his shoulder bag and gave it to her. She scanned the list. Most were shops she'd planned to visit herself, so she could at least do her own shopping while tackling the touchy subject of missing rings.

"I'll meet you back here in the lobby in fifteen minutes."

"You'll come with me?" He brightened.

She cast a pointed look at the sweatpants he wore. "You should not be allowed to dress yourself. And your stylist will kill you if you come back with yet more jeans and sweatshirts. You need me."

His answering grin was cheeky. "I know I do."

They hit the Avenue Montaigne first – Dior, Lacroix, Valentino, Ungaro.

Most men she knew would have wilted within half an hour, but Christian, the Energizer bunny, kept on going. Not that she'd ever been shopping with a man before, but she was sure most would not have had the patience to wait while she directed the stream of attendants and made their selections. Christian teased and flirted with the attendants who waited on them, tried on suits and shirts and pants when instructed and drank seemingly copious quantities of champagne.

And though this was Christian Taylor the Joker in full character, he seemed to be enjoying himself.

She was too. Much as she enjoyed shopping at any time, being with Christian brought out the sunlight and the laughter. She no longer fooled herself that it was the champagne.

They lunched at L'Avenue on lobster salads and more champagne.

Without an audience, he was himself again. At ease, quiet, not trying so hard. She only wished she'd had more time to get to know this version of him.

Tessa sipped her cappuccino and eyed him across the table. If there was ever a moment to ask him straight out about his ring, this was it. But she couldn't bring herself to do it. She didn't want to break this golden moment, this last bit of time they'd spend together.

They headed back to the Rue du Faubourg St Honoré to tackle Ferragamo and Yves St Laurent, but the sunlight was no longer there. The sky turned grey and heavy.

"Your stylist will be proud of you," Tessa said, as they stood outside the last store and watched the chauffeur load their purchases into the car. Snow had started to full again. She lifted her face to the snowflakes drifting down and closed her eyes. Then, unable to resist the temptation, she stuck out her tongue.

Christian laughed, a throaty, reverberating sound. "When we first met, there's no way you would have done that."

She blinked. The princess she'd been trained to be couldn't just stick her tongue out. At least, not where any camera might see. But she wasn't going to be a princess, was she? She could do anything she wanted. She smiled at the revelation.

"Thank you for today," she said. "I had fun." And she'd especially enjoyed spending an entire day with him without having to worry about how he made her feel or how she would keep him at a distance. She was glad she'd come.

This was a much better way to end things.

Even though she didn't want it to end.

Christian grinned as he held the car door open for her. "I should thank you. But my credit card doesn't."

She stepped into the car. She hadn't asked him about the ring. And she didn't care.

Christian opened the French doors of his suite wide, but it didn't help. The blood in his veins seemed to have reached boiling point. More than a month since he'd last gotten laid and his obsession with Teresa was nowhere near at an end. He stood on the balcony, whiskey tumbler in hand, and enjoyed the sensation of the snow falling about him, settling on the grey rooftops all around.

Even in nothing but shirt sleeves, the wintry air could do nothing to quench the fire inside him.

What kind of a future was Tessa signing up for? A future with an absent husband, with whom sex was *highly over-rated*?

She needed to be the person she'd been today: a young woman with laughter-bright eyes who stuck her tongue out to catch snow-flakes. Because that woman would never settle for a life without adventure and passion.

His grand plan for the weekend had involved letting her see her soon-to-be-husband tonight. Tomorrow he would look in her eyes and he would know. But tomorrow, if she still looked at him with the banked inferno in her eyes, then he would make his move.

It had been a good plan, a sensible one. A plan designed to not scare her off or overstep any boundaries until he was sure.

A responsible plan.

But he no longer needed to wait for tomorrow. How could she not see that she was making a terrible mistake?

He downed the drink.

He couldn't let her make this mistake and he couldn't wait. Tomorrow was a lifetime away and he wouldn't endure another tortured night.

To hell with the plan.

Sticking his key card in the back pocket of his jeans, he left the suite. Though the elevator's machinery worked with soundless modern efficiency, it moved as slowly as it no doubt had when the hotel was built a hundred years ago.

Tessa couldn't have put any more distance between their rooms if she'd tried. He found hers at the end of a very long corridor, at the furthest end of the hotel from his.

He knocked on the door, impatient.

The door opened and Tessa's eyes widened. She wore a hotel dressing gown and smelled freshly showered.

"Do you need something?" she asked, voice breathy.

*Yes. You.*

The banked fire was there in her eyes. He pushed past her into the room and slowly, reluctantly, she shut the door behind them.

Now that he was here, he didn't know the words to say. He caught her hips and dragged her against him. His lips crashed down on hers. This kiss was neither soft nor slow as their first kiss had been, but hard and demanding, punishing.

She kissed him back, fighting fire with fire. Her mouth opened, letting him in. His hands were on her lower back, sliding lower. Hers were in his hair, sliding down his shoulders, to his chest.

With an anguished groan she pushed him away, breathing heavily. When he held her fast, she pummelled at his chest and he let her. He could take it. Not for nothing had he spent a lifetime of taking abuse in the gym.

At last she sagged against him, her forehead against his chest, the fight gone out of her. He cradled her against his body, stroked his hand through her hair, silky soft, soft as her lips.

He raised her chin and looked into her eyes and something welled up inside him, something fierce and pure that he couldn't name because he'd never experienced it before.

"Are you done?" he asked.

She lifted her stark gaze to his. "What happened to scout's honour? You promised you wouldn't do anything I didn't want."

"But you want this."

For a long, suspended moment their gazes held. "We shouldn't do this. We can't do this. I need to meet Stefan and his colleagues at the restaurant."

Christian frowned. He wanted to jump her bones and he'd been with her every day for the last four weeks. Her fiancé hadn't seen her in just as long and the one evening he got to spend with her, he took her out to dinner with his colleagues?

"You're very big on *shoulds* and *shouldn'ts*, but be honest with me. You're scared. I understand that. But look me in the eye when you tell me you don't want this."

"It doesn't matter what I want."

His frown deepened. "That's not what I asked."

"Want is a dangerous thing. It's self-serving and destructive."

"Denying yourself is destructive. One of these days you're going to implode. Why the hell are you going ahead with this marriage? Surely you must have realised by now you were on the rebound when you agreed to marry him? You were barely over Prince Fredrik when you jumped into this engagement. What you *should* be doing is ending this mistake before it gets even worse."

"It's not a mistake. Stefan and I... what we have isn't like that."

"Then tell me what it *is* like. Because from where I'm standing it looks like you're about to marry someone you don't love and who doesn't love you back. And I don't understand why."

"Of course you wouldn't understand. Stefan and I... we have a shared vision."

He held her gaze, dared her to look away. Dared her to acknowledge the truth. Surely she wasn't so blind she actually believed her happiness was worth sacrificing just because they both wanted to be noble and make a difference in the world?

Desire flickered in her eyes, and something else. It wasn't just him she wanted, but everything he represented, freedom, indulgence. All the things she'd denied herself. And for what?

He pressed his advantage. "If you were mine, I'd say to hell with dinner and you'd be in that bed already. Naked." He fully expected her to come back with a sassy rejoinder, something about '*then just as well I'm not yours*' but she stayed silent.

"Your lips say one thing, but your eyes say something else."

Slowly, painfully slowly, she slid her hands beneath his shirt, gliding over his skin, exploring, setting his body alight. He moaned.

With shaking hands she began to unbutton his shirt.

To hell with the buttons. He yanked the shirt up and over his head and tossed it on the bed.

Her eyes were wide, her pupils dilated, as they'd been the night he first kissed her. But this time she wasn't tipsy. She knew exactly what she was doing.

She ran her hands over his chest, skating across his hardened nipples, down over his abs. He captured her wrists as she reached his waistband.

First he needed to be sure…

There was only one thing more he still needed to hear from her. "Do you love him?"

If she told him she loved Stefan, then this was the end. He would walk away.

But if she didn't…

He could practically hear her heart beating in the pregnant silence. Her lips parted to speak and he held his breath.

A knock resounded through the room.

"Did you order room service?" He held her gaze, not willing to let her free.

She shook her head, slowly, as if mesmerised.

The knock came again, louder. Followed by a voice. "Teresa, are you in there?"

She blinked, waking from her trance, and paled. "Oh my God – it's Stefan." She looked around wildly, as if searching for an escape. "I can't see him now! Not like this."

"Do you want me to get rid of him?"

"Definitely not!" She sucked in a breath, more a gulp, "You've got to get out of here."

"I'm not leaving. Not until you give me an answer."

"He can't see you here!"

It was the closest to panicked he'd ever seen her. Even that first night when he'd vaulted into her car, she'd shown more control.

"I'll wait in the bathroom."

Another knock. "Teresa, if you're in there, please let me in. I need the bathroom."

*Shit.*

"Under the bed or in the closet," she said. "Those are your options."

The closet would be airless. He swore and got down on his knees. As he rolled under the bed, Tessa threw his shirt in after him and headed for the door.

Oh God, he'd become the ultimate sitcom cliché.

"I'm here," she said, unlatching the door and letting Stefan in.

"Thank heavens. I didn't expect the traffic to be so bad coming across town." Hurried footsteps entered the room.

From his vantage point under the bed, Christian could see little more than a frame of bed-covering and the carpet. A pair of expensive patent-leather shoes appeared, and a smart attaché case was placed on the low coffee table just within Christian's line of vision. Then the shoes crossed the room and the bathroom door closed.

Tessa followed Stefan to the door. "This is a surprise. I thought we were meeting at the restaurant later!"

"I got off early and wanted to see you. I thought we could have a drink downstairs before we go meet the others for dinner." Stefan's voice came indistinct through the closed door.

Through the lacy bed frill, Christian could see Tessa's reflection in the mirror across the room. With her eyes closed she breathed in deeply, pulling herself together, bottling up all those emotions she'd only just unleashed. The transformation twisted a knife in his gut, as *his* Tessa disappeared.

"I'm glad. Because we need to talk." She sounded back in control, calm as ever. She moved away, out of his line of vision, and Christian squirmed to get a better view of the distant mirror, curiosity about this other man, his competition to all intents and purposes, over-ruling his caution.

The bathroom door re-opened and Stefan stepped out.

Christian could see the appeal. Stefan was good-looking, in a preppy, clean-cut kind of way. He wore a navy suit that looked as if it had been tailored in Milan and carried himself with the suave confidence that only a man born to wealth and privilege could have.

Christian hated him on sight.

Stefan wrapped his arms around Tessa and pulled her close. Christian closed his eyes. Not that it helped. He couldn't close his ears and he knew exactly what was going on out there. They were kissing.

His hands fisted as he suffocated the urge to get out there and plant one in Stefan's face. How dare the man claim ownership of Tessa when he hadn't even seen her in weeks?

When she hadn't yet chosen between them.

He calmed his breathing as the two broke apart.

"I'm so glad you could come to Paris," Stefan said. "It's been so long since I've seen you."

"Four weeks and two days."

"It's been awful, I know, but we're nearly done. As soon as I get back from Stockholm I'll be all yours. I'm just so sorry I have to do this business dinner thing tonight. I'd have liked to have you to myself."

"Do you really have to leave tomorrow?" she asked. "It's Sunday. We could spend the day together."

Stefan shook his head. "I have to go. The sooner I get these negotiations over and done with, the sooner I can come home. Besides, it's not as if we'd see each other anyway. You have your work thing tomorrow."

"Only in the evening."

Stefan pulled Tessa down beside him on the sofa and wrapped an arm around her.

"I have a gift for you. That something new from Tiffany's I promised."

He took a package from his suit pocket and handed it to her. Tessa opened the box. Christian could see nothing but a reflected glitter.

"Thank you. They're beautiful."

"You're looking good. What with the wedding preparations and this damned job of yours, I thought you'd be frazzled. But you look… different. Are you ready to tell me yet why your father wanted you to take this job baby-sitting Christian Taylor?"

Unseen beneath the bed, Christian stiffened. What did Stefan mean? What did Tessa's father have to do with her coming to work for him?

Tessa pulled away from her fiancé and rose, putting space between them. Christian relaxed a little – or as much as his cramped position allowed.

"It's been good for me." She paced towards the French doors to the balcony, where the gauzy curtains were drawn shut against the darkened sky. "Whatever my father's reasons, I needed this job. For me." Her voice rang clear, confident. "I've lived my whole life inside a protected bubble. I needed to get out and face a few of my fears."

Christian couldn't see her face, but he could see Stefan's – and he could see that her fiancé didn't really get what she was saying. Stefan leaned back on the sofa and rested an ankle on one knee. "He's a smart man, your father. You look… more alive. Radiant."

Christian inched forward. The damned bed frill blocked half his view, but if he laid his head flat on the carpeted floor, he could see a little more of the room than just the mirror.

Tessa laughed nervously. "That's only because you're here now."

But there was a catch in her voice that Stefan didn't appear to notice. Christian did.

He wriggled sideways, so he could see her profile. Not just her profile. She held her hands behind her back and he could see what Stefan couldn't.

Her fingers crossed behind her back.

His breath hitched. She'd just given him his answer. She wasn't radiant because her fiancé was now here. She didn't love Stefan, and it didn't take a genius to see that there was zero chemistry between them.

She was radiant because she'd just been thoroughly kissed moments before by the man she had a whole heap of chemistry with.

If he hadn't been wedged under the bed and unable to move, he'd have done a victory dance.

Tessa hugged the dressing gown closer around her. "I need to dress. Why don't you go downstairs and have a drink at the bar while I finish getting ready?"

"It's fine. I can wait here. Don't mind me."

Tessa blushed and Christian grinned. He didn't think for half a second that she was shy of her fiancé watching her change. She was flustered because she knew Christian was watching.

And he really didn't mind watching.

"Could you do me a favour?" she asked Stefan.

"Of course. Anything."

"I forgot to pack toothpaste. And you know I can't stand to go out without brushing my teeth. Would you please go down to the lobby and see if they have any?"

Stefan frowned but he shrugged and headed towards the door.

As the door shut behind him, Tessa whirled and headed for the bed. She lifted the bed frill for Christian to roll out. Once he was out, he used the bed for leverage and stood.

He couldn't stop grinning.

"You have to go!" she hissed, as if Stefan might still hear.

"I'm not going anywhere. You don't love him." He said it triumphantly.

But Tessa only glared at him, unmoved. "That doesn't matter. You've got to get out of here before he gets back."

"Why are you marrying the man if you don't love him?"

"Because he asked." She gave him a push in the direction of the door, just as the door handle rattled.

"Shit!"

It was the first time he'd heard her swear.

With a surprising amount of force, she propelled him in the other direction, towards the French doors. She unlatched the door to the balcony and held it open for him.

"I'm not going out there," he said. "It's freezing."

The door handle rattled again. "Let me in, Teresa. We can call the concierge desk and ask them to send up toothpaste."

Great time for him to figure that out.

Tessa swore again and shoved Christian out the door, onto the narrow wrought-iron balcony that was less than a third of the size of his rooftop one, then yanked the door closed behind him. This time he let her.

He wasn't going to get what he wanted from her by stressing her out more than she already was.

He pressed his ear to the glass pane and listened, but he could hear nothing. Tessa let Stefan back into the room again and Christian turned away.

Damn, it was cold out here. And his shirt was still under her bed. He was naked from the waist up. And it was snowing harder and thicker now.

He shivered and shifted his feet, almost slipping on the frozen snow that glazed the balcony. Bloody hell, if he slipped and fell… he peered over the ledge. She might be on one of the lowest floors, but the drop was still at least two storeys high here at the back of the building. At least the garden below was deserted. He'd hate to have to explain this to the gendarmes. Or the papers.

"Nice night for stargazing," said a voice out of the darkness.

He spun, nearly slipped again, and grabbed hold of the railing.

"What the hell are you doing out here?" he asked as he made out Dominic's face in the darkness, one storey up and several

211

rooms over.

"Same thing as you, I expect." Dom leaned forward, out of the shadows of the overhang of the balcony above, his arms crossed over his chest, as casual as if he did this every day. As if he weren't turning blue from the cold. He wore even less than Christian, for he'd lost his pants and shoes too.

Dom jerked his head towards the doors behind him. "Husband came home early. You?"

"Fiancé."

Sometimes you couldn't make this shit up.

Christian peered through the glass again. Stefan was on the phone, no doubt calling the concierge desk. Tessa seemed to have gone into the bathroom. He hoped she remembered to hide her toothpaste.

He peeled himself away from the door and turned to look for a downward drain pipe.

Dominic's voice floated down from above. "I already checked. No downpipes this side of the building and the plaster's slippery as all get out. We might as well jump, but I wouldn't want you to try. You're out of practice and you have a movie to finish. The bond guarantors will go crazy if you injure yourself."

Christian peered back through the window and wished he hadn't. Teresa was now dressed to go out in a demure little black dress and nude stockings. As Stefan helped her on with her coat, he kissed her neck. Teresa leaned back against him, smiling up at him.

Christian's fists clenched. She'd let him into her room and kissed him as if there'd been no tomorrow. How could she now so casually do the same with another man?

Frig, it was cold.

He leaned forward, trying to gauge the distance to the snow-covered garden below. It was impossible to tell how deep the snow lay, though, or what might be concealed beneath it.

He and Dom had got their start in the stunt game as two gung-ho kids throwing themselves off buildings and getting paid

212

for it. But that had been a long time ago, and there were no safety mats waiting below for them now. And if his stunt-double-slash-coordinator didn't think he could make it…

"How long have you been out here?" Christian asked. He rubbed his arms.

"Long enough – I can't feel my fingers or toes."

"You're going to catch your death." Christian peered over the ledge again. "I think we can do this."

"I'm not as young as I look." Dominic said. "And my hip…"

"Your choices are simple: climb and risk an uncontrolled fall; jump or hypothermia."

Dominic shrugged and pushed away from the wall. "The snow's been coming down for a few hours now. It might provide some cushioning."

"Any idea what's underneath it? If it's lawn, we're okay. If it's paving… "

Dom shrugged. "This is my Aunt Eva's roof all over again. And I cracked my collar bone that time."

"I fractured my shin. But we survived."

"Just in case it's not lawn beneath that snow, I'd rate my chances better with two storeys rather than three. I'm coming down to you."

Agonisingly carefully, Dominic began the slow climb from balcony ledge to balcony ledge. Christian held his breath every time Dom made the leap from one to another, letting it out only when he was sure his friend had a firm grasp on the next railing.

When Dom reached the balcony directly above him, the lights in Tessa's room dimmed. Christian risked a glance inside. There was no sign of her or Stefan, so they must have left.

Dom wrapped his hands around the railing above and climbed over, hanging over the edge. Christian didn't need to ask what he needed to do. He braced himself to catch Dom as he let go. Dom's weight slammed into him and together they tumbled to the balcony floor with a crash that must have been audible to anyone inside the room.

Adrenalin and relief coursed through him. Thank heavens the ancient eighteenth-century balcony hadn't shaken loose with the impact.

Gingerly, they both got to their feet and peered over the railing ledge. Christian was the first to mount the railing. He grinned. "Do or die."

It had been their old war cry, when they'd been nothing more than teenagers who believed themselves immortal.

Dom climbed up beside him, balancing on the frozen iron railing.

"Go on, you first." Christian waved for Dominic to take the leap first, knowing full well he wouldn't.

Dom's grin lit up the darkness. "On the count of three."

One… two… With a leap, Christian threw himself off the edge, bracing for impact. The ground rushed up to meet him, the air swept about him. He whooped his delight.

Then he hit the ground. Hard. And rolled.

Bloody hell, but the snow was hard. He tasted blood in his mouth where he'd bitten his lip. He couldn't move. But at least it didn't feel as if anything was broken. Winded, bruised, shaken, but not broken. And thank heavens it was lawn beneath them after all, not concrete.

Dominic hit the ground mere yards away with a loud "oomph".

Christian raised himself up on his elbows. He couldn't help laughing at the sight of his friend, spread-eagled, nearly naked in the snow.

Dominic groaned.

"You okay?" Christian asked.

"I seriously need to find a new line of work."

"You seriously need to stop messing around with other men's wives."

Dom chuckled. "You are so not one to talk. The first time you fall in love, and she's as good as married."

"I'm not in love." Christian bit his lip. Or was he? He'd never

214

been so relentless in his pursuit of a woman before. Never wanted a woman so badly before. Never been shopping with a woman before – even his stylist.

Was this love?

"She doesn't love Stefan," he said. The joyful giddiness was back, making his head swim.

"Yeah, but that doesn't mean she loves you either," Dom said.

He crashed back down to earth. What if she didn't feel the same way about him as he felt about her? It wasn't a possibility he'd encountered before. He was used to women falling at his feet. But what if this one, the only one who mattered, didn't want him back?

He pressed his eyes shut, surprised to find an ache in his chest that had nothing to do with the fall and everything to do with Tessa.

It was probably for the best that she didn't fall for him. He only brought pain to the people who loved him. But she did want him. He was sure of it. He'd seen it in her eyes.

And he wasn't going to let go until she admitted it, until she acknowledged the passion inside her. Preferably after he got her naked and in his bed.

Or her bed. He wasn't fussy.

"Do or die," Christian repeated softly, staring up at the sky. Pinpricks of stars glittered high above. In his headlong rush towards stardom he'd lost touch with that old feeling. That sensation of standing on the edge, putting everything on the line, and just going for it. When had he last stood on the edge and taken a risk? While Dominic still lived their old motto every single day, he'd fallen into a comfort zone.

To hell with his comfort zone. He was getting too old to flit from one woman to the next. He wanted what Stefan had with Teresa. Hell, he wanted what Stefan had. Period.

"That was fun." Dominic moved his arms and legs, making snow angels.

"Yeah, but let's not do it again." Christian pushed himself to his feet. "Come on, get up, old man." He held out a hand to Dominic.

"I don't think I can," Dom said. But he reached out and grasped Christian's hand. Christian hauled him up.

"I'm getting too old for this shit."

Christian laughed. "You and me both. Let's get inside. I don't know about you, but I could do with a whiskey."

"Drinks are on me if the receptionist squeals when she sees us."

"Drinks are on me if she agrees to meet you when her shift ends."

Dominic grinned as he brushed the snow out of his hair. "Deal."

They headed towards the terrace that led into the Michelin-starred restaurant. The diners shrieked as they emerged through the doors into the classy dining room. Christian grinned and held his head high as he crossed through the restaurant and headed towards the lobby, Dominic a step behind.

When they walked into the lobby, the receptionist squealed. Christian's grin deepened. "You can make mine a double," he said to Dom, gesturing towards the bar.

His entire body ached, but he hadn't felt this happy in ages.

Do or die. He'd forgotten that mantra along the way. He wasn't going to forget it again.

# Chapter 17

He didn't see her at breakfast, nor did she answer when he knocked on her door in the early afternoon. Surely there couldn't be any shops left in the city they hadn't already visited yesterday. So where the hell was she?

With Stefan? Had her fiancé changed his mind and opted to stay in Paris to be with her? Had she rediscovered feelings for the man she planned to marry? Christian's stomach clenched into knots at the thought.

As it grew dark, he received a text from her with the time the limo would be there to collect him. Him, not them.

He stared hard at the phone, but there was nothing more.

Would she stand him up? Had he pushed her too far last night?

But when he arrived in the hotel lobby, dressed in the evening suit she'd helped him buy, Tessa waited for him. She stood before a vast oil painting hung on the wall, her back to him.

His breath caught. For a long moment he stood and simply looked. She wore an evening gown of midnight blue, which clung to her tall, slender figure. The long sleeves were made of lace and her back was bare. Over her arm she carried a short matching coat.

Then she turned and saw him. And she smiled.

No way was he going to be left out in the cold tonight.

His heart resumed its beat, perhaps a little faster than normal.

She was the most beautiful woman he had ever seen.

And yes, he was in love with her. Who wouldn't be?

She walked slowly towards him, a sensual sway in her step as she crossed the checkered marble floor of the lobby and stopped barely a foot away.

"You really should dress like this more often. You look… dashing."

"And you look stunning." Though she made the word seem meaningless. She was so much more. She was poised, sophisticated, and heart-wrenchingly sexy.

It took all his effort not to grab hold of her and kiss her right there, in the middle of the hotel lobby where everyone could see. But then he'd muss her lipstick or her perfectly styled hair – hair so artfully tumbled he had no doubt it had taken hours to achieve. So that's where she'd been all day.

She stepped close and reached up to re-tie his bowtie. "So which role will you be playing at the premiere?"

"Who do you want me to be?" He dropped his voice low, though it didn't take much to come out sounding suggestive. "Friend? Boss? Or lover?"

Her level gaze met his. "If the choice were mine, I'd want you to be *you*. The way you are right now, not the person you pretend to be when other people are watching."

Something wrenched inside him, the old pain and fear. "That person wasn't very popular, and in case you hadn't noticed I'm in the popularity business."

"You're wrong. You're not that little boy who was picked on and who kicked out in anger anymore. The world will love the real Christian Taylor even more than the fake one. But you'll never know unless you take the risk."

He frowned and shook his head, looking away, but Tessa wasn't prepared to let it go. "You ask me why I stay in my comfort zone, but you're not willing to leave yours. Want to think about that?" She stepped back, out of his reach.

"There's a crowd of fans at the hotel entrance, so we have the limousine waiting for you in the basement."

He offered her his arm and she took it, the light touch of her hand shooting an electric rush through him. Back in the elevator, he helped her into her coat, his fingers brushing the nape of her neck as he lifted the short collar. The glance she cast back at him set him on fire, leaving him in no doubt that tonight he could make her his.

If he accepted her challenge. But could he? Could he stand up before the whole world and just be himself? And if he did, would Tessa respond – would she stop hiding behind her façade of *shoulds* and *shouldn'ts* and this loveless marriage that was so clearly wrong for her?

In the basement car park, the chauffeur held the limousine door open for them. Tessa stooped to get in first and Christian followed, checking at the door. He bit back an oath.

"Bollinger?" Dominic offered, holding out a glass of golden champagne to Christian.

"I offered Dominic a lift to the theatre," she said silkily.

Great, a chaperone. Christian scowled at his friend.

"Are you getting in or not?" Dominic asked. "You're letting in the cold air."

Tessa slid onto the seat beside him and Christian climbed in. The chauffeur shut the door, closing them in.

The city lights skittered off the slick surface of the road as the limousine edged through the evening traffic down the Champs-Élysées. Paris was as grand and as beautiful as he remembered, yet Christian missed the charm and intimacy of Westerwald. He missed being alone in the back of a car with Tessa.

She sat squashed between them on the rear bench seat. When Dominic reached for the champagne bucket, she shifted to give him room, and her thigh pressed up against Christian's.

He laid a hand on her knee. She gently nudged it off, and accepted the refill of her glass that Dominic offered.

Outside the theatre they joined the cavalcade of luxury vehicles queueing to reach the red carpet. Christian drew in a deep breath, psyching himself up for the moment when the car door opened and all hell would break loose. Dominic did the same.

It was like the moment before the director called "action", when he flicked the switch and became Christian Taylor Movie Star. Fake persona in place, ready to woo the crowds.

"Whatever you do, don't look down," he advised. It was the advice he gave all his dates, the usual parade of up-and-coming starlets eager to bask in his reflected glory.

Her eyes narrowed as she gave him a withering look.

Their car pulled up at the end of the red carpet and an attendant stepped forward to open the door. The sound hit them, as hard as the ground he and Dominic had hit last night. Screaming voices, the incessant flare of camera flashes.

Tessa took the attendant's hand and stepped out of the car, smiling for the cameras. Christian followed her out, pausing a moment for his eyes to adjust to the blinding flashes of a million cameras. Beyond the barricades, his fans screamed and shoved, and waved home-made "We love you, Christian" banners.

Even if they were used to it, most people flinched at a reception like this one. Teresa didn't bat an eye. Head high, shoulders back, she stepped onto the red carpet as if she owned it. She clearly had no need of his advice. She looked as unflappably cool and calm as ever. He should have known. Dating a prince must have inured her to this kind of attention.

"Does anything intimidate you?" he whispered in her ear.

She didn't smile. "Only you."

Slowly they made their way down the endless stretch of red carpet, Christian stopping to chat to his fans, sign autographs and pose for pictures while the harried attendant tried to move him on, into the theatre where the "important" people were. But he wouldn't be hurried. These fans had camped out here in the cold to see him, and he'd make it worth their while.

As always Dominic took point, his body tensed and ready to act as his shield should any of the fans break through the barrier of security men. Christian grinned at his friend. It was good to know someone had his back.

They reached the press pit where he posed for the photographers. Tessa stayed a step behind, allowing him the spotlight, but it was no good. This was still Europe, after all, and all the society photographers knew who she was. They shouted her name and jostled one another to attract her attention.

"Ms Adler – what dress is that you're wearing? Can you show us?"

"It's an Elie Saab, from his Fall collection." She slipped off the coat and handed it to Dominic so she could pose for the photographer who'd asked the question, revealing the plunging neckline and even barer back. More camera bulbs popped, the video cameras with their built-in lights all turned towards her.

As she turned slowly for the cameras, all Christian could see was the long white line of her neck, the dip at the base of her spine. His body pulled tight.

Dominic leaned close to Christian. "I think you've been upstaged, pal."

"Are you Mr Taylor's date?" one reporter asked Teresa.

She shook her head. "No, I'm Mr Taylor's assistant."

With a poise the most experienced Hollywood actress would admire, she extricated herself from the reporters and continued down the red carpet. Unlike the women he was used to, she neither courted the attention, nor resented it. She merely accepted it. She would be wasted as a diplomat's wife. She was born for the spotlight.

She and Dominic disappeared through the theatre doors while he still had to endure the official interview, which was thrown up onto big screens above. He couldn't remember afterward what questions were asked or what answers he gave. He'd already spoken so much about this movie – a movie he'd finished shooting so many months ago he barely remembered it – that his responses had become rote.

Inside the theatre doors he was met by another army of attendants. He knew the score. Before the show inside the auditorium could start, he had to endure the one out here. The ticketholders also wanted their pound of flesh. There were more autographs to sign, cameras to pose for, hands to shake, film producers and executives and accountants and distributors to meet and make small-talk to. He posed for photographs with his co-stars and the director, all freshly arrived that morning from LA and complaining bitterly about the cold.

He looked around for Tessa. She and Dominic stood by the bar, enjoying another glass of champagne. She laughed at something he said, and Christian glowered at them. Dom caught his eye and winked.

"You must be the first member of an entourage to attend one of these do's kitted out in Elie Saab," Dominic commented as he handed Tessa a fresh glass of champagne. "You belong over there in the spotlight, not in the cheap seats with the plebs like me."

She should have refused the champagne. She'd already had more than she should, and she'd been too keyed-up all day to eat. But she accepted the glass. Her nerves needed settling.

"You're not a pleb," she said. "A pain in the ass maybe, but never a pleb. And as for me – I haven't done anything special to deserve recognition. I belong where I am."

Dominic raised his glass to her. "I like you."

"I'd take that as a compliment, but I think you say that to all the women."

He laughed.

When a bell rang, Dominic took her elbow and guided her to their seats in the auditorium. The stars always received extra tickets for their entourages, she discovered, and so they sat surrounded by assistants and stylists, film reviewers and those who'd paid premium price for tickets.

"Isn't it odd to do the premiere now?" Tessa asked as she looked across the crowded theatre. "I thought the movie released before Christmas."

Dominic shrugged. "In the States, but here they chose to release it for Valentine's. Something about it being the perfect date-night movie for the City of Love."

The woman behind her leaned forward. "The men get to watch the action and we get to drool!"

The crowd around them chatted and joked and sipped champagne until the VIP circus entered the arena, and Tessa laughed and chatted with them, as at home here as she'd felt on the movie set.

*I belong where I am.* That was truer than she'd realised.

For months she'd felt trapped in the bubble she'd tried to describe to Stefan. But she wasn't trapped, and she didn't have to stay locked inside her ivory tower like a tragic Rapunzel. She was just as happy here as among the children at the orphanage, or on the film set, or at her country club. Maybe she could be happy wherever she went.

Maybe she didn't even need to stay in Westerwald to be happy.

Or maybe she'd had too much champagne.

There was a stir through the crowd as the movie's stars took their seats. She tried hard not to look for Christian but the impulse was impossible to resist.

Among the last to enter the auditorium, his arrival was accompanied by a round of cheering and applause. The tailored evening suit fitted him impeccably. It moulded to his broad shoulders, hinted at the superb physique beneath the superfine cloth.

She couldn't even remember what Stefan had worn last night.

She was in such trouble.

The lights went out, the music soared. She'd thought it would be difficult to focus on the film, to not be bored, but it was remarkably easy. From the moment the opening credits rolled, she was hooked.

The movie may have had more visual effects than plot, but it was mesmerising. Because Christian was in it. And he was *good* in it. He was the best thing about the movie.

His penetrating blue gaze blown up four feet high on the screen, his bare-chested torso glistening. His husky voice, which made every word seem like an invitation to sex.

No wonder women camped out in the snow at the palace gates for a glimpse of him, or chased him down in the street.

And he wanted *her*?

She fidgeted in the seat, unable to ease the itch in her body, the tension in her skin. She couldn't carry on like this. For someone who'd spent her life believing lust was for other people, for weak people, it came as something of a shock to be caught in its grip.

She had lost all control of her body. She couldn't fight this physical longing for him. For his kiss, for her hands on her bare skin.

She pressed her eyes closed, but that only made it worse.

"You okay?" Dominic whispered.

She nodded, biting her lip. But she wasn't okay.

She needed this torture to end. She needed these feelings gone so she could think straight. So she could walk down the aisle at her wedding with conviction.

But was it worth the guilty conscience to make that happen?

Would "getting him out of her system", as Lee suggested, even work?

It had to. Because she was at her wit's end.

Two hours of exquisite torment and then she still had to endure the speeches. Her thoughts drifted into fantasy, so real she could almost feel his hands stroking over her bare skin.

Then Christian took to the narrow stage before the screen amid loud applause, and the fantasy was a weak shadow to the reality of him.

He looked into the auditorium, no doubt unable to see a thing past the bright lights, yet he still managed to make it seem as though he was looking at each and every one of them.

At her.

"The proceeds from tonight's premiere go to an organisation close to my heart. A charity that does great work keeping troubled kids off the streets and out of trouble. I'd like to thank the organisers, the volunteers and all of you for supporting such a life-changing project." He handed the oversized fake cheque to the charity's organisers.

Tessa clapped along with the rest of the audience.

Christian waited until a hush descended again. "When I first came to the States from the Caribbean…" Her heart began to thud erratically against her rib cage. "I was a messed-up kid with a chip on my shoulder. I could have done with an organisation like this one." Nervous laughter scattered through the crowd. This wasn't in the whitewashed version of himself he presented to the world.

Beside her, Dominic muttered an oath. He sounded as surprised as she felt.

But Christian wasn't done yet. "Working in the movies gave me the chance not only to rise above that, but to have fun along the way. Making this movie was huge fun. More fun than that little boy from Los Pajaros could have imagined. And probably more fun than I deserved. I'd like to pay it forward by matching the amount on that cheque."

Christian pulled another cheque from his pocket. Not a dummy cheque made for the cameras, but a real one. He handed it to the stunned charity organiser.

Into the charged silence, applause began, growing wilder, followed by cat calls and wolf whistles. Up on the stage, Christian's face relaxed into a smile. A real smile. Not the cheeky one he used as a shield, but a smile of genuine pleasure.

Tessa's heart swelled with pride. She'd never expected him to really do it, but he had. He'd stepped out from behind the mask, bared himself, and they still loved him.

Even though none but she and Dominic knew just how

225

momentous this revelation was for him. She pressed her eyes shut. He'd laid down the gauntlet. He'd stepped out of his comfort zone. Could she?

At last, the applause died and the auditorium emptied.

"What happens now?" she asked Dominic as he led her upstairs to a reception room lined with red-velvet drapes and dominated by an ornate gilded ceiling. He still seemed a little shell-shocked.

"There'll be a cocktail party with an open bar." He rubbed his hands gleefully together, his usual animation reasserting itself. "And where there are free cocktails, there will be easy women."

She rolled her eyes. "Don't you ever get bored of the whoring?"

"Never! Let me get you a drink."

"I really hope some woman brings you to your knees one day."

"It'll take more than one." He laughed and left her to elbow his way through the crowd to the bar.

"Did you enjoy the movie?" a smooth voice asked in her ear. She spun around, skin hot, palms clammy, head light.

"It wasn't bad. In fact, it was quite good for a gladiator movie. *You* were good." She swallowed, unable to meet Christian's gaze. "Especially afterwards."

He smiled, a wicked curl of his lips. She couldn't drag her gaze from his mouth as she remembered the feel of those lips on hers.

"I remember someone telling me that when you've seen one of these action movies, you've seen them all."

She flushed. "I was very rude the night we met. I hope by now you've learned that I'm not that intolerant and judgmental."

"No, you're not." He curled an arm around her waist. She glanced around, but unbelievably, no one watched them. "You were upset that night, I think. By more than a couple of escaped convicts or a strange man jumping into your car."

She looked away. She didn't want to talk about it.

Even though he might be the one person who'd understand, he'd also be the one person who'd use her weakness against her to get what he wanted. Especially now that he'd done what she was

226

too afraid to do – to simply be herself and admit what she wanted.

He leaned in close, his breath brushing her cheek. "Shall we get out of here?"

He should stay and court the guests who'd paid to meet him. A good assistant would remind him of that. But to hell with *should* and *shouldn't*.

She nodded.

# Chapter 18

Tension pulled Tessa's skin so taut she was surprised she didn't give off sparks. They waited in fraught silence within the theatre doors as one of the organisers summoned their limo. Then they had to make the long walk back along the red carpet, attendants hovering either side, and Tessa was careful to keep a distance between them.

If Christian seemed less enthusiastic about greeting his fans than he had on arrival, no one noticed but Tessa. She waited impatiently in the car as he extricated himself from his admirers.

"Thank God that's over!" He slid in beside her as yet another attendant slammed shut the door, sealing them inside. The roar of sound dropped instantly.

She handed him a bottle of water from the limo's fridge and he gulped it down. "Thanks, I needed that!" He screwed the lid back on. "And thank you for coming tonight." His voice was soft, curling around her heart and squeezing tight.

His hand brushed hers where it lay on the seat between them and she glanced towards the chauffeur. But this wasn't Frank's elegant sedan. This was a bona fide limo with a darkened glass partition, ensuring absolute privacy.

She turned her palm upward to meet his and he threaded his fingers through hers.

The city lights streaked past the darkened windows, a blur of colour and motion, and she felt giddy and light and reckless. She turned to him and he was watching her, his eyes no longer bright with mischief but dark and intense. And questioning.

Slowly she nodded.

And then she was in his lap, his arm around her, his mouth hot and unrelenting on hers, and she gave herself up to every emotion and every sensation she'd denied for so long.

His fingers tangled in her hair, destroying the careful disarray the hotel stylist had taken the better part of the day to create. And aside from a half second thought about what people would think when she walked into the hotel, she didn't care.

Hiking up the long skirt of her evening gown, she straddled him. He tilted her head so he could better plunder her mouth, and she drowned in the taste of him, in the smooth sensual glide of his tongue and the playful nip of his teeth on her lower lip.

Between her thighs she felt his body's reaction, the hard length of him pressing against her core. In spite of the layers of clothing separating them, her body responded. She ached for him, a pleasurable pain that started in her belly and radiated throughout her body, demanding release.

He moaned as she slid her hands down over his shoulders, over his hard, peaked nipples, to the buttons on the front of his shirt.

He stilled her hand and pulled away. "Not here," he said. His breath came out ragged. He stroked surprisingly gentle fingers across her bruised lips. "Not like this."

No shadowy basement car park for their return, though Tessa would have preferred it. The crowd of onlookers gathered outside the hotel had moved on, so the limousine edged into the hotel's narrow, gated driveway.

She scrambled off Christian's lap, straightening her dress and trying, in vain, to repair her hair.

"You look fine," he reassured her with a quick grin that lit up his eyes. "Very sexy and very beddable, but fine."

No words had ever made her feel more beautiful.

As they climbed out of the limo, Christian offered her his hand. And he didn't let go. Hand in hand, they passed beneath the iron and glass Belle Époque portico and across the vast checkered floor to the lifts. She didn't care who saw them. She was past caring about anything but that urge in her belly.

"Would you like a drink?" he asked, nodding towards the bar, where music boomed.

"I would. But not in there."

The lift pinged and he held the old-fashioned wooden door open for her to step in.

She didn't argue when he pressed the button for his floor.

And she didn't argue when he pulled her into his arms, his lips crushing hers in a kiss that spilled over into a frenzy of lips and hands.

He pressed the flat of his hand to the apex of her legs, and she rolled her hips forward, grinding against him, groaning as the lift jerked to a halt too soon. The doors slid open and Christian removed his hand as another couple entered the lift.

Tessa buried her head in Christian's shoulder, his arm wrapped around her, holding her against him as he shielded her from view with his body.

A gentleman, though he'd probably deny it.

The doors opened again and they stepped out into the wide corridor, softly lit, as the lift swept away upwards to the residents-only rooftop bar.

He held her hand as they walked the long corridor to his suite. The royal suite.

At the door, he let go to unlock and hold it open for her, and she stepped inside.

A vast living room, in softly muted shades of gold and sunshine, with French doors to a balcony three times the size of her room's overlooking the Parisian rooftops. In the distance, the Eiffel Tower rose over the city, illuminated against the night sky. No snow now. Just a clouded sky reflecting back the city lights.

But she wasn't here for the view or the décor. She had only one purpose.

Though with the memory of his hand pressed against her, she could no longer remember quite what that purpose was: make love to Christian or get him out from under her skin?

Either way, this was only headed in one direction – towards the wrought-iron four-poster bed she could see through the panelled doors that stood wide to the bedroom.

He stripped off his jacket and loosened his tie. "Champagne – or have you had enough bubbly for one day?"

"In Paris, there can never be too much champagne." In spite of all the champagne she'd already consumed this evening, or maybe because of it, the butterflies in her stomach seemed to be throwing a party.

Christian popped open the bottle of Perrier-Jouët chilling on ice, its Art Nouveau label reflecting the hotel's house style. As he poured two glasses, she stripped off her coat and laid it across the back of a chair.

Christian held out a champagne flute to her. "This is the end of the road, then. Tomorrow we go our separate ways."

She crossed the room and took the glass, letting her fingers linger against his on the delicate stem. She didn't deny it.

"Here's to stepping outside our comfort zones." She raised her glass then took a long sip, draining nearly half the glass.

Now that she had made up her mind, she would face this with the same single-minded focus she faced every decision. She would see it through. But that didn't mean she wasn't going to need a little alcoholic help to do it.

Christian raised his glass to her. "To stepping out of comfort zones."

She emptied her glass and set it down.

"So you're calling off your wedding?" he asked.

She didn't answer.

"You are calling off the wedding?"

Slowly, she shook her head. "Are you having qualms now because I have an engagement ring on my finger? It didn't stop you from kissing me before." Three times now, each more earth-shattering than the last.

He set down his virtually untouched glass beside her empty one, the light gone from his face and replaced by a storm cloud. "I'm not the bastard the world thinks I am. I thought you knew that, Tess. Of course I have a problem with seducing another man's woman."

Okay, this was not part of her plan.

He turned away, walked to the far wall and planted his fist against it, head down. So much emotion swirled around him that for a moment she wondered if he would hit the wall. But he didn't, and when he spoke his voice sounded ragged. "I'm not made of steel. I want you so much I can't behave like a gentleman with you looking at me like that. If you don't want this to happen, then you need to leave now."

The silence hummed.

She walked towards him and stroked a hand down his back. He jerked at the touch.

"Don't," he warned.

She swallowed. Asking for what she wanted was easily the most difficult thing she'd ever done. This was the closest she'd ever come to begging. "I want you to make love to me, Christian. Please."

He pulled her into his arms, rough, frantic. She tilted her head and his mouth possessed hers. He pushed her up against the wall. Hands sliding to the shoulders of her gown, he hooked his finger beneath the delicate lace and peeled the dress away.

His lips grazed the tender skin at her throat, tracing a line down flesh she'd never known was so sensitive. She shuddered and leaned back her head, closing her eyes against the assault of sensation as the gown slid down her body to pool at her feet. His hands were everywhere, skimming over her skin, down her arms, cupping her bare breasts.

232

Her breasts ached, so tender, so sensitive, so hard. He flicked his thumb across her nipple and she arched into his touch, the simple rub and flick of his fingers doing crazy things to every part of her body.

Then his mouth was there, sucking, teasing. He held a nipple in his teeth, brushed his tongue across the tip, and she cried out.

"You're so responsive." His warm breath fanned her cool, wet skin. "A volcano…"

She felt like a volcano. Magnitude 8.9 at least. The pressure blown, the molten heat rushing through her, unstoppable and inescapable and so incredibly beautiful.

Christian sighed, reverent, and lifted his head to place light kisses across her collarbone. She shivered.

"Cold?" he asked.

She shook her head. Anything but cold. She burned from the inside out.

Then he kissed her lips, his mouth warm and firm over hers, and lifted her up, one arm wrapped around her waist, the other supporting her bottom. Without breaking the kiss, he carried her through the door into the bedroom and laid her down on the bed.

She shouldn't have been awed by his strength, by the solid, capable arms that carried her as if she weighed nothing. She'd seen him sword fight and brawl for the camera. She'd seen his muscles up close and personal; even felt them wrapped around her before. Yet still, she felt awed.

And in the safe strength of those arms she felt no shame and no fear. She was naked but for the scrap of black lace panties that were all she'd been able to wear under the barely-there dress, yet she felt no urge to cover herself. No urge to turn out the lights to hide the wicked pink glow spreading across her skin like a rash, across her chest, up her neck.

Not just safe. He made her feel adored. No man had ever looked at her this way before, as if he'd discovered a treasure, as if she were priceless beyond measure.

He leaned over her and she caught the glint of silver beneath his collar where he'd torn off his tie and released the topmost button of his shirt. With shaking, hurried fingers she undid a few more buttons. And gasped.

*Oh my God.*

"Nothing you haven't seen before," he said with a quick grin.

But it was. She reached up and touched the ring that hung on a thin silver chain around his neck.

For a breathless moment she couldn't speak. Then, "you haven't worn this before."

He looked down. "Not while I was in character and working, but tonight I'm just me, remember?"

Her fingers traced over the heavy signet ring, over the intricate detail of the antique silver roses encircling a lapis lazuli stone carved to resemble a dragon's head.

"It's beautiful, isn't it?" he said. "It looks old."

It was. Hundreds of years old. And it was real.

"Where did you get it?" she asked. Her voice sounded thin and far away.

"I found it in my mother's things after she died." He frowned. "I never knew she had it. She never once showed it to me."

There was a lot he didn't know about his mother.

Christian shook his head and smiled with all the confidence of a man who knew his power over women. "I'm wounded that at a moment like this you're more interested in a piece of old jewellery than in me."

She smiled back. "Never!"

Well, not entirely true. The ring, added to her guesses, made a convincing conclusion.

But now wasn't the time to celebrate that she had finally achieved the task her father had set her. This was the moment to celebrate her own awakening.

Her fingers still shaking, she undid every last button on his shirt, while his gaze burned into her, dark and intense.

She loved him like this, his passion and his single-minded focus. And she loved when he laughed and teased, so full of vitality that he could make everyone around him smile too. And she loved the contours of his body, the smooth, hard muscle and the wiry graceful way in which he moved.

She laid her mouth to his skin, tasted him, the salty sweet desire on his skin. She ran her hands over the planes of his stomach, over his waistband, down to the bulge in his trousers.

He grabbed her hand.

"If you want me to last long enough for this to be a pleasure for us both, I don't suggest you go any further."

She wanted to laugh, so filled was she with the intoxicating power of being able to bring a man like Christian to a place of such need. But she didn't laugh. She pressed her lips to his, licked at the seams of his mouth, playing and experimenting and savouring.

He nudged her down onto her back as he kissed her. This time, when he leaned over her, the ring brushed her bare chest, cold against her heated skin.

His hands skimmed her feverish flesh, exploring her as she wanted to explore him. She closed her eyes and surrendered.

He knelt over her, legs on either side of her hips, and his kisses moved lower as he edged down the bed, tracing a line down her body towards the black lace panties. She writhed beneath him, her body already wet and needy.

He ran a finger along the lace edge and she moaned, unable to bear another moment without him *there*. He laughed soundlessly and dipped a finger beneath the lace, his touch so light she wanted to scream in frustration. Then his finger touched her clit, circled it, and she wanted to scream in a whole different way.

She bit her lip until she tasted blood.

"Let it go for me," he whispered, as his finger rubbed and teased. "Let me hear how much you're enjoying this."

She nodded and at that moment he slid a finger into her. She arched her back, pushing up into his hand, her entire body in contact with his, bare chest to bare chest. He stroked her with his fingers until she writhed and moaned and tears of pleasure pricked her eyes. And then he was gone.

Her eyes flew open.

He watched her, held her gaze, as he eased the black lace down her legs, tossed it away, then crooked an arm beneath her knee, coaxing her to open for him.

His mouth was even hotter than his hands. He licked, he sucked, he scraped her gently with his teeth.

Her eyes fluttered closed.

"Look at me," he commanded. "I want to see you come."

And she did, scorching and furious and unrestrained, and her hands were in his hair, and she shouted his name.

He moved to lie beside her, cradling her as she struggled for breath and for sanity in the aftermath. She buried herself in him, breathing him in.

"Still think sex is highly over-rated?" he whispered in her ear.

Hell no! His mouth had done more for her than any other man had ever done with his entire body. If this was what it could be like… She pressed her eyes closed.

"Don't block me out." He stroked the hair back from her face. "Look at me."

She didn't want to. His gaze stripped her bare, saw everything.

He cupped her face and pressed tender kisses to her eyelids, to her nose, to the corner of her mouth. She rocked against him.

"Ready for me?" he asked.

She'd been ready for him from the moment he'd stood on the stage and spoken the truth. No, earlier. From the moment she'd re-tied his bowtie and he'd looked at her with such fierce longing her legs had barely managed to keep her standing. Or perhaps since the night on the bridge when he'd massaged her hands and she'd truly *felt* for the first time since she was a child.

She nodded.

He rose from the bed to unhook his trousers. She lifted herself up on her elbows to watch the slow slide of the zipper. Then he pushed the trousers down over his hips and she bit her lip. Commando.

She couldn't breathe. On the red carpet, on the stage…

Then he was back on the bed beside her, and there were no longer any barriers between them, neither physical nor emotional.

Until he broke eye contact, dropped his head to her chest and moaned.

"What is it?" she asked, suddenly panicked. He couldn't stop now!

"Protection."

She didn't want even as much as a piece of latex between them. She trusted him. But clearly for him this wasn't as all or nothing as it was for her. She blinked away the hurt as he rolled off her, reaching into the nightstand.

Then he was back, rolling on the condom with an expertise she didn't want to think about. He supported himself with his arms as he positioned his weight between her legs. "This is your last chance to back out. After this, there'll be no going back," he warned.

She wouldn't back out. And she didn't care if it was stupid or impetuous. Or if it didn't mean as much to him as it did to her.

His erection pressed against her opening and she rocked against him. He needed no further invitation. He thrust into her, sinking deep, stretching her.

Then slowly he withdrew. And thrust again, deeper, harder.

She moaned and began to move with him, the push and pull within her starting a chain reaction, waves of hot pleasure building, building, dragging her deep into that blessed place where nothing existed but pleasure. And then lightning burst behind her eyelids and her entire body was alive with it. He murmured her name, over and over again until he stiffened and came inside her.

For an eternity they lay together, limbs entwined, sweat-slickened bodies heaving.

Then he kissed her temple.

She wanted to speak, but there were no words left in her. Only feeling. She looked into his face, and he smiled, exhausted, happy. Relaxed. No longer driven, no longer working to impress. No more smart comments or chip on the shoulder. Just himself.

And she had done this to him.

He rolled off her, lifting her to open the bed covers, then slipping back in beside her, pulling the covers closed over them.

"I should leave," she murmured into his neck.

He shook his head, and wrapped a possessive arm around her. "No, you shouldn't."

When she woke, the lights were still on. Tessa lay on her side and Christian lay curled around her, his chest to her back, his arm lying loose over her hip. His body warmed her, a reassuring solidity that she sank into, drew strength from.

She should feel shame at what she'd done. Or at least a little troubled. But she didn't. How could something that felt so right and so good possibly be so wrong?

She turned in his arms to look at him and he stirred. His eyelids fluttered and slowly opened.

"I slept," he said, his voice sleep-thickened.

"Is that a surprise?"

"I haven't slept this easily or this well in ages." He grinned, more awake now. "At least not since I met you."

He nudged his thigh between hers and she felt his erection stir against her leg.

"I should go," she said. But she didn't move. She couldn't seem to bring herself to move away from him.

"Don't," he said. "We still have the better part of a very fine vintage to finish. You wouldn't want to waste it, would you?" He nuzzled her neck and she sighed.

"No, I wouldn't want to waste it."

They didn't get to the champagne for a long while. When they did, the ice had long since melted, but they didn't care. They sat in the vast bed, their backs against a mountain of pillows, and they talked and kissed and sipped champagne. And then she slid her hand between his legs, and there was no talking and no drinking for another long while.

"You're wearing me out," he said at last, stifling a yawn and pulling her into his chest to cuddle her.

"With your stamina? I don't think that's possible."

"Would you think less of me if I said I don't normally hang around for seconds? Or thirds." He kissed her. "Or fourths."

She shook her head. How could she think less of him? He'd stayed for *her*. He didn't want her to go. She didn't want to go.

Sleep claimed her again and she drifted back into its welcoming arms. As she closed her eyes, unable to fight their heaviness any longer, he whispered. "Come to Los Pajaros with me."

## Chapter 19

The hard, merciless light of dawn filtered into the darkened room. Tessa stretched cramped muscles that protested at the rude awakening. They didn't want to leave the warmth and comfort of the bed.

But this morning her muscles didn't get a say. Her head was firmly back in charge, and it was saying sensible things like *get out of bed* and *get dressed* and *what the hell was I thinking?!*

The empty champagne bottle stood on the bedside table. She couldn't even remember drinking that much champagne last night. And her head felt clear as a bell. Maybe that was the difference between expensive champagne and signature cocktails.

She rolled over, pillowing her head on her arm, and watched Christian as he slept.

She knew all too well what he was like in the mornings and she didn't think she could face it right now. Not after what they'd shared last night. And not considering what she had to do this morning.

He wasn't going to be happy.

She slid from between the sheets, grabbing for the nearest item of clothing. Christian's shirt. No, that wouldn't do.

Praying he wouldn't wake, she tip-toed naked across the floor, collecting bits of clothing as she went into the living room, where she hastily pulled on her clothes. A designer evening dress was hardly appropriate clothing for... she glanced at her wristwatch as she clamped it on... eight in the morning.

Damn! The hotel was sure to be buzzing already. There'd be staff and guests all over the place.

She hovered on the bedroom threshold. Christian still slept soundly. Heaven only knows, he needed it. Last night's performance, both at the premiere and in the bedroom, were nothing short of stellar.

Should she wake him to say goodbye? It would be the right thing to do. Sneaking out was such a cowardly way to end this. But better a clean break and sweet memories than an ugly scene.

Because end it had to.

He'd asked her to go with him to Los Pajaros. She was pretty sure she hadn't dreamed that bit. What would it take to make him understand that nothing had changed?

She wasn't about to throw away everything she'd ever known to go with him to the Caribbean. What would happen when he tired of her – when he grew restless or sated or simply realised how different they were? Where would she go then: home to Westerwald with her tail between her legs and a reputation so tarnished she'd never find a decent husband and have a family of her own?

Or would she be cast adrift as her mother had been, exiled from her friends and her family and her homeland?

No, great as the sex had been – and it had been mind-blowing – it belonged now in the past. One night only; never to be repeated.

Casting one last wistful glance at Christian sprawled across the bed in the other room, naked but for the white sheet that pulled tight across his lower half, she crossed to the door, heels and handbag in hand, and let herself out.

In the corridor she stopped to brush away the tears collecting on her lashes before she turned towards the elevators.

"Hello, Teresa."

*Oh. God. No.*

Tessa pasted a smile on her face and hoped her make-up wasn't too smudged and that she didn't have bad bedhead. Or stubble burn.

Though it hardly mattered. The evening dress at eight in the morning was enough to scream Walk of Shame.

"Hello Caroline."

An old school friend, heiress of one of Europe's largest electrical manufacturers, looking as fresh as a daisy in her hot-pink Zara dress, as if she'd stepped straight from the salon. Caroline's gaze slid down Tessa's evening gown to the heels in her hand. "I didn't know you were in Paris."

"Just for a couple of nights. What are you doing here?" Teresa tried to match Caroline's natural perkiness with a fake brightness of her own.

"Shopathon. I need something new to wear to your wedding. Is Stefan here with you?" Caroline glanced over Tessa's shoulder at the closed door of Christian's suite.

"He had a couple of days in Paris." An answer without answering. Teresa's smile was starting to stretch her face uncomfortably.

"Shame! You've only had stolen moments together, haven't you? Where are you off to?"

*My own room* wasn't an option. But Teresa couldn't think what else to say. She opened her mouth, but no words came out.

"Would you like to go shopping with me today?" Caroline asked. If she noticed Teresa's hesitance she gave no indication.

"I can't. I'm flying back to Neustadt this morning."

The sooner, the better.

"What a pity. Oh well, I'll see you at your wedding. A Valentine's wedding! You two really are the last of the romantics, aren't you?"

Caroline air-kissed Tessa's cheeks and breezed off towards the elevators. It was a long time before Tessa was able to move.

Christian blinked against the bright light. He'd left the curtains open and mid-morning sunlight streamed in across the bed. He

242

rubbed his eyes and sat up. The bed beside him was empty.

He glanced towards the closed bathroom door and smiled. He hoped she didn't scrub up too nice this morning. He was rather hoping he'd get to see her looking just a little less than perfect for the first time. Though there was also a rather large chance she was naturally perfect. Skin like hers would be worth more than gold in LA.

He stretched, glorying in the protest of over-used muscles. Even though they hadn't slept much last night, he felt as if he'd had a week's rest. God, he couldn't remember when last he'd felt this way first thing after waking. Hopeful, energised, excited. Perhaps never.

With a bounce in his step, he rose from the bed and moved to knock on the bathroom door. "Tessa?"

No answer.

He frowned and tried the door handle. It was unlocked and he opened it.

The bathroom was empty.

He tried the living room. And the terrace, even though it had to be at least two degrees below freezing outside.

She wasn't anywhere in his suite. She'd left no sign she'd ever been there. Not even a note.

Perhaps she'd gone downstairs to change? Yes, that was most likely.

He pulled on the nearest clothes at hand, his trousers from the night before. He didn't bother with shoes, but he grabbed a shirt on his way out of the apartment, only buttoning it up in the elevator, to the curious stares of the elderly couple who got in beside him.

Christian banged on the door to Tessa's room. Hopefully she hadn't gone downstairs, because he really didn't want to say good morning to her with an audience. He wanted to kiss her senseless and entice her back to bed.

And then they could have breakfast together, at the little table where the sunlight streamed in through the French doors. Maybe this morning he'd even let her feed him something more than

243

espresso.

And then he would tell her he loved her. He would tell her until she believed him and dropped this stupid notion of marrying Stefan.

Lucky for him – or her – she opened the door. But before he could indulge in that good-morning kiss, she'd turned back into the room. Behind her on the bed lay her suitcase, packed and ready to go.

"What's the hurry? The plane isn't booked until this afternoon," he said.

She lifted the case from the bed and set it upright. "I've booked a commercial airline flight home. I have a cab waiting to take me to the airport."

A lead weight dropped in his stomach; a physical blow as if he'd been gut punched. He couldn't breathe.

So this was how it felt.

She'd planned to walk out on him without so much as a "*have a nice day*".

He'd done the same thing more times than he cared to remember. Yes, he was an ass. And a bastard in more ways than one. But that didn't mean he didn't at least deserve a 'good morning' after the intimacy they'd shared last night. Or a 'goodbye'.

Better yet, she shouldn't be leaving him at all.

He grabbed her arm, stopping her, forcing her to look at him. "Don't go."

"Why are you here, Christian?" She sounded tired. And not in the "*I didn't sleep last night because I was having too much fun*" way he was used to from women. "I have to go. It's better this way."

"Wasn't last night special for you? Didn't it mean anything?"

"It was special."

"So come back to bed with me. And after that, come to Los Pajaros with me."

She looked at him as if he'd grown two heads. "Have you forgotten I'm getting married in a few days? What happened last night doesn't change anything."

"You're still going to marry him? Why?"

"Because this marriage is bigger than just him and me. It's for our families and our community. And Stefan will be the perfect husband."

"But he's not perfect *for you*. I saw the two of you together. I'd have to be blind not to see that neither one of you is in love. What amazes me is that you can't see it."

"Of course we're not in love. But a good marriage isn't based on something as fickle as love. There are other, much better, reasons for getting married."

He bit his cheek until the metallic tang of blood burned his throat. "Nothing's changed, has it? You aristocrats still all stick together, marry each other, exclude anyone who isn't like you. And I thought marriages of convenience were a thing of the past!"

"This isn't a marriage of convenience. It's a marriage between friends. Friendship is a much more reliable basis for a strong marriage than lust."

Christian frowned. "How can you shut down your emotions like that? That's just… unthinkable. You're going to tie yourself to someone for the rest of your life based on the fact that you get along? I get along with Dominic, but that doesn't mean I want to marry him. What happens if one of you falls in love?"

"That's not going to happen. Neither of us is built that way. Besides, love, lust, they're not real. This… " she waved a hand between them… "is nothing more than a chemical reaction."

"No, it's not. What we have is so much more than chemistry." He took her hands and held her gaze. "Tell me you don't feel this? After what we shared last night, I can't believe you can go back to a sterile relationship with someone who doesn't love you. Not with what I can offer you."

She pulled her hands away. "And what are you offering me?"

"I love you. I want to be with you."

She shook her head. "That's not enough. This is all just smoke

245

and mirrors. I can't trust you, Christian. One day I'm going to wake up and this will be gone. You'll be gone. It's what you do and chemistry doesn't last."

He didn't deny it. He couldn't. His track record wasn't good. Though the mere thought of waking *any* morning without her there beside him made him feel ill. Not after what he'd tasted last night. He wanted more of that.

She bit her lip. "But Stefan won't be gone. He'll never abandon me. I made a terrible mistake last night, and I can't even blame it on the alcohol. But this can never, ever happen again."

That was twice she'd called him a mistake. Her words ground salt into old wounds. That's all he'd ever been. In spite of the fans, the glory, the respect, he was still just a mistake. The mistake that cost his mother her career, her family and her home.

The mistake that Tessa didn't want to repeat.

He didn't need to look her in the eyes to know what he would see. He'd declared his love and she'd said it wasn't enough.

He'd never known pain like this existed. It blossomed through his chest, smothering him, so he could hardly breathe.

She'd said it as if his love was worthless to her. She didn't want him.

And wasn't that just the story of his life?

She might as well have slapped him, for the look on his face. The pain in his eyes stabbed into her. Tears stuck in her throat, choking her. But she couldn't take back that pain, not without hurting herself.

For Christian it was all or nothing. Most women got nothing. But with her, he wouldn't settle for less than demanding everything she had to give. More than she was willing to give.

In this one thing they were alike. When it came to her emotions, she was all or nothing too.

But where Christian would choose *all*, living loud and on the spur of the moment and living every emotion, she chose *nothing*.

Because no amount of love or phenomenal sex could make up for pain and loss.

Tessa suppressed the nameless emotion that threatened to choke her. This wasn't the moment for weak emotions. She needed to be strong. The way she'd had to be strong when her mother left and when Rik left.

Christian could never know how tempted she was, or how close she was to giving up everything she'd ever known and valued to run away with him.

She turned away, moved to her suitcase and raised the handle.

She paused. She couldn't change the way this had to end, but there was one parting gift she could give him, one tiny salve for his wounded ego: the answer he'd come to Westerwald to find.

"I know who your father is."

She braced herself for the questions. *How do you know? Who is he?*

"Why did he send her away?"

Not that one. She wasn't ready for that one. "I don't know that he did. I don't even know if he knew she was pregnant. But someone knew and they made sure she didn't stay around to embarrass him."

His face hardened. The look in his eyes frightened Tessa; so hard, so angry.

"Because she was black?" he bit out.

"Because he was about to be married."

Christian sat down on the arm of the edge of the bed as he processed her words. "So you're telling me my father was a philandering bastard?"

Ouch. Just a little too close to home.

He shook his head. "My mother believed he loved her." His voice was bitter.

She thought of Archduke Christian. He'd loved his wife. Passionately. But he was an honest and honourable man. If he'd told Connie Hewitt he loved her, then he'd believed it at the time.

"He probably did, but his marriage had been arranged. It was too important to sacrifice for his own desires."

Christian laughed, a bitter sound. "What is it with you aristocrats? This isn't the nineteenth century. Why do you all act as if your marriages have some sort of national significance?"

Her throat constricted. She didn't want to say the words aloud, but she had to.

"It does if you're the Crown Prince."

After a long moment's silence, Christian laughed. No longer the bitter, brittle laugh of a moment ago, but the kind of laugh that spilled out all his tension and frustration and anger.

"You're shitting me, right?" he said at last.

She shook her head. "That ring you wear is a royal family heirloom. It belonged to Max's father, Archduke Christian, and it disappeared at the same time your mother left Westerwald. I think your father gave it to her as a token of his feelings."

He certainly wouldn't have given it to just anyone. But did he give it to her knowing she was pregnant with his child? No one now would ever know.

"She left with nothing. Nothing but a ring."

"I think she tried to hide you. Until you were fourteen and you attracted attention. Did you never wonder where your mother got the money to relocate you to a new home where you could have a fresh start and a good education? Did you never wonder why she changed your name? She was paid to make you disappear."

"By the Archduke?"

"Probably not." Tessa knew just enough of the job her father did to make a guess at what had happened. "There are people in our government whose role it is to keep the nation's image squeaky clean. When they found out about you, they did what they always do. They tidied up."

Christian removed the chain from around his neck and held the ring in the palm of his hand, staring at it.

"It's the emblem of Westerwald," she explained. "The dragon

248

in a circle of roses. Fredrik saw you wearing it at the party before filming started and he recognised it."

Slowly Christian raised his head to look at her. "You knew." He said it like an accusation. "You knew about my past before I even told you."

"I didn't know everything."

But it was too late. He'd made the leap. In the growing hardness of his eyes she could see the pieces adding up. "Stefan said that your father arranged for you to work for me. Is that what this has all been about? Were you sent to seduce me so you could spy on me? So you could see a bloody ring?"

She shook her head, but she was too choked to speak. How could he think that? How could he believe she'd make love to him to spy on him? She opened her mouth to speak, but there was no point. She *had* betrayed him. Maybe not the way he thought, but she'd earned his trust and then given it away as if it meant nothing.

"I knew you were cold and heartless, but I never realised how much. Was everything between us a lie?"

She straightened her back and met his angry gaze. "It wasn't a lie."

She wished the bloody ring to the depths of the ocean. It should have stayed lost, and Christian along with it. She didn't want to feel this way.

"What now?" he asked. "Do you pay me to go away quietly too, the way my mother was sent away? And what if I refuse? What if I take this to the media?"

She hadn't thought this through properly. She hadn't planned on telling him at all. It wasn't like her to make such impetuous, rash decisions. Look what happened when she did.

She hadn't given a moment's thought to what this might mean for Westerwald. Oh God, she'd let her heart get the better of her and she'd betrayed her country. The country she'd once thought she loved more than any man.

But she no longer cared about her nation. It would survive.

She only cared about this man she loved more than she'd ever loved anyone.

A man who'd cracked the ice in her heart. Now she had to do the best she could to hold it together. For all of them.

"No," she said quietly. "The only thing I ask is that you think long and hard before you go to the press." She blinked against the tears burning her eyes. "Talk to Max before you do that. Please."

There was nothing else she could do, or say, without making it worse. She'd lost him now. She'd finally managed to erect a barrier between them so impenetrable he couldn't cross. A barrier she'd erected to protect herself. Except it hadn't worked. The cracks were there anyway, in spite of all her efforts.

She moved to the door.

Christian didn't stop her. He didn't even look at her.

She opened the door and paused on the threshold. "You might want to alert Pippa to the fact that she's about to get very, very busy on your behalf."

Then she shut the door behind her. Barely able to see, she began the long walk away from him.


The cab couldn't get Tessa any closer than the street corner where Christian had taken that fateful leap into her car. She passed through the security check point blocking the cul-de-sac and stood on the pavement, looking up at the familiar grand town-house before her.

The front door stood open and voices spilled out. She climbed the stairs, dodging out of the way of two men in décor-company uniforms who stumbled out the door carrying empty packing crates.

Pandemonium reigned inside, with people shouting instructions, men on ladders polishing the chandeliers, and even more people bearing packing crates.

The house had been transformed. All the furniture had been moved, and in its place was a sea of red and white. She wandered through the rooms, avoiding the workers, who ignored her as they carried on with their tasks, into the formal dining room and drawing room, which had been opened up to create one large banquet hall.

The décor was tasteful and romantic. The room even smelled of flowers, though those would only be brought in on the morning of the wedding.

It was perfect.

"You're back early!" Lee rushed towards her, wrapping her in a bear hug.

Anna approached, clipboard held tight to her chest. "Did I get it wrong?" she asked, biting her lip. "I thought you were only due back much later today?"

"I was."

Lee looked at her strangely. "What brought you back early – Paris not exciting enough?"

"Not a what, but a who, I think," another male voice said. Anton. What was her dress designer doing here? "You're not looking like the radiant bride who's just seen her beloved," he observed.

Lee pulled her back into another hug. "What happened in Paris, *chica*?"

There were a lot of things she should have said. *I'm just a little tired. How are you? This place looks incredible. Thank you so much for everything you've done.* Blah, blah, blah.

All the words that were polite and right and meaningless. The words that diverted attention away from what she was feeling and thinking.

But honesty seemed to be contagious, and she couldn't bring herself to lie to her friends. Her real friends. Truer than the Carolines of the world.

"I had sex with Christian," she blurted out.

Only it hadn't been just sex. They'd made love. The tears threatened a rematch.

"We can't talk here," Anton said, glancing around at the servants, who were busy polishing the mirrors and laying out cutlery. "Let's go somewhere private."

Tessa led them upstairs to her suite, marvelling as she did so that she was able to hold it together enough to put one foot in front of the other.

Since she'd walked out of that hotel room in Paris she'd felt the cracks growing. Like a frozen river in the spring, the water surging beneath the frozen surface was building and building, and any moment now the ice would shatter.

Lee shut the door to her suite behind them. "That's fantastic! Tell us everything."

Anna pinned him with a glare. "Has it escaped you that she's engaged to someone else?"

Lee shrugged. "It's a terrible shame to waste such a grand wedding, of course, but it can't be helped."

"And a terrible waste of one of my creations," Anton added. He turned to Tessa with a smile. "Though you can always use it for the next wedding."

"I'm still marrying Stefan," she said.

Three astounded faces looked back at her.

"So you got him out of your system?" Lee sounded disappointed.

She shook her head. "No. Now I feel worse than ever. I love him."

There, she'd said it. Though the admission made her head want to explode.

"So why are you marrying someone else?"

She was so tired of answering that question. It only made her head hurt to have to repeat it. "Because he's the perfect man for me."

The words were starting to sound rehearsed.

Anna pulled her down to the sofa and wrapped a comforting arm around her. "Because the wedding is too far down the line. The invitations have been set out, the RSVPs are in."

Tessa nodded. Wild, hysterical laughter started to bubble up inside her. She choked it back. "If I walk away from Stefan now, I'll never be able to show my face in public again."

"What does it matter what the public thinks?" Lee asked.

The one non-Westerwaldian in the room. He didn't understand.

She shrugged, trying not to let the pain scraping her throat raw break loose. "It doesn't matter why. It's over, and there's no going back. I've burned that bridge." Christian would never want her now, not with what he believed of her.

"You have to tell Stefan," Anna said gently.

Oh my God. Stefan. She'd been so wrapped up in her own anguish she hadn't given him a moment's thought. But Anna was right. She had to tell Stefan. She couldn't live a lie for the rest of her life.

He would be home in two days.

What if he wanted to call off the wedding? Then in the eyes of the world she would have been dumped twice. As far as society and the papers were concerned, she already had one failed engagement behind her. There were no second chances. Her mother was the proof of that.

Besides, Anna had worked overtime to move the rehearsal dinner. She'd even managed to book the Landmark Café.

The hysteria bubbled up and over. But it came out as tears. Scalding hot, painful tears that she had no power to stop.

"Let it out," Anna said, cradling her and patting her back. "It's been a long few weeks. You'll feel much better after a good cry."


She'd cried a lot these last two days and it hadn't helped. Tessa didn't feel better. She felt worse.

She'd barely got out of bed. She'd lain beneath the duvet, her laptop propped up beside her, and she'd watched every one of Christian's movies. Twice. Then she'd started on the TV interviews. Talk shows where he talked nonsense and charmed everyone. Red-carpet appearances where he wore a different woman on his arm every time. Charity benefits where he handed over great big dummy cheques.

She watched them all from a bed littered with tissues and

chocolate wrappers.

She checked her messages constantly, but there was nothing from Christian. Not that she expected to hear from him ever again. That didn't stop her from hoping.

There was nothing from Stefan either, though there was nothing unusual in that. There'd been a time she'd liked that he wasn't clingy and respected her space.

But she was done crying now. When she rose on the day of her wedding rehearsal, a strange new calm settled over her. A frozen calm. She was all cried out and she could feel nothing.

Just the way she'd wanted to be.

Tessa paced the pavement outside Stefan's apartment building. She knew he was home. She'd watched from the café across the road as the cab dropped him off and he'd entered the building. She'd watched the lights come on in his apartment.

A bitterly cold wind swept down the narrow street between the buildings. She shivered. She should get inside and get this over with before she caught pneumonia. A hacking cough and runny nose was not a pretty sight on a bride. Assuming there was still a wedding.

She could still walk away. She could head straight to the cathedral for the rehearsal and pretend that nothing had happened.

But that wasn't fair to Stefan. What if he heard from someone else? He deserved better.

And now that Christian had opened this floodgate inside her, the thought of being anything but honest repelled her.

Christian had warned her there would be no turning back. She'd thought he meant physically, and perhaps he had.

But there were other things that could not be undone. She couldn't erase the memories. She couldn't go back to the person she'd been before she'd bared her soul to Christian.

From the very beginning, he'd seen beneath the surface to the woman within. He'd been so determined to let her loose – and he'd achieved his goal.

No, there was no going back. She could only move forward. She had to do this.

She pressed the buzzer for Stefan's apartment and waited. She wanted to throw up with the tension in her stomach, but that wouldn't help any.

Stefan's face appeared on the video intercom. "Teresa, what are you doing here? Come on up."

He buzzed the door open, and she pushed it wide and stepped into the foyer. She'd always loved this building. It was an art deco apartment block, newly renovated but with all its original fittings. Now it only reminded her of the hotel in Paris.

She stepped into the wood-panelled lift, and remembered Christian kissing her in the lift in Paris.

She'd walked away from Christian in Paris. And now she might lose Stefan too.

But she had to do this.

Stefan's apartment door was already open and he waited for her. "This is a delightful pleasure. I only expected to see you at the rehearsal." Then he saw her face. "What's wrong?"

"We need to talk."

She stepped past him into the apartment and removed her coat. He hung it on the coat rack then followed her into the living room. Sparsely furnished, with parquet floors and bay windows. This apartment was so much like her father's office. Masculine, clinical.

Thank heavens they'd agreed to live in the Adler townhouse after they married. Though it was not much less clinical.

For a fleeting moment she wondered what Christian's beach-house looked like.

She blinked against the sudden burn and turned to face Stefan. "Are we doing the right thing?"

"I don't understand."

"All my life I've had these ideas of what my life was supposed to be, rules that I was supposed to follow, but I'm not so sure about them anymore."

255

He frowned. "What are you trying to say?"

"I met someone else. I slept with someone else."

"Christian," Stefan guessed. He didn't look particularly worried. He looked as calm and sensible as always. As calm and sensible as she usually was. "Do you plan to see him again?"

"Never."

"Have you changed your mind about marrying me?"

"No, of course not! I still want to marry you. But I'll understand if you don't want to marry me." She twisted her hands together, waiting breathlessly for his answer.

He nodded slowly. "Nothing has changed for me. I still want a marriage uncluttered with messy emotions. But I need someone who's got my back. You need to commit to this. So if you want to throw our partnership away for a bit of leg-over, then you have to decide now."

She flinched at his choice of words.

Compared to Christian's volatility, Stefan's rational and unemotional manner was a stark contrast. It was also cold and distant. Was that what she was like too?

But this was what she wanted. At least Stefan wouldn't profess his love one moment and accuse her of being a cold-hearted Mata Hari the next. Passion was fickle and painful.

So what if she never felt emotions again? So what if the world thought her hard-hearted? Better that than being thought loose and immoral. Better that than this constant pull of lust and fear and love.

She lifted her chin. "I'm sure," she said.

Stefan pulled her close and hugged her. She rested her cheek against his shoulder.

No sparks at all.

His touch made her feel calm and secure rather than lit up inside. She blinked away her tears of relief and hugged him back. And if there was a little desperation mixed with her relief, then no one needed to know.

Maybe one day Christian would understand that she'd done the right thing. She'd made the same hard decision his parents had made. Sacrificing personal happiness because it was the right thing to do.

# Chapter 20

It was snowing again, filling the footprints on the pavements and on the cathedral steps, creating a fresh slate.

Inside the old monastery buildings, a room had been prepared as a bridal chamber. Stark compared to the lavish hotel rooms most brides choose, but it was a haven compared to her own home, currently under siege by caterers and florists and musicians.

The bare little room was more than adequate for Tessa's needs. Bright light streamed in through tall arched windows, making the day appear deceptively warm.

Anton and Marie fluttered about her, fussing over the dress, touching up her make-up. Amidst their fussing, Tessa stood in an island of calm. She felt numb inside.

The scent of jasmine wafted over her from the imported buds Marie had dressed into her carefully styled hair. "You're the prettiest bride I've ever seen," she said, dabbing her eyes.

Tessa faced her reflection in the mirror and carefully fastened the new earrings from Stefan in place. The gift from Tiffany's, her something new and something blue. The gems that sparkled in the delicate gold earrings were the exact shade of Christian's eyes.

The woman in the mirror looked back at her, composed, regal. But something was missing.

She had everything she'd ever wanted, but she didn't have the one thing she needed.

Anton stepped away to answer the knock at the door.

For a moment, Tessa's heart beat a staccato rhythm. Frantic hope blossomed. Then her gaze met her father's in the mirror. He smiled, proud, happy, as he stepped into the room and she managed to smile back.

She had to remember what she'd told Christian. This marriage wasn't for her. It was for her family. Their families. Not only the hundreds of years of tradition and expectation, but the new family they'd create together. Stronger, united.

But for a fleeting moment she heard Christian's voice. *You still all keep together, marry each other, exclude anyone who isn't like you.*

She didn't want to be like that. She'd never wanted to be like that.

She wanted to hold Christian's baby in her arms.

But he hadn't offered her that. She pressed her eyelids closed against the tears. Not so numb after all.

"You are beautiful." Her father leaned forward to kiss her forehead. He so seldom showed affection that the gesture brought more tears to her eyes.

*Don't cry, don't cry.*

"It's waterproof mascara," Marie said, smiling knowingly. "You're allowed to feel emotional today."

"We'll be waiting for you inside the church, darling," said Anton. He squeezed her hand as he passed, then he and Marie were gone and it was just her and her father.

"Are you happy, Tessie?"

He hadn't called her that since she was a little girl, still young enough to crawl into his lap whenever she was scared.

She was scared witless now.

She nodded.

"Look at me." He lifted her chin. "This is your last chance to back out. Once you walk down that aisle, there'll be no turning back. Are you sure Stefan is the right man for you?"

She wasn't sure. But what she was sure of was that Christian hated her. And he would be leaving Paris now, on his way to the Caribbean.

And without him, the world just seemed grey and so cold, as if all the vitality had leached out of it.

"Of course I'm happy. I'm getting married today." This was everything she'd ever dreamed. The big white wedding to a man so perfect he was almost too good to be true. A good man, from a good family, with a wonderful career ahead of him. He was going to take her to interesting places and then they were going to have a family, and they would settle back here in Westerwald and Stefan would change the world.

Her father took her hands in his. "Space in a marriage is a good thing, but too much space… that simply means you don't have enough holding you together." He drew in a rough breath. "I should know. Your mother and I wanted such different things. We thought we could make it work if we just gave each other enough space. Instead, we became strangers who shared the same house. We resented each other. I worry that's what your future will hold."

"Stefan and I are nothing like you and her. We're very much alike. We're partners. We like the same things."

He smiled sadly. "Do you? Then why do you do them apart?"

There was no way she could cross her fingers without her father seeing. So she raised her gaze to his, prayed his bullshit radar was defective today, and lied to his face. "I want to marry Stefan."

"Then let's do it." He held out his arm and she took it. They moved towards the doors.

Tessa had stood inside Neustadt's Notre Dame cathedral hundreds of times over the years, yet she'd never seen it as beautiful as it looked today. Sunlight streamed through tall medieval stained-glass windows onto the uneven flag-stoned floor. The organ's music swelled, joined by a choir of young voices.

The scene was so breathtaking that tears pricked her eyes. She blinked them back. She didn't want to test Marie's claim that the mascara was waterproof.

Not with the cameras all pointing in her direction.

They stood in the ante-chamber, behind the flower girls and page boys, who itched to be moving, though Anna held them back until the music changed.

Tessa's hand trembled on the herringbone-wool sleeve of her father's morning coat. He turned to look at her, a mixture of love and pride shining in his eyes. She knew she was a credit to him. The perfect daughter, the perfect bride, marrying the perfect man.

It was all just too perfect.

"Connie Hewitt didn't steal the ring," she said. "It was given to her."

"What?" Her father faced her. "We can talk about this later, Teresa."

"No, we can't. There was no treason and no one close to the royal family betrayed their trust."

He frowned. "Then who gave it to her?"

"Archduke Christian."

He looked puzzled. "Why would he do that?"

"Because she was pregnant with his child."

The organ shifted into "Here Comes the Bride". She'd never liked the tune and would have preferred something less clichéd, but she'd gone with the tradition anyway.

*It's what everyone will expect.*

The assembled crowd rose to its feet, hundreds of smiling faces turned to look at her. Her father, experienced as he was at hiding his feelings, took a moment to school his features into a smile. She suspected she was the only one not smiling.

She wanted to check her cleavage. She heard the echo of Christian's advice: *Whatever you do, don't look down.*

She hadn't needed it then, but she needed it now. She lifted her chin.

She could do this. She had to do this.

By now Christian would be in the air, heading home to Los

Pajaros. No longer the bastard, but a bastard prince.

She set one foot in front of the other, matching her father's precise processional march.

She still hadn't seen Stefan. He was obscured from her by the guests. She couldn't think of them as friends and family. Most of the them were people she barely knew. Her father's business associates. Stefan's family, his friends, his business associates.

What was Los Pajaros like? Was it hot and dusty and sweaty, or did the breeze smell of coconut and flowers? Did champagne taste any different drunk on a Caribbean beach than it did in a Parisian hotel?

As they neared the front of the cathedral's nave, dominated by the ornately carved wooden pulpit that pre-dated the Reformation, she caught sight of a row of familiar faces. This time she didn't blink back the tears.

Anna. Lee. Anton. Marie. Max and his fiancée Phoenix.

She'd once believed Max would be her brother-in-law. That it would be Fredrik she'd be moving down the aisle to meet.

Fredrik, who she'd known her whole life. Just as she'd known Stefan. They'd all moved in the same elite circles, attended the same debutantes' balls, the horse races, the palace garden parties.

Fear gripped her. This was her world. The only world she'd ever known. By walking down this aisle and taking Stefan's hand she'd be safe in that world forever.

*You're scared.* Christian's voice vibrated in her head.

She was no longer scared of losing everything. She'd already lost the one person who mattered most. No, what scared her was that the things she'd wanted – the things she'd believed she wanted – would smother her.

Again, the strangled feeling gripped her, the same feeling she'd had the night of the charity banquet when Christian leapt into her car. The fear had blinded her to everything else then, but now her eyes were wide open.

The only moments she hadn't felt that fear this last month were

262

the moments when Christian had been near.

But could she do this alone?

Look at what happened when her mother left the safety of their clique. Amalie had died alone and bitter, lost. She'd died with a stomach full of sleeping pills and only been found three days later.

Stefan stepped into her line of vision. Debonair in his dove-grey morning suit, with a white rose clipped to his lapel, the ivory satin of his waistcoat impeccably uncreased.

His warm gaze met hers. He smiled.

Her step faltered.

Her father gripped her arm, steadying her. But she didn't know if anything could steady the off-balance feeling inside. The feeling that she was making a terrible mistake.

There was nothing she could do about it now.

Not with everyone watching, expectant. It was too late now.

And Christian's plane should be somewhere over the Canary Islands, heading out across the Atlantic. She'd never been across the Atlantic before. Would Stefan take her with him on his next business trip to the States?

She handed her bouquet of blood-red roses to her maid of honour, a distant cousin she only ever saw at weddings and funerals.

Her father passed her hand to Stefan, who took it with a slight squeeze.

Stefan smiled, open and encouraging. But there was something missing.

It wasn't just the spark she felt with Christian. Chemistry was, after all, nothing more than a mix of fallible hormones. Chemistry didn't last. Sparks died out.

But there was something else missing. That light she'd seen in Christian's eyes.

Stefan was a good man. He was honest and honourable. He cared for her. He'd take care never to hurt her. He'd be a solid provider and a loving father. He was a considerate lover.

He didn't treat her as if she were a treasure he'd unearthed. He didn't love her.

The way that Christian did.

Oh God, what had she done?

Christian exited the hotel behind the porter, who wheeled his luggage to the rear of the car and helped Frank load it into the boot.

Where the hell was Dominic? They were already late for their flight. Not that it mattered, since they'd chartered their own plane, but pilots got snippy about things like that.

He glanced back at the entrance of the hotel. But it wasn't Dominic he was missing.

Frank opened the door for him. "It feels strange leaving without her," he said.

Christian slid into the rear seat of the sedan. Not just strange. It felt wrong.

But he couldn't turn the clock back. He was no longer angry with Tessa. He'd had some time these last few days to shift his perspective. He hadn't planned on returning to Westerwald. The more space he could put between him and Tessa, the better.

But curiosity had won out. He'd come back to Neustadt, this time as a tourist. He'd explored this town he'd been conceived in and learned its history. He'd met Max.

He rubbed his face. His eyes hurt. He hadn't slept in days.

So Tessa hadn't seduced him for her own devious ends. It had taken him all of two seconds after she walked out to remember she hadn't exactly thrown herself at him. She'd been reluctant and he'd had to work to seduce her.

But that didn't matter.

He'd bared his soul to her, and she'd lied to him.

That did matter.

And she'd chosen Stefan over him.

She'd gone and taken with her all the light and meaning and joy in his life, and there was nothing he could do to bring it back.

Frank shut the door, sealing Christian into a warm, safe cocoon. He sank his head in his hands and waited for Frank to get in the driver's seat and fire up the engine. The door opened and shut, but the engine did not rev to life. Christian looked up.

Frank contemplated him in the mirror. "We could swing past the cathedral on the way to the airport. We still have about fifteen minutes before she walks down the aisle."

Had Frank gone insane? "I have absolutely no desire to see her marry someone else."

"I thought you might want to stop the wedding," Frank explained patiently.

"She doesn't want me. That enough information for you to start the engine and leave my love life alone?"

Frank shrugged and turned the key.

The door opened and Dominic slung his hold-all inside. "Sorry I'm late. What have I missed?"

"I suggested to Mr Taylor he might want to make a stop on the way to the airport, however it seems he's disinclined to."

"Don't bother. I already tried." Dominic flopped onto the seat beside his bag, and shut the door. "He doesn't want to listen."

Christian frowned. They had a plane to catch, and he wasn't in the mood for this.

"Just to be clear. *Tessa doesn't want me.*"

The pain clawed at his chest again, as if a tiger was inside trying to get out.

Dom and Frank exchanged looks.

"Of course she wants you," Dom sighed his impatience. "Want me to go online to Huff Post Celebrity and pull up the pictures of you leaving the premiere the other night? Cause any fool can see the two of you are hopelessly gone on each other."

"Then why is she marrying some other guy?"

"Because she's scared."

What did Tessa have to be scared of? She lived in her safe little bubble. She had respect, wealth, family – all the things he still

265

didn't take for granted.

But she'd said that Stefan would never abandon her. And Christian, fool that he was, had done nothing to persuade her he wouldn't. Or that they could make this work. Not just for a weekend, but for a lifetime.

He still wasn't sure he could.

"The thing I've learned from having four sisters," Dom said, as if discussing the weather outside the windows. "Is that girls are even more messed-up and confused than we are. And sometimes they make mistakes."

"She was very clear about what mistakes she made," Christian replied bitterly. Not so clear on the biggest of them all, though. "She believes she's better off without me. She gets to have her perfect home and her perfect family." And maybe she was right. He sighed. "I can't guarantee any of that. I don't exactly have a good track record when it comes to relationships. The people I love tend to end up hurt."

"Nothing in life is guaranteed." Frank said. He still hadn't started driving, Christian noticed.

Dominic laughed. "You have *no* track record when it comes to relationships. But you love the woman, and that's got to count for something. Tessa is not your mother. Besides, you're not the one who hurt your mother. You didn't choose to be born and you didn't make her decisions for her."

"What if I make Tessa unhappy?"

"Yeah, cos she's going to be so happy married to someone she doesn't love."

Christian glowered at his friend. He wasn't making this any easier. "I'm leaving because it's the right thing to do."

Dominic threw his head back and laughed. Long and loud.

Christian glared at him with a growing desire to plant a fist in his face. "What's so funny?"

"You've spent your entire life condemning your mother for walking away without a fight, and now you're doing exactly the same thing. You are such a wuss!"

"Am not." The retort came automatically, through long years of practice, but Dominic's words gave him pause. Was he repeating the mistakes of the past?

Was he doing exactly what his mother had done? When he'd only seen her through the eyes of a hurt child, he hadn't understood the choices she'd made. But now he knew she'd had a bloody good reason for leaving. Even if his father had married her, her position in this little country would have been untenable. She might have cost Archduke Christian his crown. And their son would still have been an outcast.

She'd done the right thing.

But she'd paid a high price. She lost her family, her career, her reputation. And she'd never loved again.

"My reasons are every bit as good as my mother's were," he said.

Teresa faced many of the same pressures his father had. Marrying an actor, and a bastard to boot, even if his father was royal, was hardly going to go down well in her social circles. She might lose the only family she had… her home. Everything.

But this wasn't the Seventies.

*Family isn't a place, it's a feeling.* His mother had said that once.

Tessa gave him that feeling. When she'd lain in his arms, and trusted herself to him, he'd found the sense of belonging he'd craved his entire life.

Could she feel the same?

"So are you going to get your head out of your ass and do something about it?" Dominic asked.

Christian looked at Frank. "How quickly can you get us to the church?"

Dominic held up his fist for a fist-pump.

"It'll be tight, but I'll do my best," Frank said. With a scream of tyres he pulled away from the hotel entrance and headed in the opposite direction from the airport.

"This is like a scene from a movie," Dom said, flashing his grin

267

at Christian. "Except in the movies, there's always a massive traffic jam and the hero has to borrow some kid's bike or a policeman's horse to get to the church on time. I haven't seen any police on horseback in this town. Lots of bicycles, though."

"This better not be like any goddamn movie!" Christian said through clenched teeth.

Then he swore.

No bicycles or horses needed, but there was a damned police cordon blocking off the entire street leading to the cathedral.

"Leave it to me," Frank said, keeping his calm. A uniformed officer waved them to a stop, and he rolled down the window. "Mr Taylor's late for the wedding. Can you give us an escort to the cathedral?"

The guard peered into the car, and Christian thanked every god imaginable that this was such a small country.

"You again," the officer said. "No fans chasing you down today, I hope?"

Christian shook his head and the grinning officer waved to a policeman on a bike complete with flashing blue lights to escort them through the barricades.


He'd never done anything this daft in his life. He was probably about to get himself on the front pages of the world's papers and for all the wrong reasons. The tabloids were going to have a field day.

And his father, the father who may or may not have known he existed, must be rolling in his grave about now.

But he would never forgive himself if he repeated his mother's mistake. He wasn't going to die alone and pining for a lost love, and he wasn't going to leave without fighting for what he wanted.

No matter how many good reasons they all came up with.

The car pulled up at the kerb with a squeal of brakes. "Keep the motor running," he instructed Frank as he flung open the door and jumped out. "I might need to make a quick getaway if this doesn't pan out."

He took the stairs two at a time, which was difficult because they'd obviously been built in a day and age when people had shorter strides. The cathedral doors, their bronze carvings blurred by verdigris, stood open. He passed between them at a run, skidding across the flagstones of the ante-chamber. The wide-eyed usher jumped out of the way as he hurried past and into the hushed nave. A few heads turned, but most remained focused on the scene at the front of the church, where Tessa and Stefan faced each other hand in hand.

Oh God, was he too late?

His heart contracted. She was so beautiful. A vision in ivory satin overlaid with lace, fresh white buds pinned in her intricately braided hair, her peaches-and-cream complexion illuminated by the ray of coloured sunlight falling through the high windows.

What the hell was he doing? Was he really this selfish?

Yes, he was.

And this wasn't only about him. This was about what was right for all of them.

"Tessa!" He shouted her name down the nave. The collective gasp of the assembled guests blew through the cathedral like an icy wind as several hundred heads turned to look at him. Only one he cared about.

Slowly Tessa turned and her gaze met his. Even across the expanse of the nave, he saw the light jump in her eyes and he knew he'd done the right thing. Even if he was too late, that light in her eyes gave him back his hope.

He walked down the aisle towards her and the closer he got, the more light and colour there seemed to be in the soaring cathedral. The crowd hushed, the air grew electric with tension, but Christian didn't care.

Tessa stood completely still, her hands still in Stefan's, her face a mask, but as he drew close he could see the pulse hammering in her throat.

He stopped a few feet away. "I love you, Tess."

269

His voice reverberated into the ringing silence. A few women in the audience gasped. Someone tittered. Cameras clicked. To his right, someone rose from a pew.

"You came here to tell me that *now*?" Her voice was low and breathy, but it carried.

"No, I'm here because I'm a selfish bastard and I can't let the woman I want to spend the rest of my life with marry someone she doesn't love." He glanced at the groom. "Sorry, pal."

Stefan shook his head. "You're too late to stop this wedding."

Christian's heart hammered so hard he struggled to draw breath. But he still wasn't ready to give up. "I'm not a knight in shining armour and I never will be. I'm probably never going to change the world, but I'm asking you to take a chance on me."

Tessa still said nothing.

A man came to stand at his right. An imposing man with greying hair who looked as though he was used to giving orders and being obeyed. Not yet evicting him, though Christian was sure his time had run out.

But he stood his ground. "I'm not going to pretend it didn't happen. I'm not going to disappear. And I'm not going to stop fighting for you."

Her hand fluttered to her throat. Her left hand. He caught the glint of gold and his heart shattered.

Tessa looked straight into Christian's eyes, those mesmerising eyes that blinded her to everything else.

Stefan's voice broke the expectant silence. "You're too late because she already stopped the wedding. Though I'd really like to know why."

With huge effort she dragged her gaze from Christian and turned on her high, spiky heels to face her groom.

His brow was furrowed. "I thought we agreed this sentimental nonsense about love was a bad basis for any marriage. Why are you changing your mind?"

She looked down at their clasped hands, then back up at him. "I'm not changing my mind because of Christian." At least, not entirely. "I'm changing my mind because I'm marrying you for all the wrong reasons. I'm marrying you out of fear and that has to be the worst basis for a marriage ever."

"You couldn't have told me this a little earlier?"

She bit her lip. "I am so sorry."

She didn't need to see Christian to feel his strength at her back. She didn't have to do this alone, after all.

She smiled at Stefan, willing him to understand. "I've only just started to realise who I am and what I want for my life and it's not what I thought it would be. If I married you, I'd be living your life, pursuing your dreams. I need to follow mine."

He nodded stiffly. "I think you're making a big mistake, but I won't force you into anything you don't want to do."

The fact that there was no shock or dismay or regret in his eyes made her decision easier. They were so much alike, too much alike. Stefan also needed to open his heart and learn to feel. But she wasn't the woman who could do that for him.

"I really hope one day you meet someone who makes you feel the way I do right now."

Alight. Alive. As if the world that had been painted in shades of grey a moment ago was now lit up in beautiful, bright technicolor.

She unhooked the earrings from her ears then slid the engagement ring off her finger, the gold band with its large diamond that still felt as if it didn't belong on her hand. She held them out to Stefan and he took them.

Then she turned back to face Christian. His smile wrapped around her, warmer than sunshine, warm enough to melt the last of the frost in her heart. Who cared if the ice cracked? Beneath it lay a river desperate to break free and plunge headlong towards the sea.

Careful of her long train, she descended the shallow stone steps to stand in front of him. "You don't need to change the world.

You changed me, and that's enough."

And then in front of everyone, in front of the cameras and the stunned guests, she kissed him.

# Epilogue – Tortuga

"I thought we'd decided on a small wedding?" Christian looked around at the crowd assembled in the clearing.

Teresa had to lean close for him to catch her words over the roar of the waterfall. "This *is* a small wedding."

He'd visualized them alone with the minister on a beach. Instead, ten of their closest friends sat on picnic blankets on the grass, sipping champagne and looking for all the world as if a picnic in the middle of the jungle on a cursed Caribbean island was an everyday thing.

Dominic, his best man.

Anna, now assistant to them both and not a whoopee cushion in sight.

Lee, hand in hand with Anton.

Robbie and his friend the screenwriter, whose script Christian had agreed to produce. Though he still wasn't sure why the hell he'd signed on so quickly when he'd barely decompressed from his role in *Pirate's Revenge*. So much for taking a break to re-evaluate his career.

Max and Phoenix. Rik and Kenzie. His new-found family.

Emotion clogged his throat. He and Rik weren't related by blood, yet Rik had accepted him as a brother. They were even going to produce this new movie together. Heaven help them and the poor investors who'd agreed to back them.

The minister cleared his throat. "I'll keep this simple. Do you, Christian Hewitt Taylor, take Teresa Amalia Charlotte Clara Adler d'Arelat as your wife?"

Christian resisted the urge to roll his eyes. He really needed to get over this aversion to all things aristocratic. Not only was he marrying one, but Max had insisted on giving him a title too. Apparently it was a time-honoured tradition for royal bastards. *Margrave of Neustria*. It sounded like something out of a history book.

He looked at his bride. Not in white today, or grey or brown or beige, but in a summery halter-neck dress the same Arctic blue as her eyes. Radiant and shimmering. He'd never seen her so happy or so relaxed.

He'd never loved her as much as he did right now. Every day he loved her more. "I do."

"And do you, Teresa…"

"I do."

Their audience laughed.

'What's the hurry?' he mouthed.

She arched an elegant eyebrow. *No shit*, it said.

*No shit* indeed. He couldn't wait to get back to the privacy of their cabin on the yacht either. He doubted they'd be seeing much of the Caribbean during their honeymoon.

"Then I now pronounce you man and wife."

It started as a tremble beneath their feet. Tessa grabbed his arm for support and Anna shrieked.

The tremble became a roar that overshadowed the thunder of the waterfall cascading into the rocky pool beside them. The ground shook, and it was all Christian could do to keep them both standing.

A champagne glass crashed to the ground, shattering into pieces.

A boulder tumbled from its perch on the bank, splashing into the river and sending a mini slide of smaller rocks and pebbles after it.

The earth's vibration rocked through him, up through the soles of his sneaker-clad feet, through his very bones. He grasped Tessa's hand and held it tight.

Then just as suddenly, the tremor stopped.

"What the…?" this from Max.

The minister was white-faced. "I've never heard of an earthquake in Los Pajaros before."

Rik stood, dusting off his jeans, his smile broad. Every face turned to him, most of them perplexed, all still more than a little shaken.

"It's the end of the curse."

Stunned silence.

Then Kenzie rose, slipping her hand into her fiancé's. "Of course. The pirate and his princess have returned to Tortuga." She sent Christian and Teresa an impish smile. "You've broken the curse."

Christian turned to his bride. His *wife*. The daughter of the Count of Arelat, betrothed to another man, swept away from the altar by her pirate lover. He laughed.

And he kissed her.